DEFIANCE

IN THE TIME OF
CHAOS AND EXISTENTIAL THREAT

BEREKET SELASSIE

Writers' Branding
(877) 608-6550
www.writersbranding.com
media@writersbranding.com

DEDICATED TO

Professor Emeritus Wole Soyinka on his 90th Birthday, in celebration of a life richly lived, a legacy profoundly cherished, and a friendship treasured beyond measure. May your wisdom continue to inspire generations, and may your spirit forever illuminate our paths. With deepest esteem and enduring friendship.

DEDICATED TO THE MEMORY OF

Óscar Alberto Martínez Ramírez and his infant daughter, Valeria Ramírez, who drowned while crossing the Rio Grande

and

The Eritrean migrants and other Africans who perished while crossing the Sahara Desert and the Mediterranean Sea.

DEFIANCE

Erecting Walls of Exclusion,
Endless Strife and Mutual Hostility

EXPRESSIONS OF GRATITUDE

I wish to express my deeply felt gratitude to the following friends:

1. Two of them, Semere Habtemariam and Daniel Teklai. Thank you, Semere and Daniel, for an excellent work done in "copy editing" and thus polishing Defiance…

   I owe you both very much for this extraordinary labor of love. As we say in Tigrigna, *"Ab KaHsaKum Yew'Elenni!"*

2. The other friend is Kiflu Tadesse. This is a belated word of thanks (with due apologies) to Kiflu who made some insightful comments and suggestions to improve my novel, Deliverance (2017). Sorry for being late in thanking you, Kiflu, but better late than never..

TABLE OF CONTENTS

Part

WHERE ANGELS FEAR TO TREAD...
"WARRIOR ANGELS"
(AKA HOLY FOOLS) RUSH IN...

Chapter One

MIGRATION—HUMANITY'S CRUCIAL CHALLENGE

The Global Context:

A Time Marked by Chaos in Government and elsewhere—widespread moral bankruptcy—corruption—threat of nuclear war—and the phenomenon of migration creating political and social problems provoking conflicts within and among nations.

In such a situation, it might help to cite some appropriate authorities to frame the issues. An authority that comes to mind is the late Samuel Huntington, a renowned American political philosopher and author. Huntington has written many books, but a book relevant for this purpose—albeit controversial—is *The Clash of Civilizations* in which he discusses the phenomenon of migration in a global, historical context. The following pithy statement is from page 198 of the book:

> *If demography is destiny, population movements are the motor of history. In centuries past, differential growth rates, economic conditions, and governmental policies have produced massive migrations by Greeks, Jews, Germanic tribes, Norse, Turks, Russians, Chinese, and others... Nineteenth century Europeans were, however, the master race of demographic invasion... Westerners conquered and at times obliterated other peoples, explored and settled less densely populated lands. The*

export of people was perhaps the single most important dimension of the rise of the West between the sixteenth and twentieth centuries

One wonders whether those people in Europe and the United States of America that have been opponents of migrants coming to their shores might read this passage and the book from which it is extracted, and change their negative attitudes toward positive acceptance, or at least tolerance of "the other." Or to use a Biblical model of the Good Samaritan, whether they might regard them as their "neighbors".

Nations in what is now called the North, i.e. Europe and the United States, are the target of migrants leaving their homelands in Africa, Asia and South and Central America, for various reasons, including war, famine, fear of persecution or even genocide. Afghanistan, Syria, Myanmar, Eritrea, Ethiopia, Sudan, Honduras, El Salvador and Venezuela are some of the examples. As the preceding quote illustrates, the migration phenomenon is part of an old story of humanity. It also provides the context for our story.

When Things Go Wrong

It was a cold morning in late November in the Shepherds Bush area of London.

In a warren of a low-ceilinged room of the basement, one floor down from the Director's office, adjacent to the "examination room," three security operatives sat around a rectangular table, poring over copies of a printout from an interrogation record. These were copies of the confessions supposedly made by a man who died under torture three days earlier. One of the three, a man with a lean and hungry look, of pallid complexion and with an aquiline nose, presumably of higher rank than the other two, looked at his watch and said: "Time to wrap up. The boss expects us in his office in an hour." The other two, whose reddened faces bore the anxiety of an uncertain fate, looked at him and at their watches and continued their readings with furrowed fronts.

One hour later, the three found themselves in the Director's office and sat on the chairs arranged in a semi-circle around the Director's desk, which was made of large mahogany with glass cover fitted over it. Two wooden rectangular-shaped file trays were placed on two edges of the desk, one to the right marked 'Incoming,' the other to the left marked 'Outgoing.'

Along the space between the Director's desk and the area where the security operatives sat, waiting for the Director's arrival, there was a medium-sized table on which there were a few magazines and a booklet with the title, *'Departmental Protocol on Norms of Conducting Interrogation of Crime Suspects.'* It can be safely assumed that the three security operatives have read the booklet or used it during their training. That some of its contents have been perused and noted carefully by lawyers engaged in the defense of criminal suspects or charged with crimes is also a fair assumption, judging by some of the dog-eared pages and underlined passages.

The Director arrived at his office one hour later than had been expected, and the three operatives had no choice except to wait. On his arrival, the Director did not apologise for his late arrival though he was known to be a stickler for punctuality. And he was unusually gruff in the way he started his remarks to his subordinates. For he threw a question at them suddenly and in a somewhat angry tone.

"I was detained at the Attorney-General's Office. Can you guess the reason for my delay?" It was considered a rhetorical question by the three operatives, so they did not respond to his question.

"I was detained at the office of my boss because of what you people did here at the interrogation room."

Looking sharply at their three faces one after the other, he continued:

"A man died while he was undergoing interrogation conducted by you men, right?"

No answer came from the three. "Is that right or not?"

"Yes, sir."

"Yes sir, what?"

"He died while under interrogation, sir," answered the supposed senior operative who looked for affirmation by his two colleagues, which came in the form of a vigorous nod.

The Director waited a while. He thought for a few moments and continued in an even tone.

"I have reviewed the printout of the interrogation and there is barely any useful information in it. The deceased did not provide any lead as to others engaged in criminal activities or co-conspirators."

He waited for a moment and continued: "So my question to you, which was also the question my boss posed to me sharply and repeatedly, is: "The wretch died in your hands for nothing. He died and you got nothing out of him. And his lawyers will howl, claiming that he was murdered by our Department... And for nothing... Am I right?" He spat the words in a barking staccato voice, repeating, "Am I right?"

"Yes sir," answered the three in one voice. "Are you saying he was murdered, then?"

This time the three answered in unison like a chorus: "No, sir."

"So, what happened at the Interrogation room, which the lawyers, and almost everybody else is calling the Torture Chamber?"

No answer.

The Director calmed down a little and returned to the subject that had become the topic of conversations and national Newspaper articles and radio and TV commentaries.

Addressing the senior operative, the Director said:

"David, you tell me what really happened. And the rest of you pay attention and think hard on what you may be telling the court because a case will be opened charging that a death had occurred under government interrogation, or torture."

David cleared his throat and began explaining how the deceased died while under interrogation.

"You are quite right, sir, that he died while under interrogation. But he died of cardiac arrest."

"Cardiac arrest? You mean the man died of a heart attack. Is that the doctor's verdict?"

"Yes sir, the doctor used the words, 'cardiac arrest.' Those are his words." "When and where did this cardiac arrest occur?"

"It occurred while being interrogated."

"I want details, David. The courts will require details. His lawyers will demand details. Haven't you heard of the saying 'the devil is in the details?'

"I have, sir."

"So give me more details. Consider my questions as though they were posed by an examining magistrate, or a defense counsel cross-examining you in a court of law."

He uttered the last phrase, "...*cross-examining you in a court of law*" spelling out each syllable with deliberate emphasis

"How did he die? What did you do to him? Answer me."

"Certainly, sir. It is simple, and I will describe exactly what happened."...

..."Well, I am listening."

"What happened was this, sir. We were trying to get information from him, information that he refused to give willingly during the earlier interrogation. As has happened in a few cases here and elsewhere in the world like the United States after the 9/11 attack on America, we used '**water boarding**' on him. We tried the method on him three times. He was kept under water for a few seconds, then brought out and asked questions. No response. On the fourth attempt, we were about to push him under water when he groaned, emitting gurgling sounds, heaved a deep sigh and collapsed in our hands. We got him out and administered the standard reviving procedure, but it was too late. He was dead."

David looked at his two colleagues and asked them if there was anything they want to add or change in his testimony. Both responded with a shake of their heads.

The Director got up from his chair and addressing nobody in particular, in a kind of soliloquy, said:

"Somebody dies under interrogation, or torture as it will be characterized, and my men have nothing to show for it. Just terrific!...Terrific!"...

After a thoughtful moment, he added, "if he died under water boarding, how can it be cardiac arrest?" Looking at David, the Director asked pointedly: "Are you sure this is in the doctor's report?"

David replied, "Positive."

"I must review the doctor's report and also talk to him."

Inquiry Commission

A Public Inquiry Meeting is taking place at the office of Inspector General of the Criminal Investigation Division of the London Police.

The meeting is presided over by the Deputy Inspector General of the Police, assisted by two clerks sitting left and right at the head able.

The meeting is open to the public and representatives of interested parties have been invited to participate with a right to pose questions. Although the meeting was called at the behest of the Attorney-General, specifically aimed at finding out how a man had died at the hand of personnel of the Criminal Investigation Division of the Metropolitan Police, the concerned authorities decided to make the meeting open to the public being aware of the fact that tremendous public opinion had raised concern about the abuse of investigatory procedures, including in particular the persistent public inquiries voiced about the use of torture in police investigation. It was, therefore, decided to hold an open public inquiry on the subject with a special focus on the case of Alamin Idris.

The occasion was used by different interested groups, including human rights organizations and civic as well as religious groups interested in the rights of refugees and migrants in general.

The Presiding Officer opened the meeting by delivering three strikes on the gavel.

"I declare this meeting open. It is a public meeting of a special Commission of Inquiry," he said.

With that the meeting was opened and the Chairman asked the detective inspector handling the subject of the investigation to make an opening statement on the agenda.

The detective inspector rises and bowing toward the Chair says:

"Thank you, sir. The case under review concerns the death of one Alamin Idris, who died while under police interrogation. I have submitted the necessary documents related to the case of the death of Mr. Alamin Idris. The doctor's death certificate is attached to the document. According to the doctor's written testimony, Mr. Idris died of cardiac arrest. The circumstances under which death occurred are described in the accompanying document..."

"Briefly, the testimony of the interrogating officers says that Mr. Idris died while under interrogation. The testimony states that Mr. Idris had been subjected to what is known as **water boarding**. He had been subjected to this procedure three times and that when the interrogators tried to use the same procedure for the fourth time, an unexpected and serious event happened. Mr. Idris gasped, and giving out a gurgling sound, collapsed. He was dead."

Gavel sound.

"Why did the interrogators use the water boarding repeatedly?" the Chairman asked

"This special procedure that has been used rarely involves submerging the head of the suspect under water for a few seconds. At the end of each procedure, the suspect is asked to answer questions regarding his own activities and those of others allegedly associated with him. He is asked to reveal names of collaborators, their mode of operation, their addresses and so on. Apparently, Mr. Idris refused to give answers to the questions put to him repeatedly and he repeatedly declined answer, whereupon he was pushed under water again with his head submerged under water for a few seconds before he is allowed out to breath and be asked the same questions again."

"I see. Please continue."

"There isn't much else to say, except to repeat that the suspect then surprised his interrogators by suddenly dying in their hands."

Loud voices from the audience. One person exclaimed loudly:

"Death delivered him from the horrible torture." Another one added: "Our laws prohibit torture in no uncertain terms. Yet, the law is flouted shamefully. For what? Are we or are we not a nation of law?" This exclamation was followed by a loud and prolonged noise of affirmation.

Gavel sound.

"Quiet!... Quiet!... No interruption please! There will be time for questions or remarks from interested parties. That is why this hearing is being conducted in public."

The detective inspector gathered his papers and declared an end to his testimony.

"That is all I have to say, sir. There is nothing more I can usefully add. And I will answer questions to the best of my knowledge."

With that statement, the detective inspector took his seat in the front row.

The Chairman looked left and right at the clerks. Receiving no answer from either of them, he said addressing the audience:

"The meeting is open for questions or remarks from any interested parties. I admonish all those who wish to speak to be brief. And first, state your name and the organization or persons you represent."

A Volley of hands shot up.

"One person at a time," the Chair said. "The clerk will write names—five names first. Then after all five have spoken, others can raise their hands and we will continue the process until everyone has had an opportunity to ask questions or raise issues of concern related to the subject at hand."

The clerk rose to do his job as required by the Chair. He wrote the names of five people and gave the list to the Chairman.

"The first on the list is Miss Evelyn Sharpe," the Chairman said.

He then addressed himself to Miss Sharpe and said: "Miss Sharpe, please tell us whom you represent and then proceed with your question or remark as briefly as possible.

Miss Sharpe thanked the Chairman and said:

"I represent Amnesty International—the Head Office here in London. My question is why the security officers used torture on a suspect when they know, or should know, that torture is prohibited by international law and many national laws, including the law of the United Kingdom. The legal advisor of Amnesty and a legal representative of the deceased, Mr. Alamin Idris, have studied the legal consequences of such acts of torture. I ask the Chair's permission to ask Mr. Idris's lawyer to address the Commission of Inquiry."

The Chair nodded acceptance of the requested permission.

A tall and distinguished-looking man of about forty, with pale eyes and long and arresting face, rose and addressed the Chair:

"May it please the honorable Chairman. My name is Jeremy Bevan. It has been my most unpleasant duty to look into the misdeeds of the officers handling the case of my unfortunate bereaved family of the dearly departed. And I…"

"Mr. Bevan," the Chair interrupted, "I would like to remind all concerned that this meeting is not for expressing a funeral oration. It is to discover the circumstances that led to the tragic death of a man, who was a criminal suspect. The police are by duty bound to find out all relevant facts, to gather all evidence connected to the commission of a crime. And to do so according to the law. Let us all stick to the point."

"I am most grateful, Honorable Commissioner, for the reminder, and I will indeed stick to the point as ordered. Far be it from me to waste the Commission's valuable time. May I also say that in addition to the discovery of the acts of the police that led to the death of Mr. Idris, I am charged with the task of establishing criminal guilt in the commission of the act and of requesting for the appropriate legal damages as a result of the crime. This in due time and at the right venue."

"Quite so," the Chairman said adding, "I take it you have completed your main statement, Mr. Bevan. Am I right?"

"Yes, Honorable Commissioner."

"Miss Sharpe, do you have any further questions or remarks on behalf of the family of Mr. Idris?"

"No, Mr. Chairman. I just want to be clear on one point of law with regard to damages. Am I right to assume that these are matters to be settled by a court of law and not by this Commission of Inquiry?"

"That is indeed a correct assumption, Miss Sharpe."

"Thank you, Mr. Chairman. I would now like to make a point, most formally, that Amnesty International, like all human rights organizations, is seriously concerned about the use of torture to extract confessions from prisoners. Such practice is morally wrong and prohibited under international law as well as in the laws of most nations in this day and age. In conclusion, I have no doubt that those who are caught on the wrong side of the law in the case of Mr. Alamin Idris will be charged and punished in accordance with the appropriate law. I don't know if Mr. Bevan has anything else to say on behalf of his clients."

Mr. Bevan said he did not have anything to add to what had already been said.

Gavel sound.

"The floor is open to anyone else who may wish to pose questions or make statements," the Chairman said, and reading from the list of names, he called on the next speaker, Mr. Arthur Sullivan.

"Thank you, Mr. Chairman," began Mr. Sullivan.

"I have been retained by families of people who have been detained for months without charge. When asked to release the detainees or to bring them to court, the authorities answered that the detainees are under suspicion of belonging the international Islamist terrorist group known as ISIS. One of the people who have retained me to represent his family is the internationally known Soccer star, Mr. Rashid Idris, who also happens to be the elder brother of the late Alamin Idris. I was given to understand by Mr. Bevan that Mr. Rashid Idris has already been questioned by the police on the activities of his younger brother, the late Alamin Idris. Mr. Rashid Idris was properly treated in the questioning and was not detained. I wonder if his celebrity spared him from the fate of his younger brother and others who have been improperly treated."

Evidently irritated by Mr. Sullivan's comment, the Chairman opined: "We are all entitled to our opinions on any matter as long as the opinions are fair and reasonable, Mr. Sullivan."

Mr. Sullivan did not expect this sharp response. So he decided to tread carefully. Instead of pursuing the previous line, he decided to be amiable. He said: "I quite agree, Mr. Chairman. And I sincerely hope that you consider my opinion as fair and reasonable."

But the Chairman did not reciprocate the amiability, for he curtly said: "And I think it is fair and reasonable to assume that the fairness and reasonableness of your opinion would be determined by resort to an inquiry on the state of mind of those who questioned and released Mr. Rashid Idris. Wouldn't you say, Mr. Sullivan?"

Mr. Sullivan noticed the irony in the Chairman's response and realised he had overstepped the bounds of propriety. He thus abandoned any attempts to indulge in debates with the Chairman on the academic issue that he had provoked.

"I bow to your superior wisdom, sir," he concluded, to the satisfaction of the Chairman, who flashed a smile of defiant satisfaction.

There was a murmur of stifled chuckling from the audience, as if to signify disapproval of Mr. Sullivan's seeming obsequiousness.

The meeting continued for a few more minutes with other members of the audience raising issues and posing questions of similar nature to those that had been raised. Accordingly, the meeting was adjourned with a promise by the Chairman to give the final determination of the Commission of Inquiry and to advise any party with other of claims or requests for damages to refer to the appropriate court of law.

Group Consultation over Lunch

Mr. Rashid Idris joined the two men who had participated in asking questions and making statements during the meeting, namely Mr. Sullivan and Mr. Bevan, for lunch at a quiet restaurant in London's Piccadilly area, off Regent Street.

The three of them decided to hold private consultations regarding some pressing issues of mutual concern. Preeminent among such issues is the problem of migrants from Africa and the Middle East that has dominated national and international news and challenging governments and societies in the European continent. The idea of having a private lunch was suggested by Rashid, who wanted to enlist the two in his ongoing project of helping migrants and destitute refugees that he had observed during his frequent travels in European cities. His observation of destitute children and women living in squalor, exposed to the elements especially during the Winter, abandoned and helpless loitering in the streets of European cities was too much for him to bear or ignore as he himself enjoyed a dream-like life of luxury of a Soccer star.

Rashid Idris is a tall, brown-skinned Sudanese in his mid-thirties, who had studied in England. Sent by his elder brother, Yusuf Ibrahim, to study in England, he was very successful in his studies. His success induced his brother to persuade Rashid to continue to do graduate studies in any area of his interest. He was thus enrolled in a Ph.D. program on African and Middle East studies at the School of Oriental and African Studies (SOAS) in the University of London.

However, after a couple of years following the program, Rashid took a drastic change in career. Rashid had played Soccer for the University of

London where he was noticed by Soccer professional scouts who noticed his unusual ability, scoring goals for his team. Thus, while he was engaged in the graduate program at SOAS, and playing Soccer, he was recruited to play for a European national team as a striker (Position Number 10) scoring goal after goal, and gaining fame and enviable celebrity.

As it happened, even before his younger brother's involvement in extreme Islamic politics and detention, Rashid had been personally affected by the problem of migrants and refugees from Africa, including those from Eritrea and his own country, Sudan. He sought counsel and assistance from like-minded people and relatives to help provide assistance to such refugees in any way he could. Prominent among such people is his own rich uncle, Dr. Yusuf Ibrahim, a businessman dealing with energy and telecommunication matters in Africa. Rashid has recently traveled to Geneva and held talks with Dr. Yusuf at his business headquarters regarding their common concern over the problem of migrants and refugees.

Rashid's generosity is legendary among people who have known him. A man of magnetic charm, he is endowed with a well-built athletic body, an ever-smiling pleasant face and a genial manner typical of most Sudanese. He had thus become one of the most popular sports celebrities in Europe. To that popularity is added a generous spirit ready willingness to come to the rescue of people in need.

These features of his character and personality provide an additional asset over and above his renowned playing skill in ball control, striking prowess and speed admired by Soccer fans throughout Europe and Africa. These qualities were known to his student-day friend, Stefan Schmidt as well as to Messes Sullivan and Bevan, both of whom followed his Soccer career and are among his abiding fans.

It was thus natural, at the end of the Inquiry Meeting, for Bevan and Sullivan to decide to go out together with Rashid for a private lunch in a quiet restaurant. But privacy is a relative concept when it concerns a sportsman of Rashid's fame. No sooner had they arrived at the restaurant than Rashid was thronged with fans who saw him approaching the restaurant. A few rushed dangling notebooks for a fan's signature, and he could not resist obliging them. He signed for five young boys who were thrilled beyond words for landing into such a boon unexpectedly in a street of London. Such was the spirit of fandom among young people in the soccer world.

Inside the restaurant, the three men began their conversation, first regarding the encounter with the five fans and general gossip concerning international Soccer games. Of great interest and one that had become the topic of conversation throughout the world was the soccer game between France and Italy in which the famous French Soccer star, Zinedine Zidane, was seen butting an Italian player on his chest and was consequently given a red flag and expelled thus causing France to lose to Italy. They talked about the varying versions of the reason why Zidane butted the Italian, including the most common version that the Italian had provoked Zidane by using vulgar Italian language. One version was that the vulgarity was targeted on Zinedine's mother, whereas the version favored by Italian fans and the victim of the butt himself was that the target was Zinedine's sister, not his mother.

VERY UNLIKELY! Was the agreed verdict among the three men, who expressed true sadness on the discipline imposed on Zinedine, although they agreed with the referee's decision. After a while, the conversation shifted from Soccer to the challenges of migration and the fate of migrants and refugees.

Europe and Migrants

While engaged in pleasantries and jokes, Rashid's mind kept thinking about the burning issues of migrants, particularly African migrants from his own region, the Horn of Africa. He was obsessed by the subject of migrants and their fate in Europe. Therefore, he broached the subject and asked his friends what they thought about it. Rashid began by telling the other two of a piece of news he had heard from a BBC correspondent regarding the fate of African migrants stranded in a vessel off the coast of the island of Malta. According to the report, Malta declined to take some 200 migrants stranded in a boat rescued by a German Charity Mission, known as The Lifeline. Apparently, Italy's Interior Minister, Matteo Salvini expressed a wish that Malta take the migrants and arrest the crew. The Maltese Prime Minister, however, defiantly declined to accept the demand saying: "We are a sovereign country and nobody should dictate what we can and cannot do."

In a similar case, earlier the same year, Spain had accepted 630 migrants at the port of Valentia. The migrants had been rescued by the rescue ship Aquarius after both Italy and Malta refused to allow the rescue ship to dock in their ports. Italy and Malta have been engaged in acrimonious exchange of words in which Italian Transport Minister accused Malta of an "inhumane" and "absurd" decision for refusing to accept the vessel. Malta maintains that the ship was under Italian jurisdiction, and that Malta provided supplies to the stranded vessel.

It was Rashid who spoke telling the stories of these stranded migrants, though both Bevan and Sullivan said they had heard about the BBC reports. Bevan then asked two questions: first, why is Italy taking a hardline approach on the question of migrants; and second, who is responsible for migrants stranded at sea.

As to the first question, Sullivan volunteered to provide the answer. First of all, he said, he was not personally favorable to the policies of the newly elected populist government of Italy. For one thing, Italy's populist government has taken a harsh stance on immigration. It has warned that it will impound the Lifeline Vessel as well as another migrant rescue ship. The populist government of Italy has accused the Lifeline Vessel of breaking the law by taking migrants onboard, in spite of a warning by the Italian authorities that the Libyan coastguards were conducting a rescue operation. Presumably the Libyan coastguard conducts such rescue operations to return migrants back to where they came from. There has been a longstanding understanding between Italy and Libya to do this, which is designed to spare Italy the burden of huge, uncontrolled migration since Italy is fated by geography to be at the receiving end of such migrants, especially from Africa.

This is connected to the second question—who is responsible for migrants stranded at sea. This question raises moral and politico-strategic issues as to what to do with people in distress in consequence of mass migration caused by different "push factors," such as war or inter-state conflict as has happened in Africa and elsewhere in the world like Syria and Myanmar. There have been international agreements signed to address the problem of refugees, and mass exodus generally.

United Nations and regional organizations have frequently made attempts to address such problems. It is to fill in the gap created by the failure of international organizations to address this issue that private humanitarian responses have been provided such as the German Lifeline noted before. Clearly, for the foreseeable future, due to the continued failure to provide sufficient response under the auspices of the United Nations or regional bodies, the fate of migrants will continue to depend on private humanitarian responses.

Inviewoftheunstoppableincidenceofmassmigrationalongthe

Mediterranean Sea, the European Union has made attempts to respond to the challenge by convening conferences. But Italy's current government has declared its reluctance to sign up to any plan unless help is provided for its country as a matter of urgent priority. It is worth noting that more than 600,000 migrants have reached Italy's shores during the past four years. And according to a BBC report, the new Italian government has declared its intention to deport around half a million undocumented migrants.

And according to the same BBC report, over 1,000 people have drowned while crossing the Mediterranean in 2017 alone. Quoting the UN's refugee agency, the BBC claims that 220 people are believed to have died in the space of several days in mid-June 2017. The drowning of over 500 Eritreans and Ethiopians a few years ago off the Island of Lampedusa, Sicily, had shocked the conscience of many people including leaders like Pope Francis who visited the sight of the tragedy and made an unforgettable speech calling upon government of Europe to provide an appropriate response to the challenge of refugees and migrants in general.

Chapter Two

DEFIANCE IN THE TIME OF CHAOS

From Lampedusa to Calais and Beyond

We can say without hesitation, that migration is the most pressing problem humanity is facing today. Social scientists employ fancy terms to describe what drives people from their homes going through hazardous journeys. "Push Factors" is one such term; it refers to causes driving people from the comfort of their homes in search of relief and sanctuary. The assumption is that people must have compelling reasons for leaving their home and country. "Pull Factors" refers to attractions of an economic nature causing people to abandon their homes because of attractive prospects of a better life. A cursory review of the cases of mass migrations in our time shows without doubt that in the vast majority of cases, people are driven because of war and fear of physical harm or even death, both of death as individuals or groups as families or even ethnic group.

It is an interesting coincidence that the central characters of our story share the core values that actuate the thinking and behavior of all good people. Among these core values are: respect and compassion toward people whatever their differences, as well as a willingness to stake one's career and interest in defense or pursuit of the core values. Activities in support or pursuit of such values have determined the progress of humanity that is sublime. To witness a disturbing phenomenon of mass exodus under horrible conditions, like the sight of Syrians fleeing war, and the Rohingya fleeing death camps and rape are among those examples that have shocked the conscience of people in recent times.

Rashid joined two of the central characters of our story for a meeting in London to work out programs for helping refugees in need. The other two are: Isabelle Negassa and Stefan Schmidt. It was a strategy meeting as well as their felt need for them to know each other better. Rashid and Stefan knew each other as students at London University, but after Rashid dropped out of his Ph.D. program to become a Soccer star, they did not meet as often as they did during their student days. Both Rashid and Stefan have known Isabelle: Stefan for a little over a year and Rashid for a few months. Stefan, who is a member of the EU Brain Trust on security matters, facilitated Isabelle's recruitment at the EU as an interpreter. Stefan and Isabelle have collaborated on a couple of cases involving migrants from West Africa. Isabelle's knowledge of French enabled her to help the migrants from Mali. Rashid has recently been involved in assisting Muslims from Syria who had been stranded in Greece, to be settled in Germany. He used his celebrity as a Soccer star in helping leap over difficult bureaucratic hurdles as well as in persuading a family to provide temporary home for a Syrian couple with two young children.

The meeting in London was convened with the help of Miss Evelyn Sharpe of Amnesty International. It was held in the Headquarters of Amnesty with several people involved as participants and a few others as observers. Messes Bevan and Sullivan attended as participants.

Having made an opening statement, covering the agenda of the meeting, Evelyn Sharpe said that she had been hugely affected by the tragedy in what was formerly known as Burma, now called Myanmar. She spoke of the tragic plight of the Rohingya people there. A normally even-tempered person, not given to emotional outbursts, Evelyn Sharpe astounded everyone by openly crying incensed by the human tragedy of these people whom the world seems to have forgotten. She was particularly enraged, she said, by learning that the military junta ruling Myanmar, calling the claims of atrocities committed against the Rohingya as "Fake News." The military government, she said, claimed that the Rohingya burned down their own villages, staged massacres, left their children for dead. The military baldly claimed that this is the story of how 650,000 Rohingya Muslims fled Myanmar and left for Bangladesh. That is really the fake news," she said adding "It is the big lie of the kind that the Nazi propaganda machine used to employ to deceive the rest of the world as they sent six million Jews to the burning furnaces of the Holocaust."

She wiped the tears and angrily asked:

"Have you seen the trail of emaciated beings, skin and bones, trudging along miles of monsoon-flooded land? Across treacherous, mud-slicked hills?"

More silence followed, which added to the compelling eloquence of her speech. She tried to keep an even tone, with difficulty, as she looked at her notes. She said in a lowered voice:

"Each village along the way held the prospect of more danger..." She said she was reading notes derived from a BBC report and continued...

"Even in the chaos, it was clear the soldiers were bent on inflicting the most horror and fear possible, boasting that the Rohingya would never see their land again. Hillsides were wrecked; livestock was killed; and entire villages were systematically razed."

If they made it to the Bangladesh border, would that country's guards at the border turn them back? Should they risk a river crossing at night? None of the options were good. Hundreds would die trying to cross into Bangladesh, their overloaded rafts jolted by flood-swollen rapids, their bodies washed up on the sodden banks...

"On reaching Bangladesh, in a few months, they were placed on a once forested terrain in Bangladesh. Thousands of Rohingya waited in limbo for their fates to be decided by countries that want to have nothing to do with them."

The concluding part of her speech expressed the condition of people in a sprawling camp where hundreds of thousands of miserable refugees waited. She reported that the sickness and hunger of the early weeks in the camp had been mostly contained as aid groups gained their footing. But camps are not a permanent home, she said as she concluded, "and a miasma of untreated trauma, fresh exploitation and apprehension about the future set in."

She sat down almost exhausted as people applauded and a couple of the members of the audience wiped tears from their eyes.

Rashid rose suddenly and shouted at the top of his voice:

"Though I am Sudanese by origin, I feel connected to the suffering of the Rohingya. I feel I am a Rohingya, just as I am a suffering Syrian and Eritrean or Congolese." Rashid's outburst of empathy moved many members of the audience. Mr. Sullivan rose and asked:

"Did I hear you right that the Myanmar military said the report on the tragic plight of the Rohingya was "Fake News?"

"Yes, they did" Evelyn Sharpe answered.

"I wonder where they got such an expression? I seem to remember that a man sitting in the White House in Washington accused all news report he disliked as "fake news."

"You mean the master of chaos himself, of course!" a member of the audience exclaimed.

"Hear Hear!" shouted another, raising laughter.

Stefan Schmidt rose and asked Evelyn Sharpe, whom he knows well, if he could speak.

She said, "of course, Stefan. Go ahead."

"Thank you Evelyn, and thank you also for convening this strategy meeting. I think I speak for all concerned that this was a timely meeting for an overdue conversation about a burning issue, an issue, I might add, that has been pushed under the rug by almost all governments."

Then he added: "I associate myself with Rashid in openly and emphatically declaring my empathy for the suffering Rohingya and other suffering people. I, too, am a Rohingya!"

"As it happens, I have been invited by the Global Peace Institute in Washington to present a paper on peace and security in the Trump era. I look forward to an interesting and controversial encounter.

"You mean 'the Era of Chaos'?" interjected Mr. Sullivan, producing laughter.

Then Mr. Bevan rose to make a lengthy speech on the international law regarding refugees and the obligations of all governments. He commended his friend Mr. Sullivan for reminding the audience about Trump's chaotic government and its impact on international affairs. Then he asked the following with flourish:

"Should it surprise us to learn that Myanmar's dictators used the same words that the King of Chaos in Washington used when denying reports about Russia's interference in the 2016 elections of the United States? He also called Russia's interference in America's democratic process 'fake news.'"

The last participant to make a statement was Isabelle Negassa. When she rose and began speaking in a quiet, rather diffident tone, there was a general unease stemming from fear that she might stumble. Stefan who knew Isabelle better than anyone else in the audience, intervened to embolden her.

"May I interject for just a second? I hope you don't mind me interrupting, Isabelle."

Blushed and a little fearful, Isabelle said, "I don't mind," and sat down. "No, please don't sit down, Isabelle. Stay standing. What I wanted to do is to tell the audience: "Do not be fooled by this beautiful young woman's diffidence. Behind that seemingly fearful tone is a person of steel…Again, sorry for the interruption. Please continue, Isabelle. *Et bon courage, cheri.*"

The last phrase of endearment voiced almost in a whisper by Stefan to Isabelle was not lost on Evelyn Sharpe, who had a decent knowledge of French. Nor was the blushing it induced, clearly visible on Evelyn's face, lost on Isabelle, who knew that Stefan and Evelyn had known each other during their student days. Was there something there not discernible to the ordinary mortals in the audience?…

…It is possible that both Mr. Bevan and Mr. Sullivan saw the blushing in the faces of the two women. Mr. Bevan whispered something to Mr. Sullivan, who laughed loudly. And Mr. Sullivan said whimsically: "As to the possibility of whether something is going on here, *'we shall see what we shall see'*, as one Dickensian character said. Amid laughter, he added: "Was it Mr. Micawber or Mr. Pickwick? It doesn't matter which one of them said…"

In any case, Isabelle smiled and began to speak…

"First of all, I want to congratulate Evelyn for convening this meeting. I think it has been a very important gathering. Secondly, I must tell you, Evelyn, that your narrative of the plight of the Muslim people called Rohingya in Myanmar was such a touching story that I could not stop my tears throughout your speech. The story certainly touched my heart; words cannot express the feeling of empathy and sadness I felt. I have seen migrants in desperate situations here in the European continent, first in my own country, France, then in Germany and Belgium. But the graphic description of wanton violence and oppression of human beings by fellow human beings was to me incomparable and incomprehensible, even to those of us who have watched pictures of Syrian women and children in distress.

The story touched my special sensibilities because I have been affected by a personal loss from my childhood that has coloured my views and attitudes toward human folly and cruelty. Only a few of very close friends and members of my immediate family know the source of my views and attitudes. But I would like to add to what Evelyn brought to this meeting an experience I had the misfortune of going through last year in France. It was at the town of Calais in Northern France. The scenes I saw in Calais at a camp that came to be known as the *Jungle* concerned the stories of migrants from countries of Africa like Sudan, Eritrea, Ethiopia and others from Afghanistan, Iran and Pakistan. The common story linking the fate of these migrants involved circuitous journeys undertaken by them to reach the so-called haven of Europe, stories that have been documented at length since the summer of 2015. The details of the various stories often fail to acknowledge the ways in which migrants are held up and forced to find more dangerous alternatives. It omits the fact that people and organizations responsible for the life- threatening conditions under which migrants move across Europe It has been recorded that over the course of eight months of 2016, the number of people who reached European shores via journeys across either the Mediterranean or Aegean Seas stood at over 268,000.

Migrants in Calais

Let me now focus on a specific, personal experience I had in Calais to give you an idea that the so called haven can be and often is riddled with hazards of a different kind and involves living conditions that are not fit for humans. I was introduced to a small French charitable organization by the name of *Calais, Ouverture et Humanite* (Calais, Openness and Humanity). The organization has two missions: the first is to come to the help of refugees (or migrants) who live in Calais under conditions that are unbearable. The assistance comprises the collection and provision of gifts such clothes, shoes, shelter, tents and food. They do also, of course, collect money.

The second aim is to fight racism and 'stigmatization.' The organization has singled out a neo Nazi group calling itself *Sauvon Calais* that spreads hate rumors seeking to criminalise migrants. The organization writes to the local government authorities and to the office of District Attorney in the fight to stop such criminalization. Utilizing a portion of the money it obtains from supporters, it also aims at establishing an International Center for Exhibition of an Alternative Habitat (*Salon International d'Exposition de l'Habitat Alternatif*).

This is a project that aims at transforming the shacks to a pleasant living quarters. The idea is to make sure that the world looks upon this place not as a place of misery but rather as one of beautiful buildings with original vivacious colors. The government authorities want to hide the migrants placing them out of sight away from the city. We want this place to become an area of creative cultural exchange, a place where the migrants will be considered not as useless but instead it will be a place of which the city of Calais will have become a place in which humanity creates and shares. It will be a means by which the migrant populations will be put under conditions of dignity, and thereby enhance the fight against stigmatization.

Isabelle finished her statement with an impassioned appeal for a united and vigorous efforts on the part of all people engaged in the fight for human dignity. A Sublime Struggle.

The strategy meeting was concluded by a resolution issued by the participants to continue advocating the cause of refugees and migrants in general. A general appeal was launched to all concerned persons and groups to "gird their loins" and "continue the fight up to victory." The appeal called upon all concerned individuals and groups to expand and refine the methodologies of their struggle. Organizations like Amnesty International and similar Human Rights Organizations are especially urged to expand and intensify their activities focussing on a selective list of priorities and to target select people and groups. Regional bodies like the European Union especially should be targeted and challenged more vigorously.

Evelyn Sharpe gave a short closing speech thanking the participants and vowing to do her part to advance the struggle for human dignity and equality.

Chapter Three

THE ADVOCATE

On a Bright Morning in mid-May, a tall and good-looking man with partially grizzled longish hair, emerged from the Metro Station in downtown Washington. He stood outside the Metro entrance, surveying the surrounding area. Then, carrying a black brief case with his right hand, he walked toward K street. Upon reaching K street, he stopped, turned left and walked again for a few minutes. He stopped again, turned around and waited a little and raised his left arm hailing a passing car. He decided to wait a little, patiently.

Aged between mid-to-late thirties, he was well dressed, looking dapper with immaculately tailored light blue suit and sunglasses. It is Stefan Schmidt, one of the heroes of our story.

At last when he waved, a yellow cab stopped by and the driver shouted: "Where to?"

"To The Global Peace Institute on M street." "I know where that is."

"Good," the man said.

And as he entered and sat on the back seat, he gave the driver a piece of paper on which he had scribbled the address of his destination; and they drove slowly along K Street heading north.

Smiling shyly, the cab driver began giving his client some information. He spoke in a distinct British accent, which surprised the passenger. The cab driver declared that the area of the passenger's destination had become a place of great interest, "I mean in the last few days."

"Oh, how so?"

"Well, to begin with, it is now surrounded by demonstrators with the police cordoning off the area and keeping the crowd from entering the part of M street where your place of appointment is located. In fact, much of M street is shut down to protesters," he said adding that they may have to take a long detour to get to the place.

"Why is there demonstration now?" the man asked in a calm, baritone voice.

"I don't know the real reason, but I think it is something to do with war and peace. And democracy or something fancy like that."

"Something fancy!… By the way you speak English very well, and with British accent. May I ask where you are from originally?"

"I am from Ethiopia. And you?"

"I am from Germany and have come to attend a conference."

"Something to do with war and peace or democracy?" the cab driver inquired with a chuckle "And by the way you also speak impeccable English, and also with a British accent. How come?"

"My mother is English and I lived in England many years, studying." "I did too…study in England, I mean."

"No wonder. And what did you study?"

"Electrical Engineering at the Imperial College, London. For all the good it has done me."

"You mean it did not help you to land into a job here?" "Exactly… Yes, here in this 'Land of Opportunity!'" "Do I detect a note of disappointment?"

"You can say that again!"

When there was no response from his client, the cab driver added: "But that is a long story and you wouldn't be interested to know." "On the contrary, I would like to hear your story."

Driving along K Street, they had gone all the way past 16th Street, turned right on 17th Street and had driven ahead for about a quarter of a mile. But the whole area around M Street was indeed cordoned off. So, the driver was forced to take a longer route finally stopping a block away from the address where Global Peace Institute is located.

When they stopped near a small crowd that stood on the edge of the larger group of demonstrators, the passenger took out a carte de visite and handing it to the Ethiopian, said:

"My name is Stefan Schmidt. It is very nice meeting you."

He patted him on the back and shook his hand, saying, "Again, I am very glad to make your acquaintance Mr…"

"Kebede Hailu," the Ethiopian responded taking the card and examining it, for a brief moment.

"I hope you will land into a job befitting your education and qualifications. Listen, any time you come to Brussels, Belgium, where I am based, please call me. I really hope you will be able to fulfil your dream of finding a satisfactory work here. I really do. You must believe in yourself and fight on. Okay?"

"Okay, thank you, Herr Schmidt"

. . . .

The noise of the demonstrators was repeated, rising in a crescendo of different slogans. Having unexpectedly and emotionally responded to the young Ethiopian's apparent frustration, Stefan persuaded him to drive as close as possible to where the bulk of the demonstrators was.

The whole area was filled with a few hundreds, perhaps thousands of people carrying different kinds of posters, several of them shouting slogans.

Here are some samples, expressing the composition of the demonstrators and their driving passion reflecting their various causes.

El Pueblo Unido Jama Sera Vincido!…

…The People United Will Never Be defeated!

This was repeated several times, alternately in Spanish and in English

A young man wearing a red cap was acting as a conductor alternately pointing to the group shouting the slogan in Spanish, then to the group shouting in English. This exercise went on and on……

Kebede drove as near to M Street as he could and decided it was time to leave his passenger to his fate and depart. He said, apologetically:

"I am sorry, sir. I must leave you here and you will have to walk a couple of blocks."

"It is quite alright, thank you," Stefan said giving him a hefty tip in addition to the fare indicated on the meter.

"Thank you very much, sir. It has been a pleasure meeting you. Have a good day."

"You too, Mr. Kebede. Goodbye."

Stefan began pushing and squeezing through some of the people going as near as possible to the front where the action was.

There were many different slogans written in different colors, demonstrating the multiplicity of the causes and groups represented as a coalition in this demonstration.

Here are some samples:

WE BELIEVE:

NO HUMAN IS ILLEGAL! ...

...LOVE IS LOVE!...

...WOMEN'S RIGHTS ARE HUMAN RIGHTS!...

...HUMAN RIGHTS HAVE NO BORDERS!...

...BLACK LIVES MATTER!...

...MR TRUMP: BUILD BRIDGES, NOT WALLS! ...

...INJUSTICE ANYWHERE IS A THREAT

TO JUSTICE EVERYWHERE!...

...JUSTICE FOR THE ROHINGYAS!

UN SANCTION ON MYANMAR!

...STOP GENOCIDE IN CONGO!

...JUSTICE TO THE PALESTINIAN PEOPLE!

[Then there were the affirmative challenges]

...WE CANNOT BE SILENCED ANYMORE!

...WE WILL NOT BE LIED TO ANYMORE!...

...CORPORATE AMERICA: Turn Your Profits to Human Development and To Peace

[And to the delight of many Americans]:

FORTRESS EUROPE: OPEN YOUR HEART AND YOUR GATES TO REFUGEES!...

PRESERVE AND PROTECT DEMOCRACY AND HUMAN RIGHTS.!...

AFRICAN DICTATORS: TRUMPISM WILL NOT HELP YOU. YOUR DAYS ARE NUMBERED!

Stefan decided he had seen and heard enough. It was time to get into the conference, where he imagined the convenors must be busy putting the finishing touches to the meeting agenda and seating arrangement.

Having shown to the policeman at the entrance of the Global Peace Institute, his passport and letter of invitation to attend the conference, Stefan Schmidt walked into a tall building in M Street, where there was a beehive of activities teeming with people wearing name tags on their lapels.

Once inside the building, Stefan was met and greeted by an usher, who asked him for his ID card and evidence of his invitation to attend the conference. He showed his passport and the invitation letter after which the usher showed him to a room where a smiling, attractive, red-haired woman was enrolling the invitees. When his turn came, once more he was asked for his ID and letter of invite. "Your name sir?"

"My name is Stefan Schmidt", he answered and gave her his German passport.

"Thank you, sir," the woman said looking at the list of invitees.

"Yes, indeed, you are one of our distinguished guest speakers. A hearty welcome, sir," she said with a broad smile and showed Stefan the way to the conference hall. She followed him with her gaze until he disappeared into the building

The conference hall is large and shaped like an amphitheater. There was a large screen on which was displayed the theme of the conference, with

a list of the participants and the title of their respective presentations. A program brochure was also distributed to the public attending the conference.

The theme of the conference was conveyed as follows:

Conference Theme: Democracy, Justice and Peace in a Globalized Age:

Sub-themes: Implications for Liberal Democracy, The Rule of Law and Human Rights, with particular reference to the Policies and Actions of the US Administration.

CONVEYORS: The Global Peace Institute, ACLU, and Americans for Refugee Rescue and Assistance

LIST OF PARTICIPANTS AND THE TILES OF THEIR PRESENTATIONS

SESSION I: PRESIDENTIAL POWER UNDER THE US CONSTITUTION

10 am – 1 pm

- Professor Charles Boyd, *"From Royal Prerogative to Democra Accountability: What the Framers Laid Down as Core Values"*
- Dr. Donald Ross, *"In Defense of President Trump's Slogan 'M America Great Again"*

SESSION II: DOES GLOBALIZATION UNDERMINE PEACE AND DEMOCRACY

2 PM – 5 PM

- **Dr. Stefan Schmidt, *"Migration, National Security and Hum Rights: Old Problems, New Challenges***

SESSION III: MIGRATION, NATIONAL SECURITY AND HUMAN RIGHTS

ROUND TABLE DISCUSSION with all the Presenters participating.

7 pm – 9 pm
- **Chair: Ambassador Alan Roberts**

IV: CLOSING SESSION 10 am –11:30 am Guest Speaker (Name to be announced).

12—1:30 Lunch to guests and speakers

••••••••••••••••••••••••••••••

[Stefan's Paper to include the following issues: Poverty amid Plenty—
Disorder within Law and Order—Autocracy Replacing Democracy—
Oppression in the Name of Liberation—Resentment and Desperation—
Revolt and Destruction—Mass Incarceration—Disconnection In the
Digital Age—Flight from Violence—Refugees Everywhere—Timor
et Tremor (Fear and Trembling)—Inhumanity—Global "Dialogue
of the Deaf!"

What Is to Be Done? This question occupies or rather should occupy
all thoughtful persons, all sensitive souls offended by the absence of reason
and compassion that are supposed to undergird the founding charters of all
communities. Or are they mere founding myths to be abandoned at will?
Is there no binding rule forcing or inducing good behavior? No authority
of the Word to admonish and cause the healing of society's wound?

It is questions such as these that brought the protagonists of our story
together, bonded in a search for some answers. Having started with the
questions, they became engaged—willy-nilly— in a journey not knowing
of the hazards and the many subliminal twists and turns—not knowing
what fortune had in store for them.

No need to write about the presentations, except a brief outline of
Stefan's speech (outlined in bold type on page 25.)

Chapter Four

FATAL ATTRACTION

IT WAS AT THE END OF THE CONFERENCE, during the reception. Stefan had noticed the Red-haired beauty who had registered his name, had approached him with a warm greeting and followed him with a lingering gaze during much of the conference, wherever he happened to be, but especially at the close of his address. She was one of the few people who rushed up to the platform to shake his hand vigorously, showering on him praises about the quality of his speech.

"And I love that cute British accent," she had said in her husky voice.

At the end of the conference as the participants were leaving, Stefan was approached by a young man who told him he had a message for him and handed him an envelope. He opened the envelop to find a short note written in clear elegant calligraphy, with a small key attached to it.

The note said: "My address is 7920 Georgia avenue, NW., apartment # 8A, in Silver Spring MD. If you think I am being too bold and reckless, so be it. I have fallen for you, Stefan Schmidt, whether you like it or not. I am Irish and will not take "no" for an answer!"

He went out of the lobby to the veranda and sat on a guest sofa. He read the note again, breathing heavily stunned by the boldness of this seductive assault: for that is what it was, a verbally consummated seductive assault. He was astounded by the military precision of the message—or was it a command—and the unerring confidence. He was fascinated and disturbed at the same time. In a matter of minutes, a red-headed, beautiful woman had come to occupy his mind, temporarily replacing Isabelle who had dominated his consciousness the previous months and especially all week before his trip to Washington.

He was confused. He even wondered if it was some kind of witchcraft, a "black magic."

"Am I bewitched?" he muttered to himself.

"No!" he countered, "That is utter nonsense. I don't believe in that stuff.

And no one can replace Isabelle," he muttered.

A couple who were sitting nearby heard his muttering and looked askance at him, which caused him to bolt up and leave immediately. He started walking with no idea where he was heading. The walking helped clear his mind. He convinced himself that whatever he does, he should not lose grip of reality. But the reality now was that he could not deny the fact that an apparently determined (or maybe crazed) woman had captivated him with her daring and single-minded attack and he did not know how to respond to this daring attack.

He went to his hotel at the Washington Hilton and asked for a double order of scotch whiskey, black label, which a waiter brought him within minutes.

"Your Black Label, sir. Enjoy it," the waiter said, placing the glass with ice on the side on a tray and putting the tray on the side table beside his bed.

He thanked the waiter and tipped him.

After a few gulps of the black label, he felt calmed somewhat and decided to call Isabelle.

He thought of it as an antidote. It was past midnight Brussel time, but he thought she would not mind; in fact, he thought she should be happy. He dialed the number and waited for a few seconds. The answering machine came on with Isabelle's soft voice with its short message: "Please leave a message."

"Shit!" he shouted repeating the word in its German equivalent and hung up.

He decided to take a shower, where he lingered for a while letting the cold water drip and drip and thinking and thinking. Then he decided to get to bed and forget the whole damned thing. He tried desperately to sleep, counting about two dozen sheep. It was no good; he counted sheep before, and it never helped. He tossed in bed sleeplessly and sat up and started writing on what transpired, trying to make sense of it.

An hour later, the phone rang and he was surprised to hear Isabelle's voice come on.

"Salut Stefan. I just saw the number from your hotel. The answering machine registered your call. I just came in from a long meeting at the office. How are you?"

"I am well, but exhausted." "Hasn't the meeting ended?" "It ended today."

How many days are you staying in Washington and what about our plan? "You mean my assignment with the Ethiopian Mission to the UN? I have not forgotten. How could I? You would kill me if I did, right? "Right. So, when are you going to New York?"

"In two or three days. But I have secured an appointment with an official at the Mission."

"Not just an official. You must insist on meeting with the ambassador. I told you he was a close friend of my father and fellow freedom fighter."

"I know. I will ask specifically for a *tete-a-tete* with the ambassador. I promise."

"I trust you. *Bonne nuit, alors. Je t'embrasse.*" "*Mois aussi. Je t'adore*"

He felt somewhat relieved that he talked to Isabelle. Nonetheless, he could not rid of the thought of the strange situation with a unique challenge, which kept hammering at him. He tried to sleep again but could not. He looked at his watch, it was a little past eight pm.

He suddenly felt that he was assailed by a strange irresistible force was tugging at him. Nagging to be exact. The invisible force dragged him out of bed and he found himself obeying this invisible force that got him to get dressed and pushed him out of his bed and of his room. It was an experience he never had before, a real challenge and he had no clue how to meet it.

He found himself walking out of the hotel lobby. He called one of the cabs waiting outside.

How far is Georgia Avenue from here, he asked the driver. The driver asked for the number of the street. When he got it, he said, "I can get you there within 25 to 30 minutes, sir."

And so he did, more or less.

He paid the fare and hesitated a little before ringing the bell. There was no going back. He had no choice now except to ring the bell of the apartment— number 8.

It is as if the red head woman had been expecting him. But to his shock and surprise, the door opened but not by a woman but by a man, a tall grey-heard man of about fifty. Stefan started apologising…

"Did I ring at the wrong door?" he asked the man who was also embarrassed.

"Dr. Schmidt, I presume," said the man with a wry smile and opened the door wide open, stepping aside.

"Do come in, please. We have been expecting you." "We?" inquired Stefan.

"Yes, indeed. The entire group of professionals has been curious to know you and perhaps learn from you," cried the man with an affable laughter.

The man walked toward the middle of the room where there were three sofas and spare chairs beside or around the sofas. He sat on one of the sofas and, with his right hand, motioned Stefan to sit on another. Seated around a table nearby, were three young men of Stefan's age whom the older man introduced to Stefan. Stefan could not remember their names, but his attention was drawn to a bearded young man with an intense look whose unblinking eyes stared at you.

Stefan could not help remembering the name of that particular young man—Maximillian, Maxim or Max for short. They all expressed quiet words of welcome. Max added some words of praise about Stefan's presentation at the conference.

"I hope I am not interrupting a meeting? I was not…" Stefan said apologetically.

"Not at all," said the older man, cutting Stefan off before he could finish his sentence "You are not interrupting a meeting. And you are indeed welcome to join us in this earth-shattering rendezvous," exclaimed the man who seems to be given to hyperbole and enjoyed it.

"And my name is Robert Wyzanski."

"Mr. Wyzanski, I like a person with a sense of humor. But…"

…"Please call me Bob."

"Thank you, Bob. I am curious to know. Would you kindly explain to me in what sense our meeting is an earth-shattering rendezvous? Oh, and what is my role in it?"

As all of the men looked at one another and smiled expecting Bob to provide the answer, Stefan muttered to himself inaudibly: "What an odd experience!" "I think I am in a dream."

As if to answer his silent self-questioning, Miss Dorothy Shaw walked into the room, wearing her inimitable smile.

"Did I say "inimitable?" he asked himself silently. "No," he corrected himself. "Rather, it is at once a cajoling and intimidating smile."

Bob Wyzanski intruded into his silent wondering: "And here is the person you expected to open the door for you Mr. Schmidt." …I give you our distinguished colleague and co-director of our organization, Dr. Dorothy Ann Shaw."

Thus, Stefan Schmidt once more found himself staring at the woman who appeared to him to be more beautiful than when he first set eyes on her. She had the appearance of beauty queen upon whom a mysterious authority had been endowed by some mystic powers. She stood there gazing at him with a combination of an amorous feeling and a curious intellect. Her voice was most alluring when she said:

"Well, hullo there, my prince charming!"

And without any fuss or shame, she wrapped herself around him. The others watched without remark or any surprise, as if they had been used to this extraordinary experience.

Stefan felt slightly dizzy as she unwrapped herself from her embrace and looked into his eyes. And she pulled him gently and seated him by her side on one of the spare sofas.

All of a sudden Bob Wyzanski must have given the other men a signal for they stood and left the room one by one, followed by Bob himself…

Left by themselves the two people—an apparently love-stricken woman and a man who behaved like captive embraced each other and kissed passionately.

"Are you okay?" she asked him in a sexy voice, breaking from the embrace and looking into his eyes. Her voice sounded to him like the voice of a creature from outer space.

Suddenly, he broke away from her embrace and sat up. After some hesitation, wondering whether he was okay, he answered:

"I think I am okay. But you owe me a lot of explanations about all this."

He had regained his voice and he addressed her firmly. As she sat on his side, he stared at her intently and asked:

"Who are you, really?"...

She listened to him calmly with her never-failing charming smile. He continued in a somewhat subdued voice: "Why are you playing this strange game on me?... What the hell is going on?... Where is this place? Whose place is this palatial mansion?... Who are these people who were here and slipped out from your presence?"

"I will explain everything, I hope, to your satisfaction. Give me time, my sweet, brilliant, charming German who speaks with a cute British accent. You have charmed all the women and raised envy among the men, obviously."

"Well, that is a start," he tried to joke.

"Inside, somewhere in this palatial mansion as you rightly called it, is a dinning hall fit for kings and I am hereby inviting you to accompany me to go there, where everyone is waiting for us." She said this with a flourish, rising and stretching her arm and giving him her hand."

He took her hand and followed her.

As they walked arm-in-arm, he cried: "This is crazy. I didn't even know your name when I found myself willy-nilly coming and knocking at your door, or rather at what I believed to be your apartment door."

"Dorothy Shaw, at your service, sir. You and I it seems were destined to meet," she said with a flashing smile. "We were destined to meet to advance a Greater Cause than our individual selves."

"Really? And what, may I ask, is your role in all this? Obviously, it is a critical role, because you brought me here, or rather you magically caused me to come here."

Suddenly, as if he was struck by thunderbolt, he stopped and cried: "Dorothy! Why have you entrapped me? Who or what is behind this Greater Cause?

She gave a short laugh that did not contain any irony, and felt the need to respond:

"You were not entrapped, my dear sir. I did not pull you by some magic."...

...Then she added slowly framing her words: "Destiny has brought us together."

... "Or the hand of God, if you wish... "Do you believe in God Dr. Schmidt?"

"I am a believer in Goodness."

"That is not an answer to my question... Do you believe in God?" "Am I facing the rack now? Are you an agent of the Inquisition?"

"You know I am not. I am not even a Catholic. My Irish ancestors came from the Protestant region of Ireland. They were thorough Lutherans. I take it you are not a believer in a Higher Being. But can I assume your belief in Goodness puts you on the side of the Angels."

"As you wish," he answered sounding like a defeated man.

"Come on, don't sound defeated. This is an exciting adventure of ideas and action that you and I will be engaged."

"All I can say is, we shall see."

She wrapped her arms around him, and they walked side by side. She is almost as tall as Stefan, without high heels.

They arrived at the door of the dining hall where she stopped and gave Stefan a quick kiss smack on the lips before opening. She declared:

"And Tonight's Dinner Event is a Preview of Tomorrow's Historic Debate."

A "Business" Dinner at the Science Academy

When the two entered the Dining Hall, those assembled in the hall, about thirty in number, rose ceremoniously and there followed an explosion of applause in the hall like a thunderclap.

"Please sit down all," cried Dorothy and pulled Stefan toward the head table. As the two of them sat at the head table where Dr. Wyzanski was seated, Dorothy stood up and clapped her hands.

"Attention everybody!" There was a murmur and Dorothy clapped her hands again and repeated:

"Dear friends and colleagues,"...

...She waited till the murmur of wonder and surprise died down. As if thirsty, she filled a glass of water and drank a little from it...

..."I am sure some of you, perhaps most of you are wondering: "Who is this gentleman I have brought with me to join us in this banquet, this special dinner convened in the name of the Committee On Social Sciences of the American Academy of Sciences.

The dinning hall was a large area inside the mansion, adorned with paintings and large portraits of former Presidents and Board Members of the Academy. At the center of the hall is an oval-shaped, large mahogany dining table. Seated around the table are some thirty people, mostly men in casual dress. At the head table four chairs are placed, two of which were reserved for the two co-directors of the Special Committee on Social Sciences, Drs. Wyzanski and Shaw. The respective names and titles of the wo officers are written in large letters and fastened to their respective chairs:

Robert Wyzanski, Ph.D., JD and MSc. (Econ. Chicago), and Dorothy Ann Shaw, LL.B. (Oxon), Ph.D. Anthropology, (Harvard).

To each are also added: "*Distinguished Fellow, American Science Academy (Division of Social Sciences).*"

Dorothy continued her introduction of Stefan:

"As I said, people are wondering about our surprise guest. His name is

Stefan Schmidt, Ph.D. (Lond) and MA in History (Heidelberg). Those of you who attended the conference this last few days at the Peace Institute couldn't have failed to be suitably impressed by his erudition and command of history and international affairs, all delivered with ease and charm in his British accent. Let me add that the women in particular, including yours truly, were absolutely charmed by his wonderful delivery in that cute accent. (Laughter)...

…What it is that fascinates American women, in particular, by the British accent, I don't really know, but I do know it does. Even in some American advertising, like that affecting little lizard with the British accent has done well for the Life Insurance company, GEICO. Other imitators have followed though not to the same degree of success…

…Anyway, we are joined here tonight by a distinguished scholar and activist who has some strong views on a range of issues as was demonstrated during his presentation a couple of days ago. Now is not the time to go there. Now is a moment of greeting, so I will not bother you all with details on that matter. I hope and trust this will be adequately covered during our debate tomorrow. I will just inform you that Stefan occupied an equivalent role in the European Union; I mean equivalent to those held by Bob and I—Not quite the same, but equivalent. Perhaps Stefan will enlighten us on that point as well."

…So, for now, please help me welcome our distinguished guest by raising your glasses to drink to the health of Dr. Stefan Schmidt.

Glasses were quickly filled with the wine in the several bottles arrayed on the table, and all raised their glasses with an expectant gaze fixed on Stefan.

"To Dr. Stefan Schmidt!" all cried raising their glasses. And Stefan, who had also been served with a glass of wine, raised his glass and smiled in appreciation. He and Dorothy clinked their glasses.

"To your health and happiness, Dear Stefan!" Dorothy said quietly.

"And to yours!" he responded simply, shyness and bewilderment overpowering him on how quickly things happened. He has not quite recovered from the spiralling way things happened in which he had been caught practically unaware, as if by magic.

Dinner was served by a trio of well-dressed waiters, presumably hired from a hotel, judging by their uniform attire. The first serving was a choice of vegetable soup or minestrone followed by salad. The main dish consisted of a choice between beef steak, Hungarian Goulash, or fillet of Sword fish—all with side dishes of vegetables, carrots. For Dessert, there was Apple pie, with Ice Cream, or variety of fruits.

Dorothy recommended the Hungarian Goulash or the Beef Steak, choosing the Goulash herself. For starters, she chose and recommended to Stefan the minestrone.

Stefan chose Minestrone and the Fillet of Swordfish with vegetables. Except for the sound of crockery and occasional clinking of the wine glass, everybody ate quietly. There was a soothing background music, mostly classical consisting of violin quartets.

After about half an hour, another clinking of a glass was sounded, and Dorothy's voice came on:

"Hullo everyone. I hope you are all enjoying your superb dinner. I thank the Apollo Restaurant for preparing a delicious dinner and the excellent service of their fine waiters."

She claps and all follow her with enthusiasm.

The young man by the name of Max raised his hand and asked to speak. "Yes, Max. You wish to speak?

"I just want to second your words of welcome, and also to say that I was particularly struck by his fine presentation at the conference. Might I ask him to indulge us in a brief statement on his work and in what way our two organizations might collaborate in the future.

Dorothy looked at Stefan anxiously and smiling with eagerness. "Speech!... Speech!... Speech" cried a few voices in support of Max's suggestion "Stefan?" inquired Dorothy quietly.

"Is this really necessary?" It was Stefan trying to wriggle out of the request, but finally got up, pushed his chair back, cleared his throat and started speaking.

..First of all, I must say that I am deeply touched by this enormous and undeserved attention showered upon me."

"It is a well-deserved attention," cried Max who might have downed two or three glasses of the wine

"Thank you, Max. I am humbled and hope to live up to your expectations."...

...Well, where to begin...

...My work at the EU Headquarters... Right now and for the past two years, my work has focussed on migration issues in relation to security."...

...I happen to believe that the issue of migrants is the most pressing problem facing humanity...

...In this respect, I believe there is one significant difference between European and American perspectives on the incidence and impact of migration, a difference grounded in history and geography...

...Historically, America has benefited from—indeed, it was built on— immigration: immigrants came from Europe and elsewhere to build this amazing nation—millions of them, bringing with them their hopes and aspirations and their various skills. The immense geographic space, and the expansive and generous mentality it involved was an important pull factor, to use the terminology of sociology. America is thus still a welcoming place with immigration laws regulating and accommodating the flow of migrants to this country...

...By contrast, Europe is geographically constrained by its smaller space. Europe is also the outcome of a long history of division, competition and wars. In view of that history of division and competition, the creation of the European Union is a remarkable achievement. There is, of course, the legacy of Judeo-Christian ethos and the culture of universally recognized core values at the heart of that ethos. At the height of their universalizing operation, such core values had indeed caused the emergence of a unified Christendom under the aegis of the Roman Catholic Church. But that proved short-lived, as the individual components of the nation states asserted their individual sovereignties and strained the applicability of the universal ethos. Thus, unified larger unity transcending national division gave way to the assertion of separate national entities. It was thus that the idea of a sovereign nation-state took a firm hold in the minds of European leaders, leading to periodic conflict rooted in competition and overriding ambition of some of the larger nation states...

...In the meantime, the industrial revolution of England, preceded and, in some respects, accompanied by political and social revolutions, changed the character of European societies forever. Driving that multi-layered revolution was the idea of individual liberty and emancipation of the suffering masses of populations, working and living in mass misery, and earning pittance as wages under inhumane conditions. The Eighteenth Century Age of Enlightenment had also produced the idea of individual self-determination as well as eventually the democratic idea and institutions. The American Revolution was, of course the

contemporary of the French Revolution, being separated by a mere thirteen years...

... All these developments were accompanied with or resulted in political organizations by the affected masses. England had become in this respect a country leading the industrial revolution with all the attendant social and economic problems I just outlined. It was also a time when great minds like those of Adam Smith, Jeremy Bentham, John Stuart Mills, Karl Marx and other philosophers and social critics, including those in continental Europe, made their immense contributions to human progress.

...Fast Forward to the Twentieth Century...I must also note in passing the devastation wrought by two World Wars, which were caused by competitions among the great European states like Germany, England and France. Complicated by the drive for imperial expansion, these competitions provoked two devastating wars, in which America played a crucial role in defeating Germany. America's role, particularly in defeating Hitler's Nazi regime is rightly regarded as saving Western Democratic Civilization. America also played an equally crucial role in stemming the tide of Soviet Communist ambition in Europe and elsewhere.

...What has all this history to do with the issue of migration?

...Well, concerning migration in Europe, we begin with refugees displaced by the 1939-1945 war, millions of them. The Geneva Convention on Refugees was signed in 1951 in response to the exodus of European refugees, who had been displaced by war as well as survivors of genocide and persons who were truly fearful of being victims of genocide...

...A key phrase in the Convention is: "Well-founded Fear of Persecution..." And the millions of refugees fleeing Syria, and many parts of Africa, especially the Horn of Africa and North Africa are covered under the provision of the Refugee Convention...

...It is worth emphasising that though there is a general commitment to the Refugee Convention and other international agreements on refugees or migrants, Europeans have been subject to a growing popular resentment and hostility toward refugees and migrants in general, complicated by security issues related to the emergence of Islamic extremists like ISIS. Coincidentally, and in some respects due to such

resentment and hostility, Right Wing extremist parties have gained ground in many parts of Europe, including Italy, Poland, Austria, Hungary and even France and Germany. It is worth stressing, however, that this development falls short of negatively affecting the major political parties in Germany and France, even though some Right Wing parties have gained seats in Germany's House of Representatives. The leaders of Germany and France are on record in opposing Right Wind political agitation against migrants, especially those from Islamic countries. The courageous statement by both Chancellor Angela Merkel of Germany and President Macron of France on this issue have been truly remarkable...

...Amid the unstoppable volume of migration to Europe, several incidents of migrants being stranded at sea, with some facing drowning, and the continuing agitation against migrants by Right Wing politicians has raised the question whether, left unresolved, such crises might lead to the demise of the EU. It is a question that has become a topic of speculation and continual commentary among European leaders, both practicing politicians and opinion leaders...

...Let me conclude by stressing that despite the problems related to migration, the governments of Europe, both individually as well as European Union are deeply committed to resolving this and related problems satisfactorily, and are determined not to let this or similar problems affect the stability or integrity of the Union...

I think I will stop here...I don't think I was expected to speak about the problem of migration as regards the United States of America. Perhaps tomorrow, and I hope some colleagues here will say something to enlighten me about the migration problem as it affects America.

Thank you. Prolonged Applause.

Dorothy, flushed with excitement, rose to speak. It was a short comment. "Colleagues, I am sure that you now understand why I was excited about this man. And I know we will all hear more from him tomorrow. Now for the questions or comments.

The dinner and the wine must have had an effect on the assembled; for no hand was raised. They were probably in hurry to go to their beds and prepare or tomorrow's meeting.

Stefan certainly felt relieved.

A Strange Affair

After the guests left, Dorothy showed Stefan to where he would sleep—to a large guest house with a Queen-size bed and well-furnished otherwise. She didn't even question in her own mind that he would show reluctance to spending the night there. Nor had he considered going back to his hotel after the sumptuous banquet and following the lion's treatment he received from these interesting people none of whom he hardly knew.

Having installed him in the guest bedroom, Dorothy expected a warm embrace. So, she went ahead wrapping her arms around his shoulders and kissed him. Her desire to spend the night with him was reflected in her expressive face which was all smiles. Alas! She was to be rudely disappointed for Stefan showed an unexpected resistance. He did not respond to her kiss, breaking away from her embrace instead. Her desire to spend the night with him, which she had assumed would be accepted by him without question, was thus coldly rebuffed. Stefan slowly and gently broke away from her. Her reaction was instantaneous, visible in her blushed and angry visage. She did not expect to be thus frustrated, an expectation based on Stefan's earlier willingness to be seduced.

"Hell hath no fury like a woman spurned!" he thought remembering his Shakespeare readings. A part of him had hesitated though he resolved in favor of stopping her irresistible advances. What will she do, Stefan silently wondered. After her extraordinary behaviour with her bold attempts to seduce him and her profusion of accolades, he too was equally surprised by his own reaction. It seemed as if some hidden force from within wanted to correct the earlier submission to seduction. It seemed that from the depth of his perplexed soul, he found the strength to reject her at least this time.

Her immediate reaction was visible in her reddened face. She made an effort not to show her frustration with a few proper words. "That is okay, Stefan dear. We will see you tomorrow morning at breakfast," she said as she left the room. But he could see her anger and frustration and felt a little sorry for her. Some two hours later, after he had just dozed off, about two o'clock in the morning, she knocked at the door twice and opened it.

She turned the light on and stood there in her yellow transparent night dress. Before she came rushing to jump in bed with him, he was awakened enough to take a full measure of this sudden invasion. Stefan gazed at her transfixed by her beautiful body. He could see through the night gown her two breasts looking like small ripe apples.

Before she slipped into the bed and covered his body with wild caressing and kissing, he caught a glimpse of her remarkably beautiful body and good looks with her fair skin and red hair. Her two breasts stood as if challenging him to a duel. She was tall and had a strikingly well-proportioned body. But more than her physical beauty, Stefan was impressed by her strong character, decisive and independent-minded with a strong sense of self-reliance. These characteristics of her character were obviously known and understood by all her colleagues none of whom seemed to raise questions about her behavior toward Stefan, including her embrace and kiss in their presence.

After a passionate lovemaking, they lay side by side exhausted and naked. Looking at her at close quarters, Stefan noticed certain details about her beautiful face. Her face was radiant with alluring freshness and vigor for a woman of her age—early thirties at most. Her mid-sized mouth with its full red lips was alluring, though when she raises her chin, she assumes an air of haughtiness and even arrogance. In fact, arrogant she is not. From the first day he saw her when she registered his name for the conference, she never struck Stefan as arrogant; to the contrary, she struck him as good-natured and very friendly.

Having passed a hectic evening at the dinner party, Stefan had looked forward to a restful night. His plan was to rise early in the morning after a restful night and go to his hotel and to phone Isabelle. He had felt a deep sense of guilt while he was carousing and had wished to make it up to her by an early call the following morning. He felt keenly the need to call Isabelle and had thought of calling a taxi service to take him to the Washington Hilton Hotel.

As it happened, Dorothy put an end to that intention by dallying most of the morning with him in bed where they made love again, before dawn and decided to linger on.

"What about the Great Debate?" Stefan reminded Dorothy, somewhat anxiously.

"It is not until late afternoon and all logistical questions have been Taken care of."

They were silent for a few minutes and she rolled over and pushing the bed sheets away, asked him nonchalantly:

"Are you ready and eager to do battle, Stefan?"

"Well, I am ready to present the case for the need of an international legal and political order."

"Your challenger is a dedicated Trump supporter as we all are in my committee on Social Science."

"You are a Trump supporter?" asked Stefan with incredulity.

"Yes I am. And tonight, my guy will give you a run for your money." "Wait a minute. You are not serious?"

"If you mean about being a Trump supporter, I am dead serious." At that point, Stefan bolted out of bed and stood up…

And he started looking at her as if she was a stranger he had never met. He looked seriously troubled. He had never expected that he would wake up confronting such perplexity. He thought of quickly getting dressed and quietly walk out of the place and forget about the debate planned for the evening.

As if Dorothy read his mind, she also got up, put on her gown and confronted him and was about to speak when he beat her to it saying:

"If you are one of Trump's supporters, then why all this intense and seemingly romantic interest in me? Or did you assume I was a Trump supporter?"

She could see he was angry and perplexed; so, she gently took him into her arms and led him to the sofa where she sat him down. Looking him in the eyes intently but using her soft sexy voice said:

"Stefan my dear, you are a brilliant man and I assume you have had some worldly experience. I also confess that I saw you as a man of great promise and wanted to recruit you to our cause. That was the political side of me. Then there is the personal. You know by now that I have fallen in love with you. We need to separate the two issues."

He told her point blank that her attempts to recruit him are vain attempts. They were silent for a moment and she asked him: "By the way, who is Isabelle?"

"She is a friend and colleague in Brussels. Why do you ask?"

"You were calling her in your sleep. You seemed to be anxious or annoyed.

Is she a girl friend or maybe your wife?"

"Not a wife. But she is dear friend, a special human being. She is an important part of my life."

"Do you love her?"

"I love her, but I am not in love with her, if you know what I mean." "Yes, I think I do. ..."

"Shall we have breakfast here in the room?" "Good idea. I am famished..."

More silence and Stefan sighed, and she turned to face him, wondering why he sighed.

"I hope you are still going to be in the great debate tonight." "What made you think I may not be in it?"

"Well, our recent conversation has not been exactly encouraging."

"Why, because I said I am not a Trump supporter? Aren't you in favor of a debate or serious conversation about such an important subject? I am ready to present my case. I expect your guy will challenge me as much as I will challenge him. And as they say in the boxing business, may the best man win."

"All I can tell you is that he will be good match, and he will give you a good run for your money."

"I am on the side of keeping the world order, imperfect as it is. Anyone who believes in separating America from the world system is not a builder. Slogans like ***America First*** are destructive of a system that has taken incredibly stupendous efforts and investment in life and treasure to build. America helped to fashion and led for over half a century a world order that has ensured peace and stability, more or less. It is not a perfect system; no system is perfect, but the alternative is nightmarish disorder."

"But Americans have sacrificed more lives and treasure to build and maintain governments of Europe and other parts of the world. And we have received in return not gratitude but resentment."

"Is that why you are Trump's supporter?"

"That and his dedication to make America great again."

"Do you really believe in that simplistic slogan—***Make America Great Again?***"

"It is simple but not simplistic. You would not dismiss this clear and concise summing up of America's problems if you know how the working half of the American population lives. America's first-class manufacturing has been taken over by China and other countries. Our once thriving industries that were once the envy of the world have suffered a fatal blow and once vibrant communities have turned into ghost towns and rust belts. I grew up in one of such communities.

He answered her: "America still leads the world in industrial production and the creativity of its people still keep her ahead in intellectual property."

After a while he added emphatically: "I am still intrigued that a highly educated person like you is a Trump supporter. I need to know what makes people like you believe in such a man."

"To understand Trump's appeal, you need to travel to areas where the condition of people's lives among the working class and 'Blue Collar' Americans have suffered. Trump stands for the forgotten working people that the Establishment politicians, both Republican and Democrat, and their financial supporters have ignored."

"Well, I doubt if you can convince people in Europe that separating America from the rest of the world, and from Europe in particular, will help what you call the forgotten people in America."

"I am sure Europe can take care of itself." "And the rest of the world?"

"Well, China, India and the other emerging economies can also take care of themselves. In fact, they should welcome being themselves uncontrolled by us and you Europeans."

"And Africa and the other parts of the world that your Trump calls shitholes?"

"Now you are being emotional and offensive."

"Offensive? Who is being offensive? Are you denying that your Trump called these countries shitholes?"

He raised his voice a few decibels when asking these questions. He also had sat up and began putting his clothes on.

"Why are you suddenly putting your clothes on?"

He did not answer her but continued dressing up and put his shoes on. She noticed that his mood had changed. His face had also flushed and he stood up as if he wanted to walk out.

"Stefan, what is going on? Why are you angry. Our breakfast is coming in a matter of minutes."

"Sorry, I must go now. I will have breakfast at the Hilton," he said walking toward the door.

She rushed ahead of him toward the door and stood between him and the door.

"Dorothy, stand aside and let me go, please."

She would not budge, so he made a gesture to push her out of his way. She resisted and when he pushed her hard, she slapped him so bad he staggered... He looked at her half in in disgust and in dismay. He shook his head and simply said:

"You are pitiful!" He then walked slowly past her, opened the door and walked out...

Dorothy emitted a cry mixed with anger and regret. She opened the door and pleaded with him calling him to come back.

"Stefan, come back right now...Stefan, please come back and let us eat breakfast together... Please, Stefan!"

He did not respond. He walked away—out of the building and to street to call for a taxi...

At the Hilton Hotel, he went into his room and rolled on his bed, deeply troubled. He thought of placing a call to Isabelle but was not sure what to tell her. He could lie saying he was detained by work. He would hate himself if he did that. Isabelle has a sixth sense like many women and would see through him. So he changed his mind. He felt that he was losing his mind torn between his loyalty to Isabelle and his strange attraction to the red- headed Irish beauty who has also obviously fallen for him as she admitted in public among her co-workers…

…He went into a reverie, remembering every detail of the previous night, especially the incredibly wonderful, feverish lovemaking, including her moaning and groaning as he penetrated her and continued through a prolonged passionate love making.

He knew that a pleasurable experience had befallen on him unlike anything he had known before. At the same time, he recognized clearly that, wonderful as it is, this experience is not really sustainable. It goes against the grain— against his basic instinct of decency and loyalty that has guided his action in all important relations both at the personal and the collective levels. He knew this to be a basic element of his psychological make-up.

He thus began to feel a profound sense of shame for having so easily fallen victim of Dorothy's seductive assault, going all the way to the consummation of a sexual relationship in a matter of hours.

"Am I being too old-fashioned?" he wondered. "After all this is the twenty- first century. Don't I have autonomy and the right of self-determination?… Ha ha!"

As soon as he posed this imaginary rationalization, he knew it was false reasoning.

"Who do you think you are kidding, Mr. Schmidt," he asked himself with a bitter laughter, being conscious of his resort to American English— who do you think you are kidding."

The most shame-inducing part of the previous night's recollection was the way he had allowed Dorothy to manipulate him into doing and saying whatever she wanted, including the long disquisition of history to explain the relevance of putting a discussion of migration in a historical context. There is nothing wrong doing that in and of itself; after all, his remarks were based on sound historical narrative and reasoning. What made it shameful was the fact that he appeared like a readily employable weapon at the hand of a woman who later turned out to be a Trump supporter.

"But you didn't know at the time that she was a Trump supporter" said an inner voice, in extenuation of his behavior. But that inner voice seeking to excuse his behaviour is countered by the opposed argument that her being for or against Trump it not relevant to the issue of his guilt.

His guilt is in being easily suckered by her seductive assault in a matter of hours without putting up any resistance.

"Should I confess all this wrong doing to Isabelle?" He muttered to himself…

He remembered that he must call Isabelle. So he put the self-flagellation and remorse to rest and picked up the phone to place a call to Brussels.

"*Salut ma Cherie!*" he said when her voice came on.

"*Salut Stefan. Comment va-tu?* I was waiting for you to call all morning. It is now past 4 o'clock our time. Are you okay?"

"Yes, I am okay, just tired and a little frustrated by some things. I will explain to you when I come back."

"What things?"

"I will explain when we meet in a few days. I will go to New York tomorrow to do my errand. By the way, I need to know the name of the Ambassador of Ethiopia at the United Nations Mission. I forgot to ask you when I talked to you yesterday. Do you know his name?"

"I used to; my mom used to talk about him. And my dad was very fond of him. Apparently, he is a very funny person, as well as kind and loyal. I will ask mom and will call you with the info tonight, or first thing tomorrow. Okay?"

"Okay. And how are things in Brussels?"

"Nothing of importance. The EU is angry at Trump's tariffs and the big guns are consulting how to respond. Can you raise a stink there at the conference and also (on my own behalf) tell the SOB to go to Hell?!"

Stefan gave a hearty laugh and simply said: "That's my girl!"…

And after another laugh, he added improbably: "I will do my best."
"Everyone is angry and some think he does not mean it. They believe

Trump must be bluffing because the tariff will start a trade war. And historically, trade wars are a prelude to real war. What do you think?"

"I am afraid he is not bluffing. He is already boasting that trade war is good for America because the other governments will submit to America's will."

"Well, Europe will retaliate as I think China and other countries negatively affected by the tariffs will retaliate. They are confident that Trump is a braggart and will finally regret his decision and pull back."

"I hope they are right, but I don't think so. His resentment and belief that the world is robbing America is deep-rooted."

"To change the subject," Stefan said: "I am going to debate these issues tonight against a Trumpist true believer who will hold forth in defense of *'Making America Great Again'* and other nonsense."

"Well give it to them Stefan Stefanovitch!" "I will Isabelle Negassovitch!"

"I will call later today or early tomorrow to tell you the name of the ambassador. Okay?"

"Okay. *A bien tot, alors.*" "*A bien tot.*

Chapter Five

FROM VERBAL DUEL TO A VIOLENT EPISODE

The evening of the same day, there was general excitement among people who had attended or participated in the International Conference convened by the Global Institute for Peace. Also affected by the excitement were the members of the American Science Academy, particularly the members of the Committee on Social Sciences. The debate was conceived and organized by the said Committee.

The excitement is related to the debate scheduled to be held on the subject: President Donald Trump's Slogan, *'America First—The Rest Will Follow'*

Speaking for the Motion is Dr. Donald Ross. Dr. Ross teaches history in one of the colleges in Ohio.

Speaking in Opposition is Dr. Stefan Schmidt. Dr. Schmidt works at the European Union. He specialises in issues related to migration and security.

Both speakers presented Papers at the recently held International Conference on peace convened by the Global Institute for Peace

Venue: The Assembly Hall of the Global Institute

Facilitating the Meeting: Dr. Robert Wyzanski. Assistant Facilitator: Dr. Dorothy Ann Shaw

The facilitators are seated in the middle of a large table at the center of elevated platform facing the amphitheater. Dr. Ross is seated on the right corner of the table. Dr. Schmidt is seated to the left corner.

Dr. Wyzanski opens the meeting by striking the gavel and asking the members of the audience for their attention.

"It gives me great pleasure to act as facilitator of this important debate. We are indeed fortunate to have two outstanding scholars with us today willing and ready to engage in a debate of great interest to us all. The first speaker will be Dr. Ross, after which Dr. Schmidt will follow with his answer. Each presenter will speak for twenty minutes, to be followed by ten minutes each of closing statement.

There will be no applause or any form of interruption during the presentations. There will be plenty of time for the members of the audience to participate in the form of questions or short statements. Assisted by Dr. Shaw, who will keep time, I will allow more time, not longer than one minute for each question or statement by members of the audience. I must repeat that there will be no interruption during the presentation; and certainly, there will be no personal attacks of any kind directed at the speakers. I expect all to observe the rule of civility and decency.

With these words of admonition, I now ask Dr. Ross to speak in favor of the proposition:

America First—The Rest Will Follow

Dr. Ross rose and bowed to the Chair

Mr. Chairman, Dr. Shaw, Honored Guests, Ladies and Gentlemen

I stand in defense of the proposition: America First and commend it to you as a historic necessity for America to look after its own affairs and let the rest of the world look after their affairs. For far too long, we Americans have been taken for granted, abused and robbed of our hard-earned taxpayer's money. And what did we get in return? What have we received for our generosity and friendship to a world that has responded in resentment and even wanton attack by citizens of nations that we helped prosper? I will not bore you with statistics of the billions of dollars of assistance we poured to their treasuries and financed the training arming and equipping of their military. Nor do I need to remind you that we saved them from tyranny and despotism by spending blood and treasure in two devastating World Wars, as well as in regional wars and inter-and intra-state conflicts.

Our leaders touted international obligations in defense of their intervention in numerous wars in pursuit of wrong policies and disastrous politics. Perhaps the most unfortunate example of our Quixotic adventure in foreign wars is the Iraq war. The Iraq war stands as a monument of the most disastrous intervention in which we sacrificed precious lives and billions worth of treasure for nothing. That it was waged on the basis of a false assumption of defense against nuclear arms should act as a warning against fake news that is also part of the armory of our politics today. The on-going war in Afghanistan is another example, as is the tragic story of Syria that we abandoned in the end inviting Russia to move in into the vacuum. Syria in particular is a tragic example of America's mindless intervention in the affairs of other nations in the name of international obligations. The case of Syria should be a lesson—an expensive one—in terms of wasted effort, lives and treasure, even though the lives lost are Syrian caused by a cruel dictator. America fumbled and gambled in Syria. And lost its prestige with nothing given in return.

All the wrong policies and disastrous politics followed by previous governments were led both by Democrats and Republicans.

Enter Donald Trump.

As a result of a historic election that has been maligned by opponents of President Trump using fake news, Donald Trump came to power to the surprise of everybody who took him as a bombastic charlatan. Whether they like it or not Donald Trump won the presidency and vowed to shake things, to drain the swamp in Washington and to make America Great Again. It will be an uphill fight because all the inertia of tradition and vested interest is arrayed against him. The globalists, the supporters of the international economic and political order, will tell you that all our financial and security interests are tied to the global order and that America, which played a key role in creating and maintaining that order, is made up of intricately connected web of interests. Ergo, America cannot separate itself from such a global order without damaging its interests in a fundamental way. That is what they will tell you. And they contend that an open and fair-trading system and open borders regulated by law must, therefore, be maintained.

Let us take open borders, for example. The proponents of open borders claim that it benefits America to allow immigrants to come regularly in accordance with the appropriate US immigration law. In support of their argument, they make reference to the historical fact that America was built by immigrants. President Trump, on the other hand, believes that such open-door policy has harmed America by allowing criminals to slip in and disturb our security and wellbeing. He wants to build a wall along our southern border with Mexico to stem the tide of such immigration. Moreover, in the wake of the attack on America on Nine/Eleven, American security has been challenged by the rise of Islamic fundamentalist groups like ISIS. These extremist Islamic forces openly say that America is their number one enemy and foster and encourage attacks on all things American, be they institutions of government or commercial and other economic institutions.

When he passed a policy aimed at controlling or restricting the immigration of people from Muslim countries, the President faced enormous challenges by people citing constitutional and legal principles in support of their flimsy arguments. It is my sincere hope that the Supreme Court will put an end to these spurious claims and arguments, now that the balance in the Court is definitely tipped toward the conservative wing. This new balance is thanks to the President's single minded efforts to fill the Court with the right people.

And while speaking of the role of the Supreme Court as guardian of the Rule of Law, the Crown Jewel of our constitutional order, let me say a few words on other matters on President Trump's domestic agenda. Even though his efforts to change Mr. Obama's disastrous Health Care legislation, the President has vowed to make another attempt to change it, if he can obtain the right number of supporters from his own party. He will definitely defeat all efforts to bring about a European style socialist health care system that diminishes private enterprise and individual rights. I also applaud Mr. Trump's heroic defense of the Second Amendment's right to gun ownership, despite the Left ideologue's attempts to use some tragic incidents in which mentally unbalanced citizens have been involved in killing innocent people.

In conclusion, I support the proposition and proudly defend Mr. Trump's policy and actions in protecting this great nation to make it greater.

The chair then asked Dr. Stefan Schmidt to present the case against the Proposition.

Stefan rises and bows to the Chair.

He then says to much laughter from the audience: "Is this the best that the Proponents of the Motion can make?—WAFFLE!…WAFFLE!…WAFFLE!!?….After the laughter subsides, he continues:

Mr. Chairman, Dr. Shaw, Honorable Guests, Ladies and Gentlemen I stand in opposition of the Motion.

With all due respect, I must say that the Proponent has failed to make a case for the Proposition, which I must say is doomed from its very beginning. Why do I say that?

First a brief historical context as to why Donald Trump succeeded in capturing the power of the American presidency where other candidates in his cohort failed. Donald Trump came to power for the same reason that other populists in Europe and elsewhere got elected. Voters were disgusted by a governing elite that seemed corrupt and out of touch from the ordinary folks. In Europe, for example, people felt swamped by waves of immigrants, frustrated by economic stagnation as well as disgusted by the cultural values of cosmopolitan elites. Instead of addressing people's problems, governments like those of Italy's Berlusconi, for example, the leaders degraded public discourse with extremist views, while weakened government structures were beset with corruption. The easy way out for them—the line of least resistance — was to call for the expulsion of immigrants, over half a million immigrants in the case of Italy. Such appeal to the basest instincts of the aggrieved members of society in Italy and elsewhere is replicated in American society with President Trump's naked appeals to bigotry and toying with racist and white supremacist slogans. The Trump administration has resorted to threats of restricting the advent of immigrants to the United States, particularly immigrants from Muslim countries.

It is a sign of the time that the US Supreme Court has allowed President Trump's discriminatory travel ban (of Muslims entering the United States) to go into effect and his administration has said it will slash the number of refugees who can be admitted to the United States in fiscal 2018. These cruel policies, enacted during the worst refugee crisis since World War

II, put the lives of tens of thousands of people in serious immediate risk. These policies have been adopted at a time when thousands of people all over the world are struggling against the waves of violence in places such as Myanmar, Syria, Central America and parts of Africa. In all these examples, governments are engaged in the dehumanizing politics of "us versus them."

Let me be clear about the legitimacy of the appeals being made by hundreds of thousands for help, appeals addressed to governments in Europe and America. Right Wing politicians in Europe as well as America have resorted to race-based arguments that simply say: "we do not owe these people any obligation or any favors." I cannot overstress the fact that such statements are contrary to the universal values codified in international agreements, values that place upon our collective shoulders an obligation to be "our brothers' keepers." We owe our "neighbors" the duty of coming to their rescue, like the Good Samaritan. These sentiments now enshrined in treaties are rooted in our Judeo-Christian values. I might also add that Islam's basic creed of decency and brotherly consideration is similar to these Judeo-Christian values. I was informed about this by an unimpeachable authority, an Islamic scholar.

A noise was heard from the audience, which forced the Chair to strike the gavel and call for order.

"No interruption is allowed." he said. But the noise continued. A short, bearded young man with a red cap on which is written "Make America Great Again" and a black shirt rose to shout loudly: "This is Islamic propaganda!"

"Islamic propaganda!" he yelled repeatedly, joined by a couple of other men.

The Chair should intervene to stop Islamic propaganda," the man with the red cap repeated standing and at the top of his voice.

"I am asking you politely to stop," the Chairman shouted back..." You have the right to raise objections in due time during the Q. and A. session."

At that point Stefan interjected: Let the man finish his point. I can answer his objection."

The Chair overruled Stefan's point and asked him to continue his speech...

...Thank you, Mr. chairman. I was trying to argue that the rights of refugees and immigrants in general is rooted in international law, which is itself rooted in basic Judeo-Christian values of helping my neighbor. I will remind the audience that it was when asked "who is my neighbor" that Jesus told the parable of the Good Samaritan. There are equivalent parables in all religions including Islam, which was my last point before I was rudely interrupted. [*There were more murmurs from the same section of the audience. But the Chair and the speaker ignored them and continued. By that time two uniformed police officers had come in and were standing behind the noisy group, presumably summoned by people in charge of security of the meeting*]

...Mr. Chairman, I cannot overstress the fact that governments throughout the globe are using the rhetoric of "us versus them" to choke off the oxygen supply of those standing up for people's rights. Such policies and actions are based on bigotry, xenophobia and hatred. Perhaps the most astounding resort to such hatred is found in Myanmar against the Rohingya Islamic minority by a Buddhist majority goaded and guided by the military government. From Russia's President Putin to China's President Xi and Egypt's President el-Sisi leaders are dismantling the foundations needed for a free press needed for a free society. By removing the right to protest, and targeting protesters with harassment, threats and even physical attacks, oppressive leaders have been causing massive exodus of vulnerable communities thus causing the number of immigrants to increase exponentially.

President Trump has added his own notes to the repression chorus—threatening journalists with retaliation, endorsing the use of torture, and tweeting anti-Muslim videos from a British hate group and, as I mentioned before, pushing for Muslims and refugees bans during the worst refugee crisis in modern times. While advocating for America's leaving the world community with his America First slogan, Trump has traded on hate emboldening repressive leaders like Putin of Russia, Erdogan of Turkey, Duterte of the Philippines among others. And lately, we have been treated to gruesome tales of immigrants from Central America who have been subjected to cruel fate. Difficult as it is to believe parents and children, some as young as four years old, have been separated from their parents under presidential order. Apparently, this incredible deed is meant to dissuade immigrants from coming to America. Is this the way of demonstrating America's greatness, or proving America's renewed power disengaged from the rest of the world? I leave the judgment to all fair-minded and reasonable people. But I need to point out that America's name as the beacon of hope and the "shining city on the hill" has suffered most grievously.

I will end by posing a few questions to Mr. Trump's right-wing supporters, including the ultra-right white supremacists:

When Mr. Trump seeks to disentangle from America's engagement as a crucial partner in the world community, calling "America First and the Rest Will Follow".

3. In his dealing with North Korea, does he have any larger goal w know about, other than to find a pretext for a military exit and momentary glory (like a Nobel Peace Prize)?

4. Having cancelled the Iran Deal unilaterally, does he have a detailed toward Iran other than to renounce the nuclear deal and vainly hopi better deal?

5. What is his policy on Syria other than letting Assad, Putin and the win? Has he considered how the US and its regional allies like Is Saudi Arabia will respond to the fallout coming from the cancellatio Iran deal?

6. Does the "America First" Slogan include a renegotiated NAFTA d Canada and Mexico? If so, does the America First Slogan co exception as regards our two important neighbors and trade partne what negotiations are under way to that effect?

7. Finally, I would like to remind Trump and his supporters of an i historical fact that the world learned on September 1, 1939 w mentality of everyone for himself—every country for itself—lea Chairman, ladies and gentlemen,

It is my firm belief that your wilful and politically wounded President is leading you and the rest of us to that fateful moment of September 1, 1939, which was the eve of the most devastating war the world ever experienced. It was also in response to that experience that in a moment of redemption the leaders of the world headed by America, created the United Nations. I ask everybody to read the Preamble to the Charter of the United Nations. I also sincerely hope that we all remember that, five years later, NATO was created by the Democratic West in answer to the threat of Soviet Russia. And now Mr. Trump is calling for the dismantling of NATO.

Would I be exaggerating, then if I say that President Trump is leading the world toward utter Chaos? I think not. In fact, I dare say Donald Trump by his words and action should be called the King of Chaos.

Shouts of "Liar!… Liar!… Islamic Propaganda!…Liar!…" was heard from the back of the hall. The short man with Trump cap rose to challenge Stefan. He began by saying: Schmidt, you are a disgrace to your race! He repeated this statement. Stefan asked him: "what is my race?"

"You are German, unless you are a Jew pretending to be German." "For your information, I am of mixed blood…I am…

"I knew it! You are a Jew pretending to be German. You are a dirty Jew polluting the pure German blood!

Completely frustrated and unable to control the disturbance, Wyzanski thought he had enough and called the police to restrain the speaker and his companions. But the red-capped speaker jumped out of his seat and rushed toward the platform, followed by two others. The two policemen who ran after him were too late. For, before they could catch him, he reached the platform where the speakers stood and pounced on Stefan planting a punch on his chin. Pandemonium broke out in the hall before the attacker could attack again …

The surprised Stefan took off his coat and landed a karate kick on the body of the red-capped attacker who went reeling and fell. Seeing their comrade falling, one of his gang jumped on the platform to attack Stefan. He was about to swing a punch on Stefan who was also ready for him and tackled him with another karate kick. Then the red-capped man who was apparently the leader of the gang, rose from the floor, took out a gun and aimed it at Stefan shaking with fury. But before he pulled the trigger, Dorothy Shaw who was near Stefan cried: No!… and came between the gun man and Stefan. The gun man fired a shot, which landed on Dorothy's chest.

…Dorothy fell sprawling on the platform…

The gunman fired two more shots that hit and felled Stefan.

By that time the policemen had tackled all three of the attackers and subdued them…

…Meanwhile, Wyzanski had called for a doctor and ambulance. A man came running from the audience shouting; "I am a doctor!…I am a doctor!."

The doctor started attending to Dorothy first and then to Stefan…

After what seemed to be an eternity, the siren of an ambulance was heard from the street. Very soon thereafter four people rushed in with stretchers and two of the men wearing white medical apparel started attending to the two patients, amid much anxiety and fearful expectations. The doctors did some acts that seemed to be aimed at stopping bleeding from both patients. They did some binding and ordered the bearers of the stretcher to take the two patients to the ambulance. The siren sounding, they were taken to the George Washington Hospital, leaving the audience dumbfounded and watching what the Chairman would do next.

Wyzanski came back to the center of the platform and made signs requesting the attention of the audience or what was left of it. At least one third of the audience had left in disgust and exasperation mixed with fear…

…"Ladies and Gentlemen," Wyzanski called to an attentive audience…

…"Ladies and Gentlemen. I am sorry to have to end this meeting with deep regret but also with a sincere hope that our colleagues who have been shot would survive this wanton attack by a group of irresponsible people…"

"Irresponsible! Did you say irresponsible?" questioned a young member of the audience.

"They are more than irresponsible. Much more…"

"My name is Max. I am a member of the Academy and I call upon the authorities to speedily bring these fascists to justice. I didn't think that they would infiltrate this lawful gathering to inject poison onto our democratic exercise of dialogue. These obviously are fascists who have used this democratic exercise to advance their evil agenda, just as they tried to do at Charlottesville, Virginia. I pray to Almighty God that our wounded colleagues will survive this dastardly attack."

There was a murmur of agreement from the audience. Wyzanski then said he and a couple of his colleagues would go to the hospital to see what is happening there.

"All our thoughts and prayers will be with them. We need your prayer and good wishes that our two colleagues will survive. I am sure the doctors at George Washington Hospital will do their level best to take care of them… Please follow matters by going to our website as well as our Facebook. You will find it on our brochure which you will find on the table…Good night and we will see you soon."

At the hospital, Wyzanski asked to speak to the doctors who took responsibility for the care of the two wounded colleagues.

After waiting for over two hours, a doctor appeared from the surgery room where the two victims of the attack had been taken. Wyzanski and his group ran to the doctor and anxiously watched him for a positive answer. The doctor asked for the group's leader and Wyzanski pushed forward with an anxious look, saying: My name is Robert Wyzanski from the American Science Academy. We convened the meeting where the incident took place. What can you tell us about the condition of our colleagues?"

The doctor spoke slowly raising anxiety among the four people expectantly waiting for his verdict …

He said: What I can tell you is that one of the patients is in a critical condition. The chances of survival are fifty-fifty. My colleagues and I have done and are still doing what we can to save her."

"Her? Is it Dorothy, then?" Wyzanski asked greatly disturbed. After a nod from the doctor, he cried: "Oh, Dorothy! My dear, wonderful friend!"

Max cried wildly pulling his hair and wailing like a child. We will avenge your death!"

"Wait a minute, please. You are already concluding the lady is dead, which makes me a bearer of bad news, a messenger of death. I am not. I told you we are doing everything possible to save her. I said the chance of survival are fifty-fifty. I said so on purpose out of a precaution of raising false hopes. If it will assuage your shock, I will revise the odds. Let's say fifty-one forty-nine. Okay?"

"Thank you, Doctor…What about the condition of the man, Mr. Schmidt?" Max asked.

His case is much better. The bullet went through his right shoulder. His condition is fair to good. He should be out of hospital in about a week. Is he a foreigner? And does he have a family member whom you can inform?

"Yes, I will call his close friends in Brussels tonight or first thing tomorrow," Wyzanski said.

Chapter Six

PRELUDE TO ISABELLE'S MISSION

The Following Morning, Wyzanski received a call from the Washington Hilton Hotel. The call came from the office of the manager of the Hotel inquiring about the whereabouts of Dr. Stefan Schmidt. The message asked for a return call, so Wyzanski called the manager's office.

"My name is Robert Wyzanski. I understand that you wished to know about Dr. Schmidt who has been staying at your hotel."

"Yes, sir. We have had calls from Brussels from a young lady who was anxious about Dr. Schmidt. She says she was expecting to hear from him but has not heard from him and so she is worried. Can you help me in this matter?" That was an assistant to the hotel manager, and Wyzanski answered her as follows:

"Thank you, Mr…

"Martin Driscol. I am an assistant manager."

"Thank you for your concern, Mr. Driscol. My colleague, Dr. Schmidt had a slight accident yesterday and he is undergoing treatment at the George Washington Hospital. Nothing serious, but he will stay under observation for a few days. If you have the name and number of the young lady, I will call her myself and explain to her. That much at least we owe our distinguished colleague."

"Certainly sir. Her name is Isabelle Negassa," he told him and also gave him her number.

Dr. Wyzanski placed a call to Brussels and found Isabelle, who was extremely anxious; so he broke the news about what had happened taking great care not to upset her.

"Are you sure he is alright?...Is he able to talk and can I speak to him?"

"He is quite alright. I will have him call you straight away. Okay?"

"Thank you, sir. I am very grateful. And I will await his call. May I have your number too?

And Wyzanski gave her his own cell phone number. Then he immediately went to the hospital and told Stefan about Isabelle's call and that she was waiting for his call...

Stefan called Isabelle and told her the whole story. She was upset and cried a little, but after she made sure that he was okay, she settled down to listen to the whole story. Then she said she was coming to Washington, waiving his objection.

"I am coming and after your complete recovery, we will go to New York together," she told him, adding "I am coming and that's final. *Tu a compri? J'ai bien comprit. A bien tot.*

"**How is the condition of Dorothy Shaw?**" Wyzanski asked the doctor in charge of her case. This was after he had talked to Isabelle on the phone. The doctor was non-committal, going instead into detailed description of the nature and extent of her injury. He concluded by a slightly reassuring statement. He said:

"I will say one thing that is encouraging in her case, that is that the bullet had scraped one of the heart valves, but did not destroy it. So there is still hope that she will pull through in the end. However, she will need more surgery in the coming days.

"Thank you, doctor. We are most grateful for the splendid job you have done."

The following day, Wyzanski was awakened from his afternoon siesta by a call from the Hilton Hotel. It was Isabelle on the line and after a momentary puzzle, and she told him her name again, he apologized profusely and asked when she would like to visit Stefan. She said as soon as he was ready to take her there.

"Now, if possible," she added, and he said he would be at the hotel in half an hour. He went to the bathroom and washed his face with cold water as he always did after his afternoon siesta. When he arrived at the hotel, he saw her waiting outside the lobby at the main entrance. He pulled up outside and cried: "Are you Isabelle?" She answered with an affirmative smile and entered the car.

"So nice of you to do this; I am grateful, Dr. Wyzanski," She said in a sincere and earnest tone. He said, "It is my real pleasure. I am only sorry that you had to come all the way from Europe under such unfortunate circumstances."

Chattering pleasantly with Isabelle, Wyzanski drove for about quarter of an hour toward the area where the George Washington Hospital is found. He was curious to know about Isabelle and Stefan's relationship. Curiosity is a natural human characteristic, difficult to resist. Delicately phrasing his question, he ventured to ask the first question.

"You were naturally anxious about Stefan when he did not return your call, right?" He said, hoping to induce the right response, which he got. He followed it with a more daring guess: "It is natural for a spouse to get so anxious." And he got what he wanted, for she answered quickly: "Actually I am not a spouse."

"Oh, really? I guess I was wrong, then. So, you are just friends or colleagues?"

"Both friends and colleagues," she answered. By that time, they had arrived at their destination.

His curiosity satisfied, Wyzanski drove silently for a while. Upon arrival to their destination, he parked the car on the street nearest to the main entrance of the hospital. He walked to the side of the passenger, opened the door ceremoniously holding it while she got out of it and led her by the hand toward the entrance of the hospital. They walked briskly for a few minutes, arm in arm, toward the main entrance. While walking, Wyzanski talked about the incident as carefully as possible while leading Isabelle by the arm.

They entered the hospital and walked along the corridor toward the surgery department and reached the ward where Stefan was sleeping. A nurse was attending to his wound, changing the dressing. When they entered the room, the nurse walked toward the door. Seeing Isabelle in tears, she told her that Stefan was alright and that the doctor would be coming to check on him soon. Kneeling beside Stefan's bed, Isabelle fell on Stefan's shoulders and wept quietly, kissing him on the cheek, holding his hand in hers. Wyzanski came beside her and comforted her, patting her on the back and saying: "Isabelle, Stefan is lucky he survived the attack with a light wound, without any vital organ being damaged. So, you should be thankful… Don't cry." He pulled her up and sat her on the chair beside the bed. He then asked Stefan how he was feeling.

"I am fine, Bob, thank you. I am lucky. Luckier than Dorothy."

All of a sudden, as if he received a blow from and an invisible hand, Stefan became emotional and cried. He cried loudly and wailed like a person who lost a comrade in a battle. He said tearfully:

"Dorothy sacrificed herself for me. She took the bullet that was aimed at me." And he went into a paroxysm of sobbing for a few minutes. Then he asked Wyzanski to go to find out what Dorothy's condition was. He pleaded: "Please Bob, find out about her fate and bring me the good news. I don't want to hear bad news. Do you hear me, Bob? I want good news." And he continued weeping to Isabelle's consternation…

…After a while, the doctor attending to Stefan's wound entered the room and asked how Stefan was feeling. He also greeted Wyzanski whom he had met the previous day. Wyzanski introduced Isabelle to the doctor as Stefan's friend and colleague who had flown from Europe that morning. The doctor shook Isabelle's hand and told her not to worry because her friend was well and was in good hands.

At that point, Wyzanski gently pulled Isabelle by the arm and took her out to the waiting room. He understood Isabelle's consternation, puzzled by Stefan's weeping, and he was anxious to help in any way he could to avoid any problems between the two friends and colleagues, whose relationship he now understood to go beyond ordinary friendship.

In the waiting room, which was filled with visitors, Wyzanski took a corner seat near the window as far away as possible from the visitors. Gently patting her on the back, Wyzanski asked Isabelle if he could get her something to drink like as soda. She said she did not need anything.

"But I am perplexed by Stefan's behavior and I want to understand what has been going on. What is going on between Stefan and Isabelle?"

Wyzanski decided to take Dorothy to a nearby Ethiopian restaurant (the Nile) and treat her to lunch. It is a very popular place in downtown Washington, not far from the Washington Hilton, where Ethiopians and other customers frequent especially in the evenings. When they arrived at the Nile Restaurant, it was not even half filled. He chose a quiet corner table and recommended to Isabelle his favorite which also happened to be most people's favorite dish—*Awaze Yebeg Wett*—and beer. Having settled on what to order, Wyzanski told Isabelle what exactly happened at the meeting the day of the attack by "some crazy people."

"Who were these people, and why did they target Stefan?" Isabelle asked in earnest. He replied: "They are some extremists who admire President Trump to the point of adoration, to the extent that they resent any criticism of him or his policies."

"And I assume, Stefan criticized Trump, which does not surprise me, knowing Stefan's view of Trump," Isabelle rejoined.

"That is correct. But they have no right to resort to violence in response to criticism in a democratic system."

"Nobody has any right to resort to violence. Right" intoned Isabelle. "Exactly, Isabelle. And that is there all tragedy that two innocent participants in a democratic process suffered because they exercised their First Amendment Right of Free Speech."

"And why did they shoot what was her name...?"

"Dorothy. Her full name is Dr. Dorothy Ann Shaw. And she is co-director, with me, of the Committee on Social Sciences of the American Academy of Science. And she was at the table on the speakers' platform assisting me to run the meeting, when the incident occurred."

"Did she also criticise Trump?"

"No she did not. In fact, she is a supporter of Trump if not of all his policies."

"I am confused. Why did they attack her then?"

Wyzanski did not tell Isabelle that Dorothy intervened standing between Stefan and the attacker for fear of a misunderstanding. He said she was simply caught in the confusion by a bullet aimed at Stefan."

He added: "This always happens to people who innocently intervene to mediate between people engaged in a fight."

"I heard Stefan weeping saying she saved him by such an intervention. Did she sacrifice herself for him?"

"Isabelle, no one can say what exactly happened and why and how Dorothy intervened. It all happened so fast and there was chaos and confusion throughout. It seems to me that Stefan was expressing what they call survivor's guilt when he tearfully said she saved him."

Isabelle seemed to be mollified a little, but questions lingered in her mind. Clearly, Stefan will be facing questions when he and Isabelle meet after his recovery. Wyzanski felt pleased that he did a decent job of explaining a difficult situation. His conscience is clear and he felt he did the honorable thing to do to a colleague who had fallen victim of an unfortunate situation.

After the lunch interlude, he took her back to the hospital because she expressed a wish to sit and talk to Stefan about the prospect of visiting New York. So he took her back to the hospital. Before he left her, he asked her if she would like to stay with him and his wife.

"It makes no sense for you to spend so much money," he told her, "when you could stay with us in our spare room," He said this smiling amiably. And she agreed.

"Good, it is settled then. By the way, my wife Wanda and I live alone in the house; our two daughters are grown up and attending college. So it will be double pleasure to have you stay with us." They agreed to meet at the hospital and drive together to their house in Chevy Chase, Maryland.

By the time Wyzanski came to pick up Isabelle, she and Stefan had a quiet and more or less pleasant conversation. The talk with Wyzanski and his 'explanation of what happened at the meeting had calmed Isabelle, though she is still intrigued by what happened and decided to leave detailed talk till after his full recovery. Wyzanski came to the hospital after 5 pm and picked up Isabelle. They drove to the Hilton Hotel, from which she checked out and they drove to Chevy Chase.

When they arrived at the home of the Wyzanski's at 4002 Woodland Road, Chevy Chase, Maryland, Wand Wyzanski received them with warm open arms. She embraced Isabelle and kissed her as if she knew her all her life, making her feel instantly at home. Wanda led Isabelle holding her hand and carrying her bag t the spare bedroom. Apologising for the mess in the room, left by one of her daughters when she was spending Christmas with them, she said: "When they leave, I leave their rooms as they left it. It reminds me of the holy mess that was part of our lives together, making me nostalgic of the holy mess.

"It is what we call *joie de la famille* in France. I can relate to that.

"*C'est ca. Exactement,*" Wanda said in excellent French. Isabelle felt completely at home and gave Bob Wyzanski a warm hug, thanking him for the warm hospitality.

"I feel at home already. Thank you Bob and Wanda, very much."

Isabelle's Story in Her Own Words

My mother had kept the secret for much of my earlier life. It was during a chat with one of my classmates that I discovered about the secret that had been concealed from me since that fateful day. My father's disappearance was apparently known to my friend Monique's parents and she had heard about it from her parent's dinner time conversation. According to Monique, her mother asked the father point blank:

"How did you know that Negassa had disappeared?" To which he responded:

"Because he did not attend a meeting at which he had been booked as the principal speaker." Her father added in a whisper that it was rumored that he did not come because he had gone to Ethiopia and was reported missing by members of his underground movement.

Like my father, Dr. Negassa, my friend's father was also Ethiopian and belonged to a revolutionary group espousing socialist ideas, aiming to bring about systematic change in their country, Ethiopia. They were both married to women who are French and whom they had met in college. Both of the women shared in their husbands' socialist ideology. My friend's mother is called Anne-Marie, she is from Marseille and is of the same age as my mother. My mother's name is Claudette and she comes from the Bretagne region. Apart from joking with each other making mutual fun about their different accents, they get on well, sharing secrets and helping each other in times of trouble like now. Ever since my father's disappearance, Anne-Marie has been by my mother's side. Monique and I have grown up like sisters spending weekends in each other's homes and exchanging gifts and secrets.

The last picture I took with my father was when I was between three and four years old.

I am fond of that picture and carry it with me. He is carrying me over his neck with my legs dangling and my hands holding his head. We are both laughing like crazy. We have other pictures of the family like one with my sister, Clara and I, sitting in the middle and mom and dad wrapping their arms around us. In the picture we are all smiling. I must have been five and Clara seven years old in that picture. I have vivid memories of how we were all laughing when that picture was taken.

It had been some ten years since my dad disappeared when Monique revealed to me about his disappearance. I remember rushing back home that day and angrily shouting at my mom: "Why did you hide my dad's disappearance from me. Did you also hide it from Clara?" My mom was startled at the way I shouted at her. She put her arms around me and led me to the armchair where she sat by my side and tearfully told me about all her efforts to find out what had happened, to no avail.

"What happened to him, mommy?" I asked her between tears.

"I don't know *ma cherie*," she said. "I don't know. I did all I could to find out what happened to him, but in all my attempts, I drew a blank," she said with bitterness. She traveled to Ethiopia and contacted everyone who knew him. She visited his relatives in the countryside, hoping they could pull strings and find a clue. Again, to no avail. Nobody was able to help; all their efforts were made in vain, and finally, they gave up. And she gave up.

That night, I had a dream in which I heard my father groaning in pain. I could not see him, and I tried to go toward the place where the groan came, but I was unable to move. I tried to shout calling "Papa!" but no voice came out of my mouth. The tortured voice continued groaning, getting sharper and sharper. He was pleading with whoever was torturing him. As the groaning went to a higher pitch, I woke up perspiring and crying "Papa!" My mom heard my cries and came around to my bed and found me breathless and drenched in sweat. She hugged me tightly and I cried in her bosom."

Later that day I asked my mom, why did my father go to Ethiopia. She said he was a leader of the Ethiopian Socialist Movement and slipped into the country to organize followers.

"Why didn't you stop him?" I asked my mother. She said, "it was his destiny, and nobody could stop him from fulfilling his mission or advancing his cause."

"You should have known it was a lost cause."

"How do you know it was a lost cause?" my mother asked angrily. And I answered equally angrily," I have been reading about it in the library. It was a lost cause, and he was following a mirage, not a dream," I said.

"Isabelle, have you any idea about what you just said? Do you know what you are talking about?"

"Yes, I do. He and his fellow revolutionaries were following a mirage. That is what people are saying and writing—people who know these things."

"What the hell do you know about such people? If you continue spreading such lies you will be committing a betrayal about your own father."

"Why do you say that? How would I commit a betrayal? You don't even know how he died and where he was buried."

"Isabelle, that is enough."

"No, it is not enough. I am not a child any more. I am almost eleven, and I know things."

"No you don't, Isabelle. You don't know what you are saying. Do you know that your father is considered a hero and martyr by thousands of Ethiopians?"…

…My mother spoke with such force of conviction, I felt that it was no good arguing with her. Besides, I didn't know anything about what happened, so I decided to keep quiet and bide my time. One thing was certain, my father is gone and nothing we say or do can bring him back. What he left us is his memory—a memory of a gentle beautiful father, who never raised his voice in argument and who was polite to the point of diffidence. That is what all his friends say, with reverence, when they speak about him.

But I swore quietly that I will move heaven and earth to find out what had really happened and where he was buried. There must be a closure even though his memory is still with us, we cannot live without knowing what happened. With the change of government, the fate of the Emperor who had been overthrown by the military was revealed, including where he had been buried. So, there must be a way to resolve the mystery of my father's death and disposal of his remains.

The following day, I asked mother to tell us about our father. What kind of man was he? How did you meet him? Mother agreed to tell the story of how they met and what kind of man he was.

She said I am glad you asked me. I have meant to do it but for some reason I kept postponing it. Your questions have now stimulated me to talk about your father. And I think we should celebrate it by eating dinner out, just the three of us.

"I was so excited that I cried: 'Goodie!'"

And so, we went to the Trocadero area to have dinner. There is a restaurant that your father and I frequented during our student days. We will remember him, and it is the right place to tell our story.

So, one fine evening the three of us went to the Trocadero and sat and ordered dinner consisting of *agno roti* as main dish, preceded with minestrone for mom and spaghetti for Clara and me, and ending with ice cream…

When we finished eating the main dish, and were eating ice cream, mother started the story of how they met.

"Where and how did you meet?" I asked mother.

"We met at the Sorbonne as students. By the way, I must tell you, it was 'Love at First Sight' and you two are the issue of a great love." We laughed at mother's wit and humor.

"Who took the first step, you or papa?" Clara asked with a smile.

"All eyes were on that very handsome man, so don't be surprised if I tell you, it might have been I who took the initiative."

"What do you mean, it might have been you? It was either you not. Which is it?" Clara inquired." I giggled agreeing with her

"So, what did you say to him? Did you say: hey I am in love with you, so let us get together?" said Clara with "a laugh.

"Listen girls, do you want me to tell you the story or are you going to keep interrupting me?"

We both said, "Sorry mom." And I said, "Please continue. You were telling us how handsome he was."

"He was one of the most handsome men I have ever known," mom said with emotion and with tears in her misty eyes...

She continued: "He was beautiful inside and out. He was tall and graceful and his patience and decency was legendary. As long as I knew him, he never raised his voice in argument, but rather waited patiently listening to people until they finished. No wonder he ended up a leader of a great movement"

"What was the first word he uttered when he spoke to you?" I asked.

"I don't remember exactly, but I remember his captivating smile and his gentleness...And the way he lingered his gaze on you always smiling. It was like magic."

Mom then went on describing how many days they dated before consummating their relationship by taking serious steps toward holy matrimony. Though modern in many ways, my mother was a strict, practicing Catholic and raised us to becomes serious practitioners of the Catholic religion. She named me Isabelle after a favorite saint **Isabelle**.

Carla quizzed her more on religion and how she and my father reconciled the potential contradiction between her religion and his political views.

"Wasn't father a Marxist?" she asked her and continued, "That is what some writers have reported according to Left Newspapers in France that have written about Ethiopian Left Groups."

"Where did you read that?" my mother quizzed Carla

"The father of one of my friends reads Socialist publications," Carla responded with confidence. She continued with pride:

"My friend knows about father and his political activities, and apparently father was widely admired by socialists in Europe."

Mom confirmed the claim that he was widely admired also among Ethiopians and other Third World socialists. He was recognized as a thoughtful and popular leader, according to mom. As to the contradiction between the Catholic faith and socialism, she said that many Catholic leaders are socialists, especially in Latin America among Jesuits. Mom believes that even Pope Francis is reputed to have been influenced by what was called "Liberation Theology", which was influenced by socialism.

I certainly did not see any conflict in our household. I think their deep- rooted love was the basis of the harmonious life we experienced as a family. I remember one of my mother's favorite sayings was: *Amor Omnia Vincit* (love conquers all). She used that saying whenever there was difficulty in people's relationships—people that is who have differing political views, though they are in love.

Fast forward.

By the time I entered the university, I had read and heard about my father and his disappearance. It had become an obsession for me, and I took courses in Marxism among other subjects, in order to understand my father's political life and work, including his role in helping create the Ethiopian Socialist Movement. I even befriended a few Ethiopians of my generation seeking to locate former members of the Movement. Lately there has been some journalistic interest in his life and death or disappearance. Even members of our family have been interviewed about my father. There has developed a fascination about him and about his mysterious disappearance, or if he was killed how and when he was killed and by whom.

In addition to my own psychological makeup and above all my silent suffering as a victim of his disappearance, deprived of a love of a wonderful father, the recent interest in my father's life has fired my political imagination. I have frequent dreams about my father. Some of the dream is benign in which he appears like a ghost and disappears as quietly as he appeared. At other times, the sound of a groaning tortured man screaming at the top of his voice and calling for help disturbs my sleep, following which I cannot sleep. Even during my wakeful moments, he comes to haunt my consciousness.

All this has led me to do the kind of work I have been doing in Brussels and elsewhere. Some of my father's idealism and commitment to human betterment, as well as my defiance against oppressive systems and people, including the current American President is grounded in my father's commitment, a commitment that sent him to his disappearance and death.

My study of my father's life and the example he set for commitment to human betterment has thus rubbed off on me. My sister Clara also missed father, of course, but I was particularly affected by his absence from my life. I missed his warm affection and the meticulous attention he paid to his children. He left us before I had enough of that warm love and attention of which I felt deprived. Mother knew I felt keenly deprived of his presence and did everything in her power to make up for his absence. She paid special attention to our needs, taking us to all social occasions at our schools and in our neighborhood. She made absolutely certain to provide us with all the material needs equal to those provided by our friends' parents, if not more than theirs.

Still, whenever we saw our friends attending school events and other social events with their fathers, we felt our father's absence. As we grew older, we made sure that our mother did not feel alone, and we went out of our ways to make her feel that we were happy. She was very proud of us and told us so all the time.

But in my heart of hearts, I felt the void, though as I grew older, I made sure not to show it; I buried it inside me. As if to compensate for my loss, I saw my father in my dreams. In many of such dreams I went on picnics with my father in some distant land where children played with their parents. But I stuck to my father and did not play with them, afraid that they might take him away from me.

I was not bad at school. Mother helped me and Clara to do our homework. When I began having problems in following lessons, being absent-minded, my mother consulted the school counselor. The counselor, a very nice woman, talked to me asking questions about my interests, including sport and subjects I liked and disliked. She also asked me if I had dreams or nightmares. When I told her about my dreams, she asked me if I missed my father, at which point I started crying...

I think I was seven or eight years old when I frequently wetted my bed. My mother had been worried and had told our family doctor about it. The counselor who was a friend of the doctor had also known about my bed wetting. She didn't mention it but obviously knew that the bed wetting was caused by the fact that I missed my father. When I cried, she put her arm around me saying some soothing words about how my father also must be thinking about me.

"Just remember that your dad is thinking of you and also misses you," she told me, and I was cheered and thanked her. From that interview onwards, I improved my performance at school. My counselor also encouraged me to play sport. She asked me what kind of game I played in school. I said I played soccer and tennis. "Have you ever played chess," she asked me one day. When I said no, she told me soccer is a good group sport, which involves individual skills and speed as well as cooperation and coordination with others. She then said among individual games, chess is a good thing for taking your mind of worries, and to help you develop step-by-step thinking and strategic planning."

She was right in all respects but especially in taking my mind off troubling thoughts. She was very helpful in reorienting me from morbid thoughts and memories toward positive thoughts. Her name is Madame Monique Legrand. I am forever grateful to Madame Legrand.

Chapter Seven

JOURNEY FROM PARIS TO BRUSSELS

Soon after I completed High School in Chantilly, in the suburban areas of Paris, I applied to the School of Languages at the University of Geneva, Switzerland. The entrance exam comprised written and oral tests all of which I passed comfortably. Among the oral tests were questions as to why I applied to study languages: what was my ultimate objective? My answer was that I had always been fascinated by languages, in part because I came from a biracial family with a French mother and an African father. As a young girl I had been exposed to people speaking different languages other than French, especially my father and his Ethiopian friends who frequently stayed with us in our home.

As to my ultimate objective, I told my examiners that I wanted to become an interpreter in international organizations like the United Nations (UN) and the European Union (EU).

In three intensive years of taking Spanish and English, in addition to advanced French language and literature as well as minoring in history and Political science, I passed the appropriate exams and received my diploma as a professional interpreter. I must also state that the courses I took included practical exercises, which involved taking part as an adjunct interpreter assisting the fulltime employees at organizations of the UN in

Geneva, including the Sub-Commission of Human Rights sitting in Geneva representing the Principal Commission that sits in New York.

During the three years of training, I visited New York twice and sat with the interpreters learning techniques of taking noted while listening to speakers and simultaneously interpreting. I also used the New York visits to develop friendships with other interpreters, with whom I remain connected.

My journey to Brussels was not all pleasant. I have had ups and downs. My connection with my sister, Carla, suffered during the last year of high school. It began with a love affair she had with one of my teachers, who was also our Tennis coach. Carla had graduated from high school two years earlier than me and was employed as an assistant coach to the girls because she was the Tennis champion of the school. The coach, named Bernard, helped obtain her the job because he was interested in her. He had a bad reputation as a flirt among many students, but he seemed to focus his amorous attention on Carla and because he was good-looking and influential in the school, he was able to persuade Carla that he was really in love with her. Mom warned her to be careful not to fall for him because she had heard about his reputation. Unfortunately, Carla did not heed to mom's advice but rather went her way. She even left our house and rented a cheap apartment near our school.

One day, he approached me during our Tennis practice and told me that I was beautiful, more beautiful than my sister. I was shocked by this and told him to go to Hell.

The following day, which was a weekend, Carla came home full of fury and confronted me with a silly question: why did I flirt with her boyfriend. I said what boyfriend? She said Bernard, and I laughed at her. She slapped me hard and we fought violently until mom heard the noise and came and separated us. She asked why we were fighting, and Carla told her that I was trying to rob her of her one lover. Mom went livid with anger and turned to me and asked: "Is this true?"

"Absolutely not," I shouted and told her the story of his attempt to begin a relationship with me by telling me I was more beautiful than Carla."

"And how did you respond?" mom asked me and when I told her exactly what I told him—to go to Hell—mom said she believed me and told Carla about her warnings. Carla stormed out of the house and disappeared for months. Mom quizzed me about the man and my response to his advances, and I reassured her that I told her the truth. Again, she said she believed me, but was so distressed she wept bitterly. I had never seen my mother, who is a strong person, weeping before, and weeping bitterly as if the incident touched within her some hidden wound. I put my arms around her and wept with her telling her that I loved her and that I was sure Carla will come back and all will be well again. She stopped weeping and wiped the tears from her face and mine with a kerchief. She broke the embrace and smiled hugging me tightly...

"I will be alright, *ma tres chere petite fille*," she said and went to make tea, her favorite drink, even before wine! I shouted after her, "Why not drink wine to drown your sorrow?"

"What?! And break the tradition of my Breton ancestors?" she shouted back turning her head and smiling.

"Ah, wonderful, your beautiful smile again!" I shouted and she giggled, putting the kettle on the stove...

...Months later, Mom gave me a bit of good news. Apparently, Carla discovered to her bitter disappointment that Bernard was dating another woman, a more mature woman who was once a teacher in the school and left the school and was employed in a Travel Agency in Paris. Mom was an amateur detective and had been following the relationship of Carla and Bernard. She used her connection with the school, including Madam Monique Legrand, the counselor who, it seemed, knew Bernard to be a flirt and philanderer. Like my mom, it seemed that Madame Legrand was herself interested in people's lives and activities. And as it happens people brought their stories and those of their neighbors to her because of her intense interest in knowing what was going on in their lives. One of the people who brought news of happenings in the school was her own colleague, the assistant counselor, who apparently did not like Bernard for some reason. He told Madame Legrand about his new love affairs with the employee of a Travel Agency. And Madame Legrand told my mother, Claudette. She also told her that she had known about Carla's romantic involvement with Bernard, and that she is now incensed and broke her relationship with him. She even threatened to expose him to the school authorities that he tried to seduce me (her sister)!...

…After learning about all this, mom decided to look for Carla and asked me to help her.

"I hope you have forgiven your sister and will help me to bring her back to her family," she said. I told her that I love my sister and would help bring her back to the family fold. So, she went out looking for her. She found out she was staying with a friend who is a student at the Sorbonne…The following day, we went looking for Carla in the student quarters, looking from one café to the next until we were exhausted. We decided to try it the next day early in the morning. Mom had taken a short leave of absence from her teaching position in the area elementary school where she had been employed for many years…

Two days later, Madame Legrand called to tell mom that she met Carla and convinced her to call home and talk to her mother and sister.

"I impressed upon her as strongly as I could to call home and make up with her family. She said she would. I tell you she is full of remorse and will come home soon. She misses her mom and sister. So dear Claudette, be gentle and forgiving. Do you hear?"

"Don't worry about that, we will," mom told Madame Legrand.

In the evening of the same day, Carla called and tearfully said sorry and will be home.

"I am sorry, mom. I miss you and Isabelle. I am coming home tomorrow."

So, all was well that ends well. We kissed and hugged each other, and things went back to normal after a nasty interlude…

Soon thereafter, I left Paris to go to Geneva to begin my study of languages. The three years of study in Geneva were pretty uneventful. There were not much extracurricular activities; the study schedule was intense with not much time left for anything else. The little socialising that I did was limited to dancing on occasions and occasionally travel over the weekend to Lausanne with Swiss friends and meeting their families. But during my last year, I traveled to Belgium to learn about the structure and operations of the EU. When visiting the various departments of the EU, I was introduced to a handsome man who was deeply interested in issues of migration. His Name is Stefan Schmidt and he is German but speaks perfect English. I was fascinated by this intelligent man and wanted to find out why he is interested in migration. I found out that he was a member of the German Social Democratic Party (SPD) and that during his political activist days as a young member of the SPD, he came in contact with many young African refugees who impressed him with their exemplary dignity and dedication to their people back home. He made a modest contribution to sensitize leaders of the

Party on the problem of immigrants from Africa and elsewhere.

That experience in his native Germany as an SPD activist, led him toward the job in the EU. Ultimately, Stefan convinced me to join the EU as an interpreter.

During the short time I have known Stefan, he impressed me as a sincere friend and a dedicated human rights activist, who sees himself first and foremost as member of the human race, who by biological and historical accident, was born in Germany, to a German father and a British mother. That fact of accidental birth did not constrain him from considering himself first as a human being, before his nationality. For that reason, he chose to work for the European Union (EU), which though not perfect, he regards as the right step toward creating a European human family built on common values of decency, freedom and democracy. Above all, he stressed our common humanity with people in other lands as brothers and sisters and fellow travelers in this incredible earthly journey. That belief was what motivated him to work in the EU, an organization that he sees as the egg of a new Europe. Now, any egg can addle, and there are countervailing forces opposed to the aims and methods of the EU.

In discussing problems connected to this matter, he refers to the Preamble to the American Constitution, which refers to the ideal of building "A More Perfect Union." Like that ideal to which Americans have been striving to reach, Europeans also will work hard toward creating a better continental organization uniting Europeans in a common effort to achieve better lives for their peoples in peace and harmony. The recent challenges facing Europe as a collective human community and Europeans as individual human beings have tested the tenacity and historic role of the Judeo-Christian ethos on which European civilization was grounded. The response of some of Europe's leaders like, specifically that of Chancellor Angela Merkel of Germany, in providing a balanced response to the challenge posed by the advent of Muslims in large numbers, especially those from Syria are a testimony of Europe's commitment to "the better angels of our nature," to borrow a phrase from the great Abraham Lincoln, is as thought provoking as it is heart-warming.

In this respect, Stefan is a new prototype of a universal citizen who is aware of his own human frailties and limitations as does the organization in which he works toward an ideal. In his latest essay toward that goal, he traveled to Washington and ventured to make critical assessment of the policies and politics of the new Trump Administration. What happened in that meeting is a matter still a mystery to me. Stefan fell victim to some extremists who aimed a gun to kill him, but another participant of the conference, a high-ranking member of the American Science Academy took the bullet and fell and was in a critical condition the last I heard of the incident. I reserve comments on the incident for now, sincerely hoping that the victims of the shooting will survive and recover speedily. *(**End of Isabelle's Story in Her Own Words**)*

Defiance of a Special Kind

Two weeks had passed since the shooting incident. Isabelle had visited Stefan three times during that time and was struck by how much Stefan had changed since she last talked to him before the incident. During those two weeks Stefan called Isabelle only twice and she called him almost daily. Though he had recovered enough to be released, the doctors kept him in hospital to make sure he was safely out of danger.

When he recovered fully, Stefan called Isabelle about his full recovery but said he was not yet ready to go to New York with her on the special mission that he had promised to do before. When she asked him why, he told her of the sad news that Dorothy Ann Shaw did not make it. She passed away the day before he was released from hospital, and he was informed about it a day later.

Isabelle asked Dr. Wyzanski about Dorothy's death and he confirmed her death without further comment, which intrigued her. He just said morosely:

"Yes, Isabelle, she didn't make it," he added after a few minutes that he spared me the bad news because he was distressed as were all her colleagues, who were still in shock. But he apologised for not telling her the news.

"Though we were badly affected by Dorothy's death," he said speaking slowly," it was wrong to hide it from her. He said, "I must tell you we are still in shock."

Wyzanski and Isabelle were in the lounge and Wanda joined them and guessing that her husband must have told Isabelle the bad news, she went over to her side and saw her sniffing and dabbing her eyes. She also saw her husband looking crestfallen and downcast.

Wanda hugged Isabelle and at the same time said to her husband:

"Bob, we cannot undo what has been done and bring back Dorothy. What happened was unexpected and horrendous, but we should deal with it with reason. We also need to do our best to comfort the parents and siblings of Dorothy. By the way, Bob, has the Academy reached out to them?"

"Yes, we have. I talked to her father who is crushed by his daughter's death. They were very close, though they disagreed on politics."

"When is her funeral?"

"Her remains were flown to Ohio and then taken by car to her birthplace, where she was buried in a quiet ceremony, following the wish of her parents."

"What about the Academy?"

"There is going to be a Memorial Service organized by the Academy next week. By the way, Isabelle, Stefan is going to speak at the Memorial. Would you like to attend?"

"I expect Stefan would want me to, don't you think?" said Isabelle.

"I am sure he does. Your presence will help him deal with his grief…I think he feels that he was responsible because the bullet had been aimed at him," Wyzansky said.

"Yes, I am sure he does feel guilty. She took the bullet for him, didn't she?" inquired Isabelle. It was a question loaded with irony mixed with pathos. The couple looked at each other and Wanda said something about a cup of tea would be good for everybody, and went to the kitchen to put the kettle on…

When they were having tea with some biscuits, Wanda asked Isabelle if she knew whether Stefan would like to stay with them for a while.

"I forgot to tell you," Bob told Wanda, "Stefan is planning to go to New York, and prefers to stay in the hotel until he travels to New York. He told me this when I asked him if he would like to move in with us."

The eyes of both Bob and Wanda fell intently on Isabelle's face, as if they were thinking the same thought. Isabelle felt their intent gaze and somewhat awkwardly shifted in her seat and averted her gaze looking toward the ceiling. It was an uncomfortable moment and thanks to Wanda's presence of mind and gentleness, the conversation was changed.

"Isabelle," Wanda said, "Have I told you about an interesting Play being staged at the Kennedy Center. It is a new Play by an upcoming playwright. Would you like to see it?

"I would love to, thank you. When?" "This coming weekend, in three days."

"Okay, I look forward to it very much. I think I need it. And now I would like to go to my room and rest a little."

"By all means. Go and rest. See you later."

Isabelle went to her bedroom. As she lay on her bed, she drew a deep breath, remembering what Bob had told them. Stefan had not used any terms of endearment as he usually did in his communications with her. At the time, she considered the traumatic experience he had just gone through and, in her mind, composed excuses or extenuation on his behalf. She had not thought of blaming him at all. In retrospect, and considering what had happened to Dorothy and why, she began imagining something sinister must have happened between Stefan and Dorothy—something amounting to guilt. After all, she thought, why would a woman who hardly knew him suddenly decide to step between him and a gunman shooting at close range. There is no doubt about it: they had become lovers. *Oh God, they had become lovers overnight*! They had just met, and that idea pierced her like an arrow…

"And he said he was going to New York," she said, laughing. "The New York mission was supposed to be on my behalf," she cried as if speaking to Stefan, "and here he is telling them he was going to New York. And he preferred to stay in the hotel until then! Why?"

And she answered herself…"

"…Because he would not face me here at the home of these good people," she concluded bitterly, with a little hysterical laughter. She was restless and decided to phone him at the hotel. She had written the number in her notebook and in her cell phone.

She called the hotel and asked for him…She was connected instantly.

Without any greeting, she asked him point blank:

"Why didn't you accept the kind hospitality of these good people?" He was taken aback and mumbled, "Isabelle…How are you…?…I felt I needed some quiet moment…I hope you understand."

"Why? You cannot face me…Is that it?"

"Don't judge me harshly, Isabelle. Don't judge me, before giving me a chance to explain everything," he blurted out before she cut him…He cried: "Isabelle!…Isabelle!…"

She had ended the call… He called again and again…until she finally answered him.

"*Cherie!*…" he cried "Don't call me *Cherie*!..

"You know I love you, but…"

"But what!?…But you made a mistake…? Yes you did, and it was a fatal mistake…And it ended in an innocent woman's death." She said in a harsh but trembling voice…"

…"Give me a chance to explain… I love you, whether you believe it or not, and I want to save our unique relationship… I will redeem myself and make it up to you. You will see. I will go to the end of the earth to do what you desire…You know that…And I have not forgotten our New York project, our special mission…"

She ended the call again, cutting him off…

He got out of bed and went to the lobby and ordered a black label at the bar—double order. He took the glass full of the whiskey, walked to a nearby table and sat alone. There were a few people in the lobby where soft jazz music was playing. He sipped twice in quick succession and sank into a state of gloom…

"The woman is certainly entitled to be angry with me," he thought. "…Fair is fair…I didn't exactly jilt her, but there was a betrayal, definitely… Didn't I go into a state of excitement…at Dorothy's bold and daring seduction?…Ha ha!…Hm…And spend a glorious night the first night of our meeting!…And she knows that Dorothy sacrificed her life to save me!… And Isabelle knows this now…poor Isabelle with her sad, gentle eyes…I didn't even stop to think of those gentle eyes, that beautiful face…that rare beauty, issue of a mixture of French and Ethiopian blood!…God, why didn't I resist as I did before?… And now I am in a mess"…

He took another two sips, again in quick succession…

But this time he started reliving the memory of the glorious night of love. He immediately relented and wiped out the reverie, wiping his forehead with the palm of his hand as if to emphasise his wish to delete the memory of that night. Again, he tried to focus his thought on Isabelle. And what better way to do that, he thought, than to think about the special mission in New York— talking to the Ambassador of the Ethiopian Mission about Isabelle's father. From what he could remember, out of the fragments of the conversations he had with Isabelle, her aim was to find ways of discovering what happened to her father.

It may be a wild goose chase, he thought, but Isabelle is fixed on doing it to the point of obsession, and nothing will stop her from doing it. I had promised her to be part of her mission which may well be 'Mission Impossible,' but there is not getting out of it. And I promised her, and I will keep my promise, come what may.

Wanda and Bob made a decision to include Stefan in taking Isabelle to the Play. So, the four of them spent a pleasant evening. After the show, they went to a restaurant in the Kennedy Center area for a cheerful dinner where the hosts succeeded in persuading Stefan to check out of the hotel and join Isabelle to stay with them until their joint trip to New York. Although Isabelle and Stefan appeared on better terms than earlier, the hosts thought it more appropriate to prepare a separate bedroom for Stefan.

At breakfast the following morning, Bob Wyzanski asked if there was anything his office of the American Academy of Social Sciences could do to help expedite the New York Mission, or rather Isabelle's project of discovery

of her father's disappearance. He said that Isabelle had been kind enough to share the idea behind her project and he thought there may be ways in which his office could be of some assistance. Both Isabelle and

Stefan said it is a wonderful idea and they accepted the offer gladly and with appreciation. Wanda said she once worked in Ethiopia as an assistant to the Dean of Science in one of the colleges of the newly opened University, and that she still maintains connection with her former colleagues and friends there. She said she would be happy to use her connection to help in any way possible. She ended with a rush of good memories about her time in Ethiopia. She exclaimed with warm sentiment:

"There are no better people in the world than Ethiopians, and no better country than Ethiopia. Ask any Peace Corps Volunteer who served there," Wanda said and added, "I wish I could join you to go to Addis Ababa, Isabelle."

"I don't see why not, if Bob can also join us…But that would be asking too much of both of you," Isabelle said. And Stefan joined in the conversation by agreeing about Ethiopia and Ethiopians being wonderful. But he added a note of realism in the challenge facing the project and that it is good to be prepared for surprises in the twists and turns involved in politics of any country.

"I am not trying to pour cold water on your enthusiasm, but am just being realistic," he cautioned. There was no disagreement. And the following day during breakfast, Bob and Wanda assured Stefan and Isabelle of their readiness to assist them in their endeavor of discovery. We have had occasion to meet Bob Wyzanski briefly but without revealing the depth and variety of his scholarship, including his knowledge about African peoples and cultures including those of Ethiopia's various people and their varied and fascinating history and culture. Dr. Wyzanski is well known for his modesty and his support of young African scholars, many of whom have attained places of academic honor. Above all, Bob Wyzanski is blessed with a warm sense of humor. His reddish-brown hair is half gone and he keeps the remaining half cut short. His ever-smiling face with his good humor keeps his students and colleagues at ease. His bright blue eyes have a twinkle when he smiles. His rimless glasses that often slide toward the tip of his long nose, and when that happens, he assumes an owlish aspect. In his mid-fifties, he is of medium height and rather stout, but his regular swimming and tennis game keep him fit and full of energy. He tends to be low-key to the point of shyness, and rarely intrudes into other people's affairs, unless he is asked to intervene. For example, when Stefan and

Dorothy became romantically involved in a matter of hours, he might have been astounded with the speed of the development of their affair, but he did not utter a word about it —for or against their affair...

Wanda is in her early-to-mid fifties, and full of life and verve, always laughing and joking with friends and co-workers. Now in early retirement, Wanda was an active member of women's causes and is an admirer of Ms. Gloria Steinem, whom she regards as an unsung heroine and prophet. She and her husband share all the core values like equality and human rights under the rule of law. But during electoral politics, her votes are more for Left or Liberal causes, whereas Bob leans toward the right, principally Republican causes. Their diverse views lead to some "civilized" debates and disputes without bitterness.

Endowed with a round face with high cheek bones, Wanda is a tall, pallid skinned, fairly good-looking woman with a winning smile. She has an easy laugh, which she deploys during disputes, generally having a pleasant outcome. Bob teases her saying she should be in politics, a notion that she dismisses instantly.

It should not be surprising that the Wyzanskis are a popular couple among friends, co-workers and neighbors. Their quick adoption of Isabelle and their eagerness to help restore harmony between her and Stefan was a crucial contribution to helping them resume their normal relationship.

Part

ISABELLE'S MISSION— A CALL

FROM THE GRAVE

Chapter Eight

PREPARATORY STEPS

On a Sunny Morning, the Wyzanskis took their guests to the Reagan National Airport. At the airport, Isabelle and Wanda hugged and looked at each other tearfully and bid the travelers bon voyage, with Stefan and Bob looking at each other and pumping each other's arms with warm handshakes.

"This is au revoir, not, goodbye. Do keep in touch, do you hear?" Wanda warned the departing guests.

Isabelle responded: "We will see you in DC one more time because our flight back to Brussels is from Washington, so we will stay one night with you."

"Oh, that will be lovely," Wanda said.

It was a short flight and they landed at LaGuardia Airport at midday. They took a taxi from LaGuardia to Manhattan and checked in a hotel three blocks from the UN Headquarters. After checking in the hotel and a short rest, they went out to walk toward the UN. Isabelle knew the area very well from her student days in Geneva; so, she assumed the role of guide which Stefan accepted gladly with good humor.

They walked toward the UN and having entered the gate and received the proper security permit, went in, to the Delegates Lounge. They bought two cappuccinos and sat there enjoying the sight of the comings and goings of the UN employees as well as visitors like themselves.

They lingered a while, visiting the different department offices. They ate lunch at the Cafeteria. After lunch, they decided they had seen enough and went out of the UN building and headed back to their hotel, where they googled the address of the Ethiopian Mission to the UN: 866 2nd Avenue # 3. New York, NY 10017.

From the time they spent the night in Washington DC, their conversation had been proper, fairly formal and cordial but did not go beyond. A thaw had not yet occurred in their strained relationship. This condition continued through their journey to New Nork as well as their brief tour of the UN.

Back in their hotel, Isabelle took out her night pajamas and gown as well as other personal effects. She put on her pajama and made preparations to sleep on the sofa, leaving the King size bed for Stefan. Stefan saw what she was doing and instantly protested loudly. He said that if they must sleep separately, then he will sleep on the sofa and proceeded to remove her things from the sofa and placed them on the bed. She protested and he counter- protested, with Isabelle holding on to her night gown and he pulling it away from her with intent of placing it on the bed.

This went on with Stefan taking her things to the bed and she taking it back—back and forth, back and forth until they were both exhausted. Suddenly Stefan threw his hands up and burst out laughing. She looked at him and joined him in the laughter. They both laughed loudly. Then he looked at her fondly with a smiling face. She looked desirable in her pajama which revealed her tall shapely figure and ripe breasts. His face changed to a soft and appealing pose, a pose that he knew she liked. Suddenly, he went down on his knees in front of her, took her hand in his. And gently begged for forgiveness, vowing his undying love… She gazed at him wistfully, teared up… wept and pulled him up from the kneeling position saying:

"Get up from that ridiculous position… Or are you proposing to marry me?"

He got up and said: "Why not, if you are ready to make the vow?"…

She said, "you know I made a vow to myself to find out what happened to my father. No marriage before then…After that we will see…"

…"I know. I just wanted to make sure," he answered and took her in his arms. They kissed warmly, sat on the sofa in embrace. Then he took of his clothes threw his arms around her and they went to bed without a word…

…They rose early the following morning and phoned the Ethiopian Mission asking to speak to the Ambassador. The telephonist said he was not in yet, but he would be in about half an hour…

…They rang the bell and the intercom answered with a buzz opening the door. They went to number 3 and were welcomed by the receptionist who said His Excellency was expecting them and will see them in a couple of minutes. They waited about ten minutes before they were ushered in, to the Ambassador's office, where a smiling ambassador rose to welcome them. He hugged Isabelle warmly for a long time, almost choked in emotion…He said: "Isabelle…! I knew you when you were a girl of three in Paris when I came to visit your father in those crazy, wonderful times…

Isabelle said: "Dad talked about you and his other comrades with great respect and affection. It is as if I know you all…

"Yes, I know…Those were wonderful times of idealism when we were ready to sacrifice our lives for the cause. He stopped speaking and gazed at Isabelle in warm emotion and took out his handkerchief and sobbed unexpectedly for a little while. Then he realized that he was affecting Isabelle, who after all had lost her father "for the cause." The Ambassador recovered from his touching emotional reaction on seeing Isabelle. He apologised a little and went on to ask her how she was and how her mother, Claudette, was. Isabelle who was moved by his emotional reaction said calmly: 'We are all well, thank Your Excellency." He admonished her not to be formal; he considers himself as her uncle and patted her on the back affectionately.

The Ambassador was a short and wiry man in his mid-to-late sixties. His hair was almost completely grey, and he sported a well-trimmed beard and sideburns. His large eyes were shimmering with the tears that appeared when he had wept a little. Age had not affected him, and he seemed happy with his life as a diplomat. But he said he missed the era of struggle. And he especially missed "The Great Negassa, our Revered Leader."

He suddenly sat up and called the secretary and asked her to order tea or coffee for his special guests…

"What kind of Ethiopian am I, who forgets his guests!" he exclaimed with a smile.

While waiting for the refreshments, they broached the subject of their visit. Stefan began by thanking Ambassador Taddesse for his kind welcome and for agreeing to see Isabelle and him at such a short notice. Stefan said:

"And now, without taking too much of your valuable time, we would like to tell you the reason for our visit. Isabelle told me that you and her father were very close friends and comrades in the struggle for democracy and human rights in Ethiopia…"

"We were indeed, and I promise to do anything to the extent of my ability to help in whatever project you are engaged." Isabelle spoke next. She said:

"Thank you very much, uncle Taddesse, for this promise. On behalf of my mother, Claudette and my sister, Carla, I wish to thank you for your warm reception and promise to be of assistance to us.

"Just tell me what you need and in what way I can be of assistance," the Ambassador asked.

They then told him that they were interested to know first of all, what happened to Dr. Negassa. Secondly, they wish to discover where he was buried. Isabelle spoke movingly of how traumatic his disappearance had been to the family and his disappearance is mystified by a long silence, which they want to end. The family wants closure, and for that they need answers to the two questions:

1. What happened to him. If he is dead as is likely, how did he die; and

2. If he is dead where is he buried. Can we cause a discovery and if can we disinter his remains and arrange for a proper Christian burial?

This would lead to a closure to a mysterious disappearance of a great human being lost in the mist of historical struggle that has haunted the minds of many thoughtful people in Ethiopia and beyond.

The Ambassador went back in his thoughts to the time of struggle, when Negassa used to organise meetings and conduct seminars that were incomparable in the range of issues covered and the depth of the discussion as well as the passion displayed by the members of the Movement.

After being lost in thought for a few seconds, the Ambassador came back from his reverie of some moments of the past and asked his visitors if they knew about the alliance in which the movement that Negassa led was involved in.

"I mean the temporary alliance we were involved in with the military government." he elaborated on his question. Both Isabelle and Stefan said they had read about it.

"I am sure you have read about it…Mostly negative comments, I am sure… blaming our movement of a sell-out to the military dictatorship… Let me tell you that it was a risk our leadership took in the belief that some of the patriots and progressively inclined members of the military would help in turning the revolution toward a better direction, better for the people…It was a gamble we had taken hoping for better results. As I said it was risky, a gamble…We gambled and lost!"

"Why didn't your movement cooperate with the other civilian revolutionary movement?" Stefan asked, having read some accounts about the fallout between the two movements.

"It is a long and sad story of misunderstanding, of mutual suspicions, some petty ambitions disputes and so on. Both sides must share in the blame, and historians will sort it out in the long historical perspective where more of the blame lies. But it is of no use to dwell on the past engaged in the blame game; instead we need to learn from our mistakes and look ahead to a better mode of mutual understanding in erecting a better system of governance for the good of the people as a whole.

After a longue pose, the Ambassador went back to the project that Isabelle talked about and asked: What is your real objective? Is it a personal family wish to find and recover Negassa's remains?"

Yes, said Isabelle; "It is as simple as that," which caused a small chuckle from the Ambassador, who cast his eyes to the floor.

"I don't wish to demean your questions and your legitimate request," Mr. Taddesse said apologetically, being anxious lest his chuckle might be misinterpreted.

"On the contrary," he continued, "I respect and admire your determination and filial devotion. And I will do everything I can to help you. Your father's memory is important not only to you close relatives, but to his large circle of fraternity of political comrades and extended family."

"I am delighted to hear you say so, uncle Taddese. I feel sure my dad is smiling at all this as we speak," Isabelle said with a quivering voice, overcome with emotion. Stefan stretched his arm and held her hand in his, patting her back with the other arm. Taddese was also touched by Isabelle's reaction and got up and stretched his arms toward her, which Isabelle accepted walking to his embrace; they hugged for a long while, both caught in the emotion of the moment.

Taddesse broke from the embrace and said:

"We must celebrate this meeting and have lunch and drink to the success of your worthy mission of love," Taddese said. "My wife is away back home to attend a wedding of her nephew; so, I cannot host you at home, I am afraid. But we will have dinner in a nice restaurant owned by a young Ethiopian in town. I will ask my secretary to book a place for us in the restaurant. She will also tell the driver to pick you from your hotel and bring you to the restaurant. Okay?"

"*Ishi* uncle Taddese," Isabelle said with a smile. "Ah, you speak Amharic!"

"Just a few words I picked up from some Ethiopian students I knew in Geneva."

"You should learn more."

"That's what I keep telling her," Stefan said

"I may have to find an Ethiopian boyfriend, which is the best way of learning language," Isabelle said, tongue-in-cheek, teasing Stefan." Stefan blushed and kept quiet. And Ambassador Taddese, being a good diplomat, kept silent believing silence to be the best way, following an Amharic saying about silence-"*zim aineqzim*."

Finally, Ambassador Taddese said he had an appointment at the UN. So they all rose and bid one another au revoir until dinner time. Taddese saw them to the door.

At the dinner in the restaurant, Taddese summed up his idea in which he would provide help. He said he will draw up a list of members of their movement who have joined the current government who can help the project in all respects—logistics, connections, legal issues, translations or interpretation, and assistance in case of emergency. He ended with a promise: "I will have this ready for you to pick up first thing tomorrow, Insha'Allah, as our Muslim brothers say."

Back in Brussels, Isabelle and Stefan resumed their regular employment and met with friends and colleagues and briefed those who are intimate among them the essence of their respective activities. The first person both contacted by phone was Rashid, who had himself just returned from a trip to Bangladesh where he made a brief study of the conditions of Rohingya migrants, interviewing some leaders and also made representations to local Bangladeshi authorities about what he found. Rashid said he took a short leave of absence from his soccer game commitments, and also visited friends and relatives in Sudan on his way back.

"Did you meet people in Sudan who might help us in our especial mission?" Isabelle asked him

"Not particularly, but I met Sudanese businessmen who travel back and forth to Ethiopia. Do you have any special reason for asking me this question," Rashid asked Isabelle.

"Yes, I have. It occurred to me after conversations I had with a couple of wonderful Americans who hosted us during our brief stay in Washington. Their names are Robert and Wanda Wyzanski. Robert is head of an important division of the American Academy of Sciences and was involved in the Washington International Meeting that Stefan attended; in fact, he chaired the meeting where a sad incident occurred as you might have heard.

"The one in which a woman was killed?" Rashid asked, and when he was told it was, he said that Stefan had briefed him about it.

"So what is the special reason about your interest in Sudan?" Rashid asked her and she said this is a matter she and Stefan would like to discuss with him in their next meeting when he comes to Brussels. "By the way, are you coming here soon?" she asked him and he said he was coming in three days' time.

"Good. We will have a lot to talk about and I look forward to seeing you; I miss you, Rashid."

"I miss you too Isabelle, and we have a lot to talk about," he said, and they ended their conversation…

…A few days later, Rashid came to the EU office where Isabelle worked. The two of them called Stefan and agreed to have a coffee meeting in a café not far from their office. It had been almost a month since they had a meeting at the Amnesty office in London. So, they gave one another brief reports of what they had been doing since the London meeting. A quarter of an hour later, Isabelle announced that she had an idea or rather an outline of an idea about their mission. Stefan was surprised she had not intimated her idea with him before, which he thought was unlike her. Both waited for Isabelle to tell them about her idea. Rashid said: "we are all ears."

"Well, as I said it is just an outline and it goes like this," she began. "The first point about the idea is that we will need money to bring off our ambitious project. So what do we do to obtain the money?"…

"Is that a question to us?"…That was Stefan, who had felt a pang of resentment for not having been consulted. "No, not a question; it is just an introduction," she told him boldly, being conscious of a slight change of mood on his part judging by the tone of his question.

"So, don't keep us in suspense, girl; common, give!" Rashid egged her on with a laugh.

Isabelle apologised for being slow and told them her idea was born in Washington when she stayed with the Wyzanskis as a guest. Stefan knows these good couple. Wanda Wyzanski, the wife, a very thoughtful person, brought the idea of creating a temporary research project, to be underwritten by her husband's organization, the American Science Academy.

She suggested a tentative name for the research project, like "*The Economics of Volunteerism in Ethiopia: A Modest Research Project.*" From her own experience as an expatriate in Ethiopia, she observed that there are local, community-based voluntary organizations in the country that can be used as models for the project. One such voluntary organization is the *Idder* that local people use as an informal banking to help meet emergence situations like funerals and weddings.

Both men listened attentively becoming intensely interested, wondering where Isabelle was heading. Stefan, for one, kept wondering why she had not spoken to him about all this, especially during their New York sojourn

As if sensing his thinking, Isabelle continued: "I know Stefan may be wondering why I had not shared this with him when we were in America and since our return. I am sorry, Stefan. I was turning the idea in my head and was only convinced a couple of days ago that it would be useful. I hope you understand, Stefan, dear," she told him gazing into his eyes intently for a few seconds. He told her that he understood and that there was no problem. So she continued her expose.

"The Wyzanskis are wedded to the idea of the research project, he more professionally as head of a department of the American Science Academy, and she being deeply interested in our mission on a personal level. I seem to have touched a nerve—a humanitarian nerve, so to speak—in her."

Stefan chimed in: "Yes, I noticed that Wanda Wyzanski was taken to Isabelle from my brief encounter with her. Leaving aside everything else just at a human level considering the nature of the mission, involving as it does, a touching human factor of a disappeared father and a daughter deprived of a father's love, and now wanting to recover his remains. What sensitive person could fail to be touched by such a story?"

"Thank you Stefan dear, for eloquently expressing it."

"Please continue, Isabelle, before I start crying!" Rashid exclaimed half in jest and half in earnest.

Well, the idea of a research project needs to be fleshed out in detail with financial and logistical factors taken into serious consideration. In this respect we will need the assistance of professional people, and the three of us need to put our heads together to recruit people."

Isabelle suggested that Stefan can speak or write to Bob Wyzanski for that purpose and she can do the same to Wanda, or both of them could send a joint letter to the Wyzanskis. She suggested that this and other related issues need to be discussed in more detail. She also raised the possibility of conducting a similar project in Sudan and asked Rashid' view on that point.

The idea is to create a regional context for the idea behind the research project and thus persuade interested people of the salience of the idea and its practical value for ordinary people. A regional context will also appeal to Bob and Wanda Wyzanski in that it can enable them to secure sufficient financial backing from potential funding sources. Again, Isabelle expected Rashid will offer his own views on the possibility of starting a similar project in Sudan.

"Finally, I wonder whether the appropriate departments of the EU might also provide assistance, either logistical or financial, or both. This is of course Stefan's area of interest and I would like him to offer his views on this point. I have finished the outline of my ideas, and I thank you for tolerating my meandering thoughts."

Rashid was first to respond, agreeing that a regional approach would be useful. However, in the prevailing environment of mutual suspicion between Western-based institutions and those in Muslim countries like Sudan, he thought it unlikely that we can succeed in creating what Isabelle suggested at the present moment. "But I think the idea as concerns Ethiopia, will be very helpful to enable us to obtain funding," Rashid said.

Stefan also agreed wholeheartedly with Isabelle's idea of a research project as outlined in her remarks. He promised to consult with the heads of some relevant units in the EU, both in terms of logistical and financial support for the project. He added a well-deserved tribute:

"Let me also say, at the risk of embarrassing Isabelle, who is well known for her modesty, that I am amazed at her intellectual acuity and insight in coming up with the idea and giving us a clearly stated expose…"

After a short pause, and watching Isabelle's face, he added:

"I told you; there she goes blushing! But I am used to this, which by the way, is, in my view, one of Isabelle's lovable qualities."

"So where do we go from here?" Rashid asked and answered his own question by suggesting another meeting in a week or so, when the three of them perhaps with a couple of additional people could go through Isabelle's idea in more detail and also workout a timeline and budget for the project.

"I also think we can request funding from sympathetic individuals and groups. To that end, I am hereby making an undertaking to make available for the project an initial sum of $100,000 Euros.

"Wow!" Isabelle cried loudly, drawing the attention of a few people sitting at a nearby table. Isabelle rose to give Rashid a kiss on the cheek…

And Stefan looked at Rashid in amazement and quietly said: "wow indeed!"

They decided to call it a day and agreed to meet in a week's time. Isabelle agreed to specify the time and place of the meeting and act as coordinator.

Isabelle had a few days left from her leave of absence, so she stayed in her modest apartment and sat on her sofa reflecting on the next moves, including helping to provide details to the outline of the ideas that she presented to her friends. Her apartment was of medium size, furnished with a large bed in her small bedroom, a living room with a large sofa, a writing table that stood before the sofa and four chairs and a book case in the corner. A door leads to a small washroom with a sink, a lavatory and bath and a shower room, where she spent considerable amount of time lingering playfully under the warm shower pouring over her head and the rest of her lissome, light brown- skinned body. That day, she had risen from her sofa, disrobed and gone to the shower room for a warm shower, and lingered in it as usual. Then she wiped her hair and her body with a large towel. She dried her long and black hair that hung loosely on her chest spread over and around her shoulders...

After washing and drying, she put on her pajamas and her long, loose African gown that Rashid had given her as a present the previous Christmas Day. She poured herself a glass full of Burgundy and sat on the sofa, sipping the wine and slowly and savoring it...

...For the first time since conceiving of the idea of resolving the mystery of her father's disappearance and recovering his remains to give them a decent Christian burial, Isabelle felt justly proud of herself. She even fancied herself a special heroine and mentally patted her shoulder, looking herself in the mirror and smiling. She playfully winked at herself, thinking she is beautiful but laughing at this fanciful "silliness."...

...Her thoughts wandered from one subject to another and thought of one man and then of another, comparing Stefan with Rashid...

"Oh Rashid! How wonderfully generous you are!" she intoned... "And handsome, with that brutal charm...Sometimes, I fancy him as a future companion for life," she half-whispered to herself, and then dismissed the idea as fanciful and disruptive of a magical relationship among the three of them.

After she had lunch consisting of salad and spaghetti with spiced Ethiopia sauce that her mother had taught her to prepare, and cheese. She finished off with Colombian coffee and prepared to work on her assignment for the mission. Her self-assigned duties concerned mainly preparing a rough budget proposal for the mission, as well as a list of personnel need for the accomplished of the mission.

Budget Estimate.
The main items of expenditure are:

1. Round Trip Air fares Brussels - Addis Ababa for three people, p and/or bus fares within Ethiopia for three months
2. Hotel Expenses for three people or alternatively a house rent for all three months.
3. Food and bottled water expenses for three people for three months
4. Clerical and related expenses, including translation of documents
5. Car rental—a large vehicle for use of all personnel for three months
6. Incidental expenses, including health services.

7. A reasonable amount of stipend for three people, amount to be determ

8. Hiring of a local house manager and cook

9. Hiring of an all-purpose person to act as guide, interpreter and counselor sensitive issues.

10. Hiring of a driver/mechanic for three months-to a year

[An estimate of the expenditure for the ten items listed above is attached.]

List of Personnel:

1. Isabelle Negassa
2. Stefan Schmidt
3. Rashid Idris
4. A sociologist
5. A lawyer/Linguist

The budget estimate is attached. As for the personnel, in addition to the three initiators, two more are needed, preferably a sociologist or an anthropologist and a lawyer/linguist (who speaks Amharic and Oromifa. Isabelle thinks the sociologist or anthropologist should be chosen by Dr. Wyzanski with a stipulation that the American Academy might foot the bill for him. The other person, the lawyer/linguist should be chosen by either Stefan or Isabelle in consultation with Rashid.

Isabelle also thinks that Dr. Yusuf Ibrahim, Rashid's uncle and rich businessman should be recruited to help in two ways. One is to help in the project if it is started in Sudan. The other is to help in using his wide contacts in Ethiopian government circles. Dr. Ibrahim's Ethiopian wife is also well connected to important people in Ethiopia and could be helpful in cutting bureaucratic hurdles, especially when it comes to discovering Negassa's burial site. This is also a matter that will have to be considered in consultation with Rashid. Rashid is in constant contact with his uncle Idris and he may perhaps take this matter up with him when he next talks to him, preferably directly when they next meet in Geneva or elsewhere. It cannot be overstressed that personal intervention by influential people can expedite matters. Closed doors are opened and in sensitive subjects involving the disappearance of a well-known political figure in mysterious circumstances may occasion difficulties when such issues are probed because it is hard to know who might be opposed to the discovery that is being sought and a demand for retrieval of his remains.

Chapter Nine

VOYAGE TO ADDIS VIA GENEVA

Isabelle and Stefan met briefly and agreed on two matters, and Isabelle also called Rashid and secured his agreement on it. The first is that the additional two members must be recruited locally in Ethiopia. Second, the trip should be made via Geneva Switzerland in order to have extensive consultations with Rashid's uncle, Dr. Yusuf Ibrahim, on his assistance in the project. The consultation should also include Dr. Ibrahim's Ethiopian wife who has connections with influential people in Addis Ababa.

The other change on which they agreed flows from the first, that is to say, the budget will be reduced: the fare Brussels - Addis will be for three people instead of five. Also, the stay in Addis for the group will be three months instead of five, and only Isabelle will stay there all three months so that Rashid and Stefan would return to Brussels within a few days. This too will reduce the budget considerably. Isabelle will lead the project with the assistance of the two professionals recruited from Ethiopia as well as with whoever Dr. Ibrahim and his wife can provide.

The stay in Geneva will not be more than two or three days. Dr. Ibrahim has kindly offered to host the group in his large house in Geneva, thus helping in reducing expenses. Rashid has also promised to persuade Dr. Ibrahim to make contributions for the project budget. On the whole, therefore, the budget will be adequately funded, especially if Dr. Wyzanski's American Academy office will secure funding to defray the expenses for the two professionals to be recruited from Ethiopia.

109

The Voyage Begins

Our three heroes flew from Brussels to Geneva on a slightly chilly morning in October and were met at the airport in Geneva by an employee of Yusuf's company, a cheerful and talkative Eritrean driver, named Mesfin, who said he had lived in Switzerland most of his adult life. He spoke excellent English, and French is his first language next to Tigrigna, his mother tongue. He also knows spoken Arabic, which he picked up in Sudan when he stayed there as a refugee in his late teens and early twenties. All this information was provided to the guests in rapid succession during the short drive from the airport to the Ibrahim house in 65 Rue Athene. Geneve Mesfin brought the group to the Ibrahim home and helped in carrying their bags to their respective rooms, and told them he has been instructed by Dr. Ibrahim to do whatever they asked him to do, like driving them anywhere in Geneva.

Dr Ibrahim's villa was situated in a highly valued residential area of Geneva, populated by professional people like lawyers and doctors as well as well-to-do businesspeople. The house is two storied stone building with six bedrooms and four bathrooms. Four of the bedrooms are located in the top floor while two bedrooms are situated at the two ends of the ground floor, with a large dining room and lounge in between. The lounge is furnished with two large sofas. The lounge walls are graced with large pictures of the smiling couple and several pictures of members of the extended family.

Dr. Ibrahim was out in town on a business meeting, his wife said welcoming her guests warmly with a charming smile. "My name is Azeb, and I welcome you to our humble residence," she told them, adding that after a while they would be treated to a meal at their convenience. She did not wish to rush them, but the meal would be served any time they are ready. If they want to rest a little, please do so and take your time. "Please consider this house as your own," She said with big smile. Going toward Rashid with open arms and embracing him in a warm hug, she said:

"Rashid, please tell your two friends to feel absolutely free and treat this humble place as their own. As for you…you have not called for over a month. What is going on, *ya shifta*?"

"She always calls me shifta, which in Amharic means bandit," Rashid said with a smile and putting his left arm round her shoulders. "I ask you; do I look like a bandit? "Yes, the two said in unison!"

"Ah! You see, she has already charmed you in a few minutes. Now you see how she charmed my uncle out of a Sudanese marriage into marrying her in record time!"

"He is exaggerating as he always does."...

Azeb is a middle-aged woman with a beautiful face and coiffure. She is endowed with a fairly large figure and large bosom. Her graceful manner accompanied with an ever-smiling face and large bright eyes makes her a commanding presence.

...The guests were shown their respected rooms. After a while, they changed into more casual clothes and came out to the living room.

Yusuf Ibrahim came home from his meeting and joined the group for tea, following their siesta which they had after lunch. Ibrahim is a short and rather stout man in his early seventies. He has a pleasant roundish face, light brown and clean-shaven. He spoke English very well with a tinge of British accent, learned first in school and in Omdurman College and later perfected during his stay in London studying at King's College London. He is affable in manners and progressive in his thinking, a result of having been influenced, during his college days in the Sudan, by Left Wing politics dominated by the communist party of Sudan. He fell afoul with the communists during the Nimeiry era when he secured a British Council scholarship to go to England to continue his studies. Even after he ventured into business, in the energy and communications sector and made much money, Ibrahim kept his progressive politics, remaining in contact with former comrades and school mates. Ibrahim's influence in Rashid's education and intellectual development is found in much of Rashid's thinking and worldview, exemplified by his empathetic attitudes toward the question of migrants in Europe and elsewhere. He condemns most emphatically the policies and politics of American President Donald Trump. And he uses his extensive business contacts in European countries to effect changes in their respective governments' immigration policies.

During the tea break with his guests he told them about some of his travels and actions with respect to refugees.

"Recently, I visited a refugee camp in Calais, a place in northern France, where there is a place the refugees called The Jungle," he told them. "I was told about it by a French friend who knew some Relief organizations doing relief work there. I traveled incognito, and I met refugees from several countries, including Sudan, Eritrea, Ethiopia from our region as well as from Afghanistan, Pakistan, Iran and Iraq."

"I have known about it; it is a horrible camp," Isabelle said.

"It is indeed a horrible camp. But I saw another side to the Jungle,' Ibrahim said." Because of the work of some wonderful relief workers and the extraordinary humanity in which the work of these relief workers is grounded, the Jungle demonstrated a positive side. The refugees themselves wanted us visitors and, through us, the world to know the positive aspects of their lives in the Jungle: their close and loving families; their pleasure in and commitment to education; their beautiful countries; their determination to survive in those countries, on their own in the Jungle, and in their new home countries; and their commitment to finding safety, working, and helping others."

"Did you talk to the refugees and did you hear these words from them?" Stefan asked.

"Yes, I did talk to them at length. I also talked to some of the French relief workers as well as to some students from East London University who were engaged in a research project in Calais," Yusuf answered with feeling, reflecting the extent to which he had been affected by his visit. He could not stop talking about the subject. He told about the obstacles they had to overcome, first getting out of their homelands that were involved in war: childhoods in violent places, living as adults amid conflict, genocide and persecution...Yusuf stopped as though he was assaulted by memories of what he saw and heard at the Jungle... "And then there was their dangerous journeys," he continued, "across mountains, deserts and seas...followed by the abject conditions of the Jungle, where they were dumped... like refuse... Until help arrived from people who treated them like brothers and sisters."

Ibrahim rose to go to the bathroom and said as he started moving: "Let us change the subject to a more pleasant topic for a change."

"He is quite right," Isabelle said, and Stefan agreed: "How about talking about Geneva and what we can see as tourists for today? before we begin talking about the matters for which we came."

Azeb said she would be glad to take the group to the center of Geneva. "And then we can then see what you would like to see in Geneva."

"I would like to visit the University where I studied, first, if you would be so good to take me there. And the Palais de Nation, and WHO and ILO, after that. How does that sound?"

"I am game," Stefan said and Rashid and Azeb nodded in agreement. "Speaking of the WHO, I want to visit the newly appointed head who is

Ethiopian and is, I believe, the first African to head the organization.'

Azeb said, "that is a capital idea, and I for one have a duty to visit my country man."

Ibrahim returned from the bathroom and was briefed about the agreement of the visit and tour and he readily agreed.

After the Geneva tour the group was treated to an evening meal consisting of delicious Ethiopian food—Doro wat, fifit, Gored-gored and Awaze Beg, which everyone enjoyed. Stefan thanked the gracious hostess and Isabelle said she liked above all the Doro-wat and wanted to know how it is made… Then Dr. Ibrahim brought forth rare bottles of French wine and invited everyone to help themselves. "In this household, wine is *Halal,* and even Rashid is now a convert to wine drinking.

All three guests helped themselves to the wine.

"Today is a day of greeting," Ibrahim said. "Apart from my little speech about refugees, I promise to steer away from talking about the business for which you have come to visit us."

"Here! Here!" Rashid chimed in, raising his glass to stress his agreement.

Everyone raised their glasses.

"What is the cause for celebration," she asked with a smile.

Ibrahim answered his wife: "Rashid raised his glass in agreement with my statement that we shall not talk about business tonight; we will do that tomorrow."

"So, dessert and/or coffee everybody," Azeb asked, adding, "We have ice cream."

They all wanted ice cream to be followed by coffee…

…Having passed a good day and after the wonderful dinner and wine, they were all ready to go to bed…

The following morning, they met at breakfast at 8 o'clock, after which they sat at Ibrahim's studio for a meeting.

The four sat around a rectangular table. Ibrahim sat at the head of the table. Isabelle and Stefan sat on one side of the table, and Rashid sat opposite to them. Rashid said: "I would like to welcome you to our home. I am honored to be consulted for a noble objective. Rashid has briefed me in summary about the object of your endeavor, and I wish to assure you that both my wife and I will do everything we can to help in this endeavor. I have asked Azeb to join us and she will join us shortly.

Azeb came a couple of minutes after Ibrahim's statement and sat by Rashid's side, apologizing for her late arrival. Ibrahim started the ball rolling, so to speak. He said:

"Well, we can now begin. I understand that you need our advice or assistance in finding how and why Isabelle's father disappeared, what happened to him, if he is dead where is he buried. Am I right?"

"Yes, Ibrahim, that is briefly the object of our search," Isabelle said.

"Well, Azeb can speak for herself, and I will for myself. Azeb, do you want to speak now?"

"No, you go ahead, I will speak later."

"Well, I have heard of Dr. Negassa and his organization, the Ethiopian Socialist Movement, if I have got the name right. I never met him, but I have heard Ethiopians and some Sudanese speak of him admiringly. I heard of his disappearance in connection with the conflict between his organization and the leadership of the military government, especially Mengistu Hailemariam, as a result of disagreement on some issues. I don't know the details on the conflict, only that they disagreed and that some of the leaders of Negassa's organization were liquidated." …

… "I have no way of knowing exactly as to whether Negassa was among those liquidated first, or how and where he was killed. But that he was killed by some means is beyond question. The question is where and when and how. And of course, where his remains are, which is the heart of Isabelle's search, as I understand it."

Yusuf Ibrahim then went on to relate how he heard of Negassa's death from some Sudanese sources. He had little doubt that he was killed, probably at the order of Mengistu who obviously saw him as a formidable rival, just as he had seen General Aman Andom as a rival and had him eliminated a year or two before.

Ibrahim then spoke about what can be done to find out answers to the questions. As to whether he is dead, there is no doubt, Ibrahim said again. He also said that Azeb has some information about where and how he died, which gives a clue as to where he was buried. He asked Azeb if she wanted to speak now.

"Yes. My information is based on two sources," Azeb began, "one is rumors from friends who knew Negassa and also that there was a fallout between the Derg and MEISON, Negassa's organization. I also heard that some of the MEISON leaders had made attempts to flee and were caught and executed immediately. I don't know if Negassa was among them. I don't think so…"

Azeb went silent for a bit and took up the narrative from where she left off. "My other source is Girmachew, my former husband who was a high- ranking officer and knew Mengistu and his close friends. Girmachew told me that Mengistu and Negassa had a row during a special meeting in which Negassa told Mengistu that the revolution was going on a wrong direction. Mengistu abused Negassa and told him he did not need any lecture from a so- called educated socialist or words to that effect."

She stopped for a minute and continued to inform the group that she knows people who were connected with the present government and that one such person told his sister who happened to be a friend of hers that he heard from a top government official that Negassa was tortured severely and that he either died as a result of the torture or he was subsequently executed at Mengistu's order…

Azeb was half embarrassed because she had not told this story to anyone, including her husband, Yusuf Ibrahim…

"Did the informant say where my father was buried?"

"I don't think so. At least my informant did not say so." Azeb lowered her head gazing at her feet for a while. Her forehead was furrowed, and her face changed color and she showed signs of disturbance, as she wrung her hands and covered her face with her hands trembling.

"Are you okay, *ya habibti*?" Ibrahim asked her.

"I am okay…Just some bad memories, that's all. Can we have a break for coffee?"

"Of course, *habibti*, we will have a break. Shall we say half an hour's break?"

They all agreed and left the studio and headed to the living room…

Stefan whispered on Isabelle's ears, and she nodded. He then asked loudly if it is okay to meet after lunch instead of now. Stefan got closer to

Rashid and said that he thought that he noticed some signs of disturbance in Azeb's behavior and thought it may be a good idea to consult with Dr. Ibrahim as to how to proceed. For example, he thought it a good idea for Dr. Ibrahim to talk to Azeb and asked her if she wishes not to participate in the meeting, or at least she may be excused from being asked to speak unless she wants to. Ibrahim agreed, though he did not feel that Azeb was disturbed.

Isabelle spoke agreeing with Stefan's concerns and volunteered to speak to Azeb quietly— woman to woman. Almost immediately, Isabelle poured coffee to a cup and, holding her cup, walked toward the parlor where Azeb was sitting also sipping coffee. Azeb rose and smiled. Isabelle did not waste any time. She went straight to the point.

"Azeb, dear, may I speak to you as a sister, woman to woman?"

Azeb said: "Of course Isabelle," and screwed her brow gazing at Isabelle with curiosity.

"It may be woman's instinct or perhaps silly fancy. But I thought you were deeply affected when you spoke about what your informant told you about my father's death and burial place. Am I imagining things?"

Azeb again held her head in her hands rubbing her hair and waited a little while before she responded. Finally, she turned toward Isabelle and looked straight into her soft and sad eyes and started sobbing. Isabelle put her arms round Azeb's shoulders and said quietly:

"You don't have to say anything if you don't want to, you know," she said in a quivering voice.

"I didn't tell you the whole story," Azeb said and, facing Isabelle and holding her hands, she said:

"The informant told me that your father was killed after his torture and was buried in an unmarked grave at night, with only a few of Mengistu's fanatical followers participating in the burial."

"Did he say who they were?"

"He did not know them, but Mengistu's fanatical followers are known to the current government. If they are not dead, they must be in prison.".…

They sat there in silence for a while, and Isabelle thanked Azeb for telling her the true story… She then said:

"So, now it is a question of whether the current government can do the right thing to help us discover exactly where my father is buried in the unmarked grave."

"You are quite right. It is up to the government to do that, and both Dr. Ibrahim and I have a few friends with contacts in the government. We shall do what we can. We must."

"Again, thank my dear sister; I am deeply touched."

Isabelle briefed Stefan and Rashid the essence of her conversations with Azeb. Stefan worried whether this might create problems between husband and wife, and Rashid said the love of the couple is very strong. All that is needed is for Azeb to explain to Ibrahim why she did not tell him the story before. "A few feminine tears and a warm embrace and a kiss will do it. Believe me," Rashid said. "I hope you are right," Stefan said, adding," maybe we Europeans have much to learn from our African brothers in these matters."

"And maybe also the other way around, in some other matters," Isabelle interjected, and both Stefan and Yusuf Ibrahim laughed joined by Isabelle.

After lunch and a short siesta, the group met with Dr. Ibrahim, but minus Azeb. Dr. Ibrahim said that Azeb had a bad headache and asked to be excused for not attending the meeting. Isabelle spoke for the others when she said: "Oh, I am sorry she has a headache, but we can brief her of our proceedings, won't we?" Isabelle said turning her gaze at Stefan and Rashid one after the other. Yes, of course they said yes, one after the other.

So, the meeting continued with the four of them. Yusuf Ibrahim gave his own correct assessment in line with the conclusion arrived at between Isabelle and Azeb and shared by Stefan and Rashid, namely that they would now focus on the current government in their attempts to discover the unmarked grave where Negassa was buried by the Mengistu regime.

Yusuf Ibrahim must have had a talk with Azeb during the siesta for he did not raise any questions. Nor did he challenge the desire of the group to apply whatever influence was available, including his own influence and that of his wife.

"So, now we are all ready to go to Addis, right?" Rashid queried, adding, "Insha'Allah."

"Yes, Insha'Allah" Stefan said, looking at Isabelle with a sly smile.

And Yusuf Ibrahim gave a soft laugh with a shake of the head and final agreement:

"Yes indeed, Insha'Allah!"

Chapter Ten

ADDIS ABABA: HERE WE COME

Addis Ababa is the seat the United Nation's Economic Commission of Africa as well as several other international and continental organizations, notably the African Union (formerly the Organisation of African Unity) and the UN's Economic Commission of Africa. For this reason, some people call Addis Ababa Africa's unofficial capital. The fact of the presence of so many important political and economic organizations in Addis Ababa has made it a magnet for investment from many countries of the world, which in turn has helped considerably in its growth in size and population. Like all developing countries, urban growth attracts the youth of rural populations to flock to the towns and cities thus creating overcrowding and attendant social and political problems. The inordinate, unplanned growth of shantytowns is like a festering sore in the urban corporate body. A day's visit, each to Lagos, Cape Town (the Cape Flats), Nairobi and Addis Ababa, and a tour around the shantytowns of these great cities is enough to show the fact of uneven (unplanned) growth of African cities. And the majority of the mass of their populations live in or around these shantytowns. It is also a matter of common sense for revolutionaries like Negassa to have lived among the people of such places for the simple reason that when they worked underground, they would not have lived or worked in the areas with better conditions where they would be spotted and arrested.

Thus, that Negassa must have lived in such places stands to reason, but whether he was caught there is unlikely. As Ambassador Taddesse explained to Isabelle and Stefan, Negassa's group had entered into a *"Faustian Bargain"* with the military regime, a bargain that did not last long and did cost his life and the lives of many of his comrades. This means that he and his comrades had lived and worked in better parts of the residential areas, where he was probably caught.

All this speculation is not relevant to our story, except that from the example of other revolutionaries working underground in urban areas, it is among the working class population that they lived, considering the people as "the sea" and themselves as the fish swimming among the people, to paraphrase a known writer on revolution.

Preparation for Addis Trip

Stefan took the responsibility of obtaining entry visas to Ethiopia for himself as well as for Isabelle and Rashid. He took the three passports to the Ethiopian Mission to the EU in Brussels. The consular officer asked him the reason for the visit to Ethiopia and, in accordance with their agreement, he wrote on the form: Reason for visit—Research on Ethiopian Voluntary Organizations. When asked who is funding the research project, Stefan said it is mainly funded by private voluntary organizations and interested individual donors.

The visa was granted for one year, without problem, and Stefan and Isabelle consulted with Rashid on the date of travel, which was to be via Geneva. On the last day of their stay in Geneva, Azeb told the three while they were having dinner that they will stay in their Large villa in Addis Ababa. She told them that a driver would meet them at the Bole Airport and take them to the villa. When Stefan remonstrated about this being too much, Azeb said: "It has been decided by Dr. Ibrahim and myself that you will stay in the villa as our guests. And there will be no argument, okay?"

So, after three days' enjoyable and productive stay in Geneva, the three left to Addis Ababa. They changed plane in Rome and took an Ethiopian Airlines direct flight to Addis Ababa. Dr. Ibrahim also told them he was going to call some influential friends and business clients to receive them in their offices or homes and provide all necessary assistance. All will work out, he reassured them. Just believe that you have a just cause and you will succeed, he told them emphatically.

The non-stop flight from Rome was pleasant. The Ethiopian Airline hostesses showed their famous hospitality with shy smiles. The sight of the city was spectacular and the landing was faultless. The captain himself came on and announced their arrival, declaring: "Ladies and gentlemen welcome to our beautiful city…It has been our pleasure to have you fly Ethiopian and we wish you a wonderful stay in Addis Ababa or wherever your destination may be. We hope to see you in one of our flights again. Goodbye!"

The entry process at the Customs and Immigration desks was smooth. They had nothing to declare, so they were ushered speedily out to the reception area. They waited for their luggages at the Luggage Claim Area for some fifteen minutes Having retrieved their luggage, they gazed toward the crowd of people carrying signs of names. They noticed one with Isabelle Negassa written on it. Isabelle smiled and waved at the man carrying the sign, who waved back with a wide smile. He was a young man in his twenties, tall with black hair and a mustache.

He came forward pushing a trolley. He greeted all three with typical Ethiopian bows and also shook everyone's hand. He said: "Welcome to Addis" and placed their bags on the trolley and led them out to the parking areas. He put the bags inside in the back of the SUV Toyota and opened the doors for them to go in.

Unlike Mesfin, the Ibrahim family's driver in Geneva, their driver in Addis Ababa was a quiet man who only spoke when he was spoken to, or when asked a question. His name is Kassa and he said he had been instructed by Madame Azeb to look after the guests and do whatever they ask. The drive from Bole to the villa took about half an hour. A large door made of iron was opened by a guard, who duly bowed to the guests and helped Kassa taking their bags from the car to the front parlor. Kassa called the housekeeper and introduced her to the guests.

"This is Beletech, the housekeeper, he told them. She too bowed deeply and stretched her two hands to shake each one's hand. She is in her early twenties and very shy but has a charming smile.

"She speaks English fairly well," Kassa told them, and also that she is a close relative of Madame Azeb who raised her. Beletech led them to the first floor and showed each one to their respective rooms, and Kassa brought the bags and left them near the door of one of the rooms. Each one of the guests then took their bags and put them in their rooms.

They had arrived in Addis.

Beletech informed the guests about the house rules on meals and coffee or tea service in the Villa Ibrahim. Breakfast is served between seven and nine in the morning. Lunch is served between 12:30 and 2 pm. Coffee and tea can be served whenever asked by any of the guests and Beletech will serve them.

On the day of their arrival, because they arrived late, they were welcome to have a snack with tea or coffee or (Ambo) mineral water.

There is a well-furnished studio with telephone and TV. The house is served with WI-FI for internet services. In short, the villa is fully provided in the manner of a first-class hotel, with the difference that most of the service is free in the Villa Ibrahim to these lucky guests.

Isabelle was first to wake up in the morning. Beletech who rises before 6 in the morning heard Isabelle walking from the first floor to the kitchen. They greeted each other and agreed to have an early breakfast in the dining room, where they were engaged in conversation. Isabelle told Beletech that she couldn't sleep. Beletech told her that many people coming from Europe for the first time find it difficult to sleep during the first few days.

"They say it is because of the high altitude," Beletech said. "I suspected as much," Isabelle said confirming her suspicion or guess. Apparently, both Rashid and Stefan slept well. When they came down for breakfast eventually, Isabelle told them she had not slept well and asked them both how they slept. Rashid said he slept like a log, and Stefan said he slept well, though it took him an hour or so before he dozed off. "I can understand Rashid having no problem because I am sure he has been to Addis before, but you, Stefan didn't have any problem, though you have not slept on this high altitude before," Isabelle wondered.

"But I have been to the mountain area of southern Germany may times," Stefan said, adding, "I am sure you will get used to the altitude in about a week." He called Rashid to join him for breakfast in the dining room. "Isabelle has had her breakfast already."

The two had breakfast and later joined Isabelle in the kitchen, where she was deeply engaged in conversation with Beletech. "You two seem to have hit it off. Is it the gender fraternity?" Stefan observed and Isabelle said: "She is a lovely person, warm and quite bright. She knows a lot about history and has lived in many countries, and speaks Italian and French in addition to her perfect English.

"Where did she learn these languages, do you know?" Stefan asked. She told me she went to a French-speaking school here in Addis and has lived in Italy when her aunt was living there with her husband who was a diplomat there. Rashid said he admired Beletech and also Isabelle's ability to garner so much information in such a short time. "Not a bad beginning," he complimented Isabelle, who returned the compliment by a graceful bow *a la Etiopienne.*

"And before you complement me on my graceful bowing, let me remind you, in case you have forgotten, it is in my blood; I am half Ethiopian."

"Quite so," Rashid said with a deep bow.

Stefan interposed: "okay you two. Let us move from the ritual of mutual admiration and plan our agenda for today and the following few days. Where do we begin?

Isabelle said she has a preliminary list drawn up for discussion. Here it is:

Azeb gave me the name of the nephew of her former husband Girmachew. His name is Getu and she gave me a number, which m changed. Getu works in the Ministry of Interior, which exercises sup function over security matters as well as on the Police and Administrations. I think that would be a place to start with. Getu ma to other institutions of the government that are relevant to our inquiry

Another place is the Ministry of Justice. Again, Azeb has relatives w there as lawyers. One matter on which we may find information con recruitment of the two professional members of our group.

There are also former members of the leadership of MEISON, or me sympathisers of the organization. It will not be difficult to find p other communications of former MEISON members. Some of them involved with the military regime and are therefore unpopular. We cast our net widely to catch a few of them and that catch will be h getting at the crux of the matter, namely Negassa's unmarked grave.

I am ready for questions and comments, Isabelle said and waited for the two to speak.

"And I will also phone or email Ambassador Taddesse in New York," she said, "and ask him if he can give us some names of former MEISON members, or he has thought of any other kind of assistance."

"I was just thinking about Ambassador Taddesse," Stefan said, and it is a good idea to call or email him. As to your list, I agree. But I think we should start with the office of the Prime Minister and his advisors.

"Why do you know of anybody who works in the Prime Minister's office?" Isabelle asked.

I know an Eritrean friend who lives and works in Brussels who was doing research on MEISON and he told me that he knows of an advisor of the Prime Minister who knew Negassa and may have information about how he was killed."

"That would be very helpful," Rashid joined in, going further to add, "I also think it is a good idea to start with the Prime Minister's office. If I were the Prime Minster, I would want to know more about what the military regime did to its enemies like members of MEISON and EPRP that had been caught and imprisoned."

"Okay, I think I see your points, both of you. So we will start with the office of the Prime Minister. But access to that office is not a cup of tea, as the British say."

"Stefan said his Eritrean friend knows someone who is an advisor of the Prime Minister. Does he know the name of the advisor?" Rashid asked.

"Yes…I wrote his name down…It is Zekarias."

"Well, we are lucky, then. So we will begin with meeting Mr. Zekarias," Isabelle exclaimed gleefully.

"Not Mr. Zekarias. Doctor Zekarias," Stefan corrected.

The Prime Minister's office is in the complex building built by the military government between the Old Menelik Palace (the Ghibi) and the Parliament building. The architecture of the building reflects the state of insecurity under which the military government lived and governed. By contrast, the office of the Prime Minister under Emperor Haile Selassie's government, was an open inviting place, with no security details planted all around its perimeter like an occupying army guarding a foreign invader. The security details are placed at two different points some distance from each other, so that it takes a lot of time and painful negotiations to pass from one point of obstacle to the next. At each point a security man would frisk you meticulously while two of his comrades watch him and his work, to see if he missed anything. And this is repeated at the next level. You are asked to produce IDs again and asked the same questions ad nauseam. It is as if it was designed to discourage citizens from approaching the head of their government, a condition that must be rooted in a profound sense of insecurity and alienation. It inevitably leads the person being subjected to such form of humiliation to wish to end it and go back where he came from...But then any person who goes through such process does so out of a felt need to see the Prime Minister or any one of his close advisors enclosed in that monstrosity of a building.

In an ideal situation, the architecture of government buildings should be a welcoming place, not one that frowns at you or tells you to go back where you came from. In this respect it is tempting to speculate why a Prime minister's office during the imperial government was one that was not surrounded by storm troopers and there was no obstacle placed on the way to enter it. On the contrary, any citizen, whatever his or her status—rich or poor, male or female—felt a sense of welcome. A rectangular structure built during the short Italian occupation of the country, the greyish stone building had a low wall enclosing it at a distance from the building itself.

It is worth remembering, of course, that the Prime Minister during the imperial regime, worked under the supremacy and sovereignty of the Emperor, whereas the post–imperial Prime Minister combined the power of both. Moreover, the imperial palace was not as easily accessible as that of the Prime Minister. Nonetheless, though regimented, the imperial protocol was not as heavy-handed. There was a lightness of touch that reflected a deeper sense of being secure. But then, in fairness to any post-imperial successor, the need for security is a natural necessity until the regime is stabilized. Was the Meles regime stabilized any more than the Mengistu regime? The question raises issues beyond reason of state; it concerns a thorough examination of the psychology involved in revolutionary process, including the regime that issues out of the process. We leave this weighty question for historians to wrestle with and return to our immediate business.

Our group was mishandled by some of the security details at the palace gate. One of the security people was so rude to Isabelle that he provoked

Rashid to intervene on her behalf reminding him that he was rude to a lady, unbecoming to an Ethiopian gentleman. When the security man told Rashid to mind his own business and not intervene in the affairs of a government, Rashid told him that he was intervening in his own business as a lawful guest of the country and demanded an apology from the abusive security officer for being rude to a lady.

The security officer was astonished at the pluck and eloquent defence of a woman's honor by this unknown man that he felt his authority was questioned and had to respond in kind in order to retain his own authority vis- a-vis his colleagues.

"Who do you think you are, protesting against an officer of the government?" he challenged Rashid.

"I am a guest of this great country and also a citizen of a neighboring country who is here lawfully on business."

"What right do you have to interfere in the running of a government security business?" he persisted.

"I did not interfere in the running of your government work. All I did was protest against your rude behavior which is contrary to what I have been used in my dealings with Ethiopians all my adult life, as a lawful guest of this great country and a citizen of a neighboring country."

At that point, Stefan intervened, "Sir, we are sorry about all this. Please allow us just to ask a simple question."

"Yes, what is that?" the angry security man wanted to know. Stefan confronted him with calm equanimity and firmly told him:

"We have an important business with an important advisor of His Excellency the Prime Minister. My question is: are we, or are we not going to be allowed to enter his office?"

"Nobody is denying you access," the man said, "but everything has to be done in accordance with procedures and protocols, which is what we are following." He then asked for the name of the advisor.

"Dr. Zekarias," Stefan responded. The man laughed, joined by a couple of his colleagues and said with some condescension: "Sorry, sir," the man said," Dr. Zekarias is no longer working in the Prime Minister's office.

"So all this hassle is for nothing!" Rashid exclaimed in disgust and called on his colleagues to leave immediately. Which is what they did.

"So, where to now Isabelle, Ministry of Interior?"

"Let us go back to the villa and retool…revisit the whole procedure," Isabelle insisted.

"Spoken like a good leader," Rashid said

Back to the villa, Isabelle placed a call to New York and left a message with the ambassador's secretary who told her that His Excellency was at the UN attending the General Assembly meeting and that she would gladly pass her message when he returned…

The Ambassador called at nine in the evening, which was six New York time. Isabelle briefed him about what they needed from him and he gave her a couple of names of former MEISON members who lived in Addis and that one of them probably teaching at the University. His name he said was Bekele Wako. Isabelle remembered that Dr. Zekarias was also, according to the rude security operative, teaching at the University. So they decided to go there and ask.

Isabelle briefed her colleagues his new information and they decided to go to the University after lunch.

At the University, they asked for the Registrar's office and when they got there they asked if Dr. Zekarias and Dr. Bekele Wako worked at the University. Bekele was on Sabbatical leave, they were told, and doing research in Wollega Province. Zekarias was an Adjunct Professor and does not have an office at the University, but he is usually at the Institute of Ethiopian studies. He may be found about the office of Dr. Richard Pankhurst, the founding chairman of the Institute. It was the Registrar himself who volunteered for the helpful information. So they walked to the office of the Institute and lo and behold, Dr. Zekarias was found, chatting with Dr. Pankhurst. He rose from where he was sitting as did Dr. Pankhurst and both of them welcomed the three guests. They scrambled around and brought two additional chairs for the guests and asked them to sit down.

Richard Pankhurst, the only son of the legendary Sylvia Pankhurst, daughter of her illustrious suffragette mother and herself no less illustrious as a feminist progressive writer and activist. Above all, she was for Ethiopians, an indefatigable fighter for Ethiopian rights during the dark days of Italian occupation of Ethiopia. Richard was himself a notable writer on Ethiopian economic history and current social and economic issues.

Zekarias is a diminutive figure with charming manners who was a leading light during the anti-feudal struggle waged by Ethiopian students until the 1974 revolution. Not much was heard about him later, until the Derg government was overthrown by the combined Ethiopian and Eritrean guerilla forces, after which he reappeared as if from hibernation.

Isabelle began the conversation, telling Dr. Zekarias about her father's disappearance and that she and her two friends were in Ethiopia to discover how he died and where he was buried.

Zekarias was profoundly moved by Isabelle's story and told her that he knew her father during the student activist days in Addis Ababa and in the Diaspora.

"He is one of the historic but tragic figures of the country," Zekarias opined thus clearly and concisely summarising up the story of Isabelle's father. He gazed at her with renewed wonder and sadness clearly visible in his expressive face. All three and Richard Pankhurst watched Zekarias expecting more informative statements from him. There was a short silence during which nobody spoke, and eyes were levelled at Zekarias who felt the collective gaze and suspected that all wished him to speak. But he chose silence as if to digest the moment and let it give birth to anything of which it was supposedly pregnant. As a true Showan, he loved the pregnant moment of silence compressed in the Amharic saying: *Zim aineqzim*. It was an intolerant silence and it was Rashid who broke it.

"Dr. Zekarias, what do you know of Negassa's end, and if you do, where do you think he is buried?"

Zekarias smiled amiably, exposing his cigarette-stained teeth. He brought out his cigarette and was about to light it when it occurred to him that there may be people who were allergic to cigarette smoke, so he checked himself and apologised and put back his cigarette to its container.

"If you need to smoke, why don't you step out and smoke and come back" counseled Isabelle."

He said it was not necessary and began to speak by first taking a deep breath and screwed his Forehead and began.

"Well, my answer to your question how Negassa ended is that he was killed in cold blood by the order of Mengistu Hailemariam,"...he stopped, presumably not for dramatic effect, but because he wanted to be correct. I am sorry Isabelle, but I am sorry to tell you the bitter truth and I hope you won't mind. Your father was tortured for an extensive period at Mengistu' order who wanted to extract information about secrets of MEISON's plans, its foreign supporters, and the hiding place of all members of MEISON who were still at large after Negassa's arrest...

... "In case some of you are wondering how I came to know all these, the answer is simple. The current government made available for me to review the record of his arrest and torture...Reading it made my stomach turn; On a couple of occasions, I ran out to the bathroom and threw up."...

Isabelle started sobbing, so Zekarias stopped and apologised.

Stefan kneeled in front of Isabelle and held her hand and spoke to her softly appealing to her to be strong. Rashid also told her to let this good friend complete his report. And Richard Pankhurst went crimson with a combination of shock and empathetic feeling toward Isabelle. His lips quivered and he rose unexpectedly and asked Zekarias if he wanted anything from him before he left for the day. Zekarias said he didn't need anything, so Richard apologised profusely to Isabelle, shook her trembling hands and left the room.

Isabelle composed herself, wiping her face and sniffing a little, apologised to Zekarias, and asked him to continue...

Zekarias said he did not wish to upset Isabelle any more...

"In any case, I am almost finished. As for the place where he was buried, it must be one of the unmarked graves found in the Akaki prison compound. The only people who knew where the grave is exactly, are the two or three of Mengistu's trusted insiders. I am afraid, I have no way of knowing who they are, Isabelle. Sorry!"...

"You don't have to apologise, Dr. Zekarias. You have been kind and given us much of what we needed to know, painful as it is. I thank you on behalf of myself, my mother, Claudette, and my sister, Clara. And on behalf of my friends who have come with me, Stefan and Rashid.

Zekarias shook their hands.

Stefan asked Zekarias if he knew of any of Negassa's comrades who escaped Mengistu's killing machine. "I mean anyone who may be alive and lives in Addis Ababa," he added.

Zekarias said he cannot remember off hand, but he will inquire and give them the information.

"What about his relatives, like siblings or cousins?" Rashid asked.

"His immediate relatives live in Wollega province, in the district of Arjo. I don't know if his parents are alive."

"My mother has made attempts to reach out to his immediate family, but without success," Isabelle informed them, and Zekarias said he had heard of newspaper stories of your mother's attempts," Zekarias said, adding, "Your mother is an admirable woman, Isabelle, one of whom you are proud, I am sure."…

"Just one more question," Stefan said: "Who would be the most likely person to order a discovery process to find where the unmarked grave is?"

"Apart from the Prime Minister, perhaps with his permission, the Minister of Interior, or the head of the Prison Administration," Zekarias answered.

"Another question, which may be out of order. Are you still in touch with the Prime Minister?" Stefan continued. "I ask this because we made an attempt to gain access to the Prime Minister's Office in search of you. We were told by one of the security operatives that you no longer worked as the Prime Minister's advisor. Are you still in touch with him?"

"I am not *persona non grata*, if that is what you mean," Zekarias answered with a smile." And all went silent. "The rest is silence!" as Hamlet put it…

The group left the Institute building and headed toward the Ministry of Interior. The climbed the stairs toward the Minister's office, reached the floor where they saw a sign "Minister" and knocked at the door. The door was opened by a uniformed police officer, who greeted them with frowning face. They assumed the frown was a question: "Who are you, or What do you want." Isabelle smiled and said: "good afternoon, sir. We want to see the

Minister on an urgent matter." His frown changed to a more welcoming pose. "Well, everyone wants to see him on an urgent matter. What is your issue?

Isabelle answered: "It concerns the death, under torture of a man... my father," she answered going straight to the heart of the matter. The policeman's face registered a change that might be generously described as: "understandable shock." Actually, his face, which was of a fair hue, went red. He asked her for her name and her father's name. She told him and he went inside to the Minister's office. He came back after some five minutes, and, to their surprise, led them into the Minster's large office. The first thing they noticed was a large picture of the face of the leader of the time hanging on the wall behind the Minister's desk. The desk was very large and was burdened with a huge pile of documents to the left of the Minister and a few number of files to the right, presumably those that had been seen and are ready to be taken to their destination.

The Minister rose to receive the guests pointing to the chairs around his desk. They said thank you, sir and sat on the chairs. In his early forties, the Minster, named Berhanu Bogale, had a slightly balding head, and a serious but easy manner. His English was perfect and he used the appropriate language of a person who might have been schooled in diplomacy. As it happens, he was a college graduate when he went to the "Field" to fight against the Derg government. He did not ask them why they wanted to see him because he had been told by the officer. But he began the proceedings by saying, "I hear you have a serious matter to discuss with me. I hope to be of assistance, so please go ahead and tell me about it...

Isabelle told him the whole story and asked him whether it was possible for him to facilitate the discovery of the unmarked grave. He asked whether the other two people had anything to add to what "the young lady" had told him. Stefan said there was nothing that he or his colleague can usefully add... "Except to add a word of thanks for receiving us straight away. What a contrast with what we experienced at the Prime Minister's office.

There was a change in the facial expression of the Minister. What Stefan had intended as a compliment picked the Minister apparently raising concerns that his better treatment than the Prime Minister might create problems with the latter. The minister interrupted Stefan and was anxious to know what had happened at the Prime Minister's office. The Minister asked gruffly: "What are you talking about? What did the Prime Minister say or do to you?"

Stefan was taken aback and before he could respond, Rashid, who understood the concerns of the Minister, came to the rescue: "Your Excellency, it was a misunderstanding between me and a security detail at the gate. We were not allowed to gain access. That was what Stefan was referring to."

"Oh, I see. I am sorry about that," the Minister said in remorse. Rashid wanted to gain on the advantage that he believed he had secured. He continued: "Your Excellency, my sister Isabelle has said what we need. I wonder if it is possible for you to order a search for the unmarked grave of her late father, a man that I feel sure you may have known."

"What was his name again," the Minister inquired. "Negassa," Rashid answered, and the Minister's face lit up.

"Of course I knew him," the Minister answered. "He was a great man, a great leader of MEISON," he said with enthusiasm. And gazing Isabelle with renewed interest, he queried: "You are Negasso's daughter?!... Well bless your heart!"...The Minister smiled at Isabelle and rose from his chair, walked round the desk and stretched his arms to which Isabelle immediately threw her body sobbing not for the first time. The eyes of her two companions turned toward the Minister, who had disengaged from the embrace and was returning to his chair. Their hopes of better outcome were indeed high, and Isabelle watched the two with wonder. Could this be the hour of triumph, she thought...So did her friends. Could the Minister have the answer to their quest?

"Your Excellency," Rashid went, "We are in your capable hands. We do not know how to go about our simple quest: to discover the unmarked grave where Isabelle's dad is buried."...The Minister took his time before he pronounced his decision:

"I will do what I can...I will begin with consultations with the security department and the office of prisons. Give me a week." He said and rose from his chair stretching his right hand toward Isabelle, which she took in both hands and said, "Thank you, sir."

Part

THE QUEST CONTINUES AND THE PLOT THICKENS

Chapter Eleven

ENCOUNTERS OF A SPECIAL KIND

Isabelle and her friends were thrilled by the promise of the Minister of Interior.

It was hard to believe what success they scored instantly, especially given what had happened to them at the gate of the Prime Minister's office. Isabelle laughed at the "folly" of speculating that the project would take at least three months; indeed, her original reckoning was six months to a year. And here they were accepted by a nice Minister who promised he would do what he could and asked them to give him one week. So the three of them thought of doing some touring during the week of waiting. Gondar! Lalibela! Axum!..

What else? Maybe Harar, the medieval city in the east of the country. Isabelle had a different idea. Why not go to Wollega to meet her cousins, nephews and nieces? When the other two heard of this, their hearts sank. They were not mentally prepared to go on a long journey on Land Rovers or Toyota SUVs. But neither of them had the guts to tell her so. Stefan was the first to speak, as he considered himself a kind "relative" to Isabelle's people and, as always, wanted to impress her.

So he said: "If you think it is worth it, I am game," adding," I don't know about Rashid, but I am game," hoping that Rashid would desist. Rashid didn't oblige, however. He too was interested in impressing Isabelle.

He said: "I think it is a capital idea. Isabelle needs to create a link with her kith and kin." He said it with a sly smile gazing Stefan's disappointed face.

Isabelle exulted: ", Thank you my wonderful friends and companions!" And added: "And now my courageous fellow travellers! She gave each a warm hug and then said: "We must celebrate with a bottle of wine. My treat," she said scanning their smiling faces…

So, they went to a liquor store, downtown, and she bought a bottle of Chianti and some ham and cheese and Italian bread. They headed to the villa where they opened the bottle of Chianti and drank and ate bread with ham and cheese. They invited Beletech to their celebration, and she joined them with pleasure …

Isabelle told Beletech about their decision to go to Wollega and asked about a good guide who could take them there safely. Beletech said she had a friend at the Ethiopian Tourist Organization (ETO) who can advise them. She did not waste any time; she placed a call to the ETO and spoke to her friend who said he had just the right man, an Oromo from Wollega who is a favorite guide among tourists. Her friend said he would speak to the guide whose name is Amanuel Bera, Aman for short…

…The friend called and said Aman had agreed to act as their guide. "He knows the place like the back of his hand," her friend assured Isabelle. "And he is a good Christian, a practicing Protestant and member of the *Mecane Yesus Church*," her friend said, adding in a lowered voice that his expenses are very reasonable.

"When is he ready to go," Beletech asked her friend. "He is ready to go tomorrow, if need be," the answer came, and Beletech conveyed it to Isabelle. Isabelle announced the whole conversation and asked her friends if they were ready to start tomorrow. Both readily agreed.

"So, fellow travellers, is it going to be: "Wollega, Here We Come?!" Rashid raised his glass followed by Stefan and they both cried: Here is to "Wollega." …

Stefan added: "And to Isabelle, our fearless fighter for the rights of all human beings!"

"Here! Here!" cried Rashid, "And may our tour be crowned with success."

Beletech saw to it that the travellers were sufficiently provisioned with plenty of *yesiga fitfit*, Italian bread and cheese as well as several bottles of mineral water. Kassa was informed of the voyage and he was ready to go with them. The first thing Kassa did at the instruction of Beletech, was to bring Aman Bera, the guide, to the villa early in the morning.

They started at nine o'clock in the morning and drove all the way to Ambo for a stop to fill gas and rest a little.

During their brief rest, Aman, who is an amateur historian (he majored in history and literature at Addis Ababa University), spoke about the history and geography of the area. He knew the district administrator and sent for him with a message that he had special tourists from Europe. The administrator, a sprightly and gregarious young man of about thirty-five, welcomed the guests warmly assuring them that he would be of assistance for any need. When Aman told him about the reason for the group's visit to Wollega, the administrator told them about the local administrator of the Arjo sub-district of Wollega and said he is a good man who would readily help them in their project. He even said he would write to him with a special commendation. "The more of such help, the better," Stefan whispered to Isabelle who nodded in agreement. He withdrew to a small room and wrote the letter, put it in an envelope and gave it to Isabelle. Isabelle thanked him in the only word in Oromifa that her dad had taught her: *"Waqan sia kenny gofta!"* and the man went ballistic with joy, laughing his head off and responded volubly in Oromifa, which Isabelle did not understand a bit accepted with her arms thrown up and around. But her smile was sufficient response to his generosity and he rose to go back to his work. Wishing the group a pleasant trip and success in their endeavor.

After Ambo, they travelled without stopping for hours and arrived in Neqemte, the capital of the province of Wollega. They spent the night in Neqemte. The next morning, Aman insisted on meeting the regional administrator, who also happened to be a close relative of his and a fellow Protestant. "A very good man of God," Aman adjudged him, so that there was no way of leaving without paying respects to him. And they did pay him due respect by visiting him in his office, not far from their hotel. They were treated to coffee and chechepsa, a local specialty that is now one of the Ethiopian Cuisines. True to Aman's characterization of the administrator, he gave a length prayer in Oromifa as well as in English, of which he is fluent, as a graduate of the Protestant seminary. On parting from them, the good man of God wished them well and told them he would pray for their safety and success in their noble quest.

So they started on the way to Arjo, which someone had described a long time ago when the road was bad, as arduous Arjo. Our travellers did not find the journey as arduous, for there had been a lot of improvement in the region over the previous two decades, according to Aman's explanation.

Arjo district is on an elevated highland and so appropriately colder than Addis and Neqemte. So Aman had advised the group to bring woolen clothes as well as bed covers for the cold nights. As they climbed higher and higher in the Arjo highland, they could feel the cooler air greeting them. When they arrived at their destination, Aman announced that the best hotel is not exactly Hilton Hotel, but he would do his best to warn the owners that he had three special guests from Europe so that they would do all they could to provide a good service.

The hotel was modest but clean and well-furnished in firm beds as well as clean linen and bed covers. That is all we need, Stefan judged and Isabelle was ecstatic to breath the air that her dad had drawn when he was born and for many years of his youth. She felt light-headed and wanted to cry, but she struggled to hold her tears out of consideration of her good companions. She was touched by a strange feeling mixed with nostalgia and a sense of loss that was difficult to articulate. As she gazed at the hills around the hotel, she imagined her dad running up and down the hills around the town when he was growing up.

"Well, journey's end!" Cried Rashid, who was also touched by similar sentiments as those of Isabelle, though not the same by any means. And Stefan threw his arms around Isabelle and murmured something inaudible, which made her laugh.

Aman told them he would go to the administrator and deliver the letter of the Ambo administrator. I will also, with your permission, Miss Isabelle, inform the administrator why you are here and to help in tracing as many of Dr. Negassa's relatives as he could. Is that okay?

Isabelle said it was okay, "but please stress the fact that I need to see my grandmother and grandfather if they are alive."

"I understand Miss Isabelle. I will impress that upon him."

"Yes, please do that, and thank you, Aman" Isabelle said and dismissed him. She then attended to the needs of her friends, in the spirit of the hospitality of her people. "I will find ways, with Kassa's help, to warm the fifit and we will have our dinner," she told Stefan and Rashid, adding: "You must be famished." She spoke to Kassa and he went about helping prepare their dinner. All was ready within a half hour and they sat for dinner in the bedroom assigned to Isabelle, which was the largest...

...They ate their fitfit using the Italian bread as support and washed it down with the mineral water, which Kassa opened and served. They then went to their respective rooms for a good night sleep.

They all rose early the following morning, with Kassa giving them the good news that there was a good coffee house within a few minutes' walk from the hotel. The hotel did not serve breakfast, so they walked to the coffee house, owned by a local VIP, whose husband had been a high government official and left her all his property including the coffee house. The information was gathered by Aman who apparently knew the husband when he was a student.

"Do you think the coffee lady knew Negassa's parents?" Isabelle asked

Aman. He said he doubted it but he would ask her diplomatically. And he did when they were having the coffee. She told him she did not, just as he had suspected. The reason was that the lady is from another part of Wollega and does not know this district. In the meantime, we await Aman's conversation with the district administrator and his report tonight, Isabelle thought. Stefan and Rashid went out for a walk after their coffee interlude. Isabelle seemed fascinated with buxom lady who was charming and talkative. At the end of every long speech she made, there was a roar of laughter, with some people laughing to tears. All this fascinated Isabelle. When she asked Aman about it, he said the woman was witty and very charming. People liked her, which was why her late husband married her so that she would charm his clients. She helped him become rich and influential in local affairs, Aman said.

When the coffee lady noticed that Isabelle was interested in her, she asked Aman who she was and why she came all the way to Arjo. When he told her the story of her father's death and that she came all the way from Europe to find out about her father's burial place, the woman was moved almost to tears. She asked him to tell Isabelle that she must be a special lady and God be with you. Aman did that and Isabelle told Aman that she too admired the lady's charm and her good rapport with the people in the coffee shop. The coffee woman appreciated Isabelle's sentiments and offered to pay for all their expenses in Arjo, including the hotel expenses. When Aman told this t Isabelle, she was so touched that she rushed to toward the woman and hugged her warmly.

They had become friends and talked much of the morning with Aman acting as the interpreter. Isabelle asked the woman if she had children, she said she did and all her children are grown up and gone to Addis Ababa. Isabelle told her that she would love to meet with her cousins and nephews and nieces in Arjo and the lady said she would do everything to help her. Aman asked her if she was in good terms with the district administrator, she said he was a good friend of her husband. Aman's suggestive question led her to volunteer to intervene on Isabelle's behalf to talk to the administrator. She said would do it tonight. Isabelle told her thank you in Oromifa, which sent her to a laughing fit.

"Was my Oromifa funny? Maybe the accent?" Isabelle wondered to know. "No, absolutely not. It was just that it sounded like a child speaking, and it is so touching. That was why I laughed, "the woman answered, touching Isabelle's hand.

Stefan and Rashid came back from their long walk and told Isabelle that she missed a nice walk in your father's birthplace. "Shame on you!" Rashid said in mock reprimand. Stefan was more reticent and Isabelle told them she had a good talk with coffee lady. She told them she is an intelligent and charming lady, who has also promised to speak to the district administrator as early as tonight. So my time was not wasted, gentlemen. As for breathing the air of my father's birthplace, I am breathing it now and as long as we are in Arjo. "So, there Rashido!" she gave Rashid a counter reprimand.

"So between the letter from Ambo's administrator and this good woman, we may obtain some positive results," Stefan rejoined. Isabelle thought that if the administrator can help trace some of her relatives, they would only need another day or two to accomplish what they came to do. "Insha'Allah," Rashid exclaimed. I must also tell you something extraordinary, Isabelle told them.

"The coffee lady liked me so much, she offered to pay for all our Arjo expenses, including the hotel expense. "Now I begin to understand why people liked her and why her husband left her all his property. Shall we move to Arjo to live near this good woman?" she said half in jest.

"Let us wait until we meet some of your relatives, young lady" Rashid warned in fake paternalism.

"My expectation is that some of them will be found and I will meet them." "What if some of the young nephews and nieces ask you to take them with you?" That was Stefan, and Isabelle turned toward him and gave him a blank look.

"You know, that never occurred to me," she said. "But what if it happens?" insisted Stefan almost in fright.

"Well, if it happens, Auntie Isabelle will tell them it is not possible. Right?" Rashid said looking at Isabelle.

"I suppose so. But it is hard, isn't it? What would I do with them?... Let us be realistic," she concluded as if she was escaping from a snare. "You are quiet, Stefan. And you brought out the question. What would you do in my place?"

"I would gather them together and adopt them at once and seek help from the EU," Stefan replied

"You are joking, of course, "Rashid asked Stefan.

"No, I am not. Bu then I am not Isabelle," he said and burst out, laughing." "Fooled you!" He exulted, as Isabelle went red with anger... She stood up and faced Stefan, and told him slowly, in a bitter tone:

"That was a sick joke, Mr. Schmidt,"...She then left the company and went to her room.

The two men were stricken with fear...Rashid tried to ease things and mediate between the two...

He went to Isabelle's bedroom and begged her to come back. She refused point blank and Rashid went back to join Stefan empty-handed. He counseled Stefan to take it easy, and that things would be better tomorrow.

"No, I will apologise. She is right, it was a bad joke. It just happened in a crazy moment. I don't know what made me do it...What came over me...I did it without thinking...

Rashid patted Stefan on the back and said "Well, tomorrow will bring better things... Let us forget it for the time being, as if it did not happen. We will not let a thing like that ruin our mission and our friendship... But I think you need to go yourself right now and apologise."

Stefan agreed and went to Isabelle's room and asked for forgiveness profusely. She kept silent for a moment. When he repeated his apology, she got up and said: "I forgive you…" and went quiet again.

Stefan left quietly back to Rashid. They went back to the coffee shop and ordered whiskey for two.

"We don't have whiskey, I am afraid, the good lady said, but we have cognac and Gin," She told them. They both settled for cognac, and spent a quiet evening trying to forget that unpleasant episode.

Morning came with a piece of good news. Aman had spoken to the district administrator who said he would visit the guests later and will invite them for dinner in his humble home. He told Aman to bring back positive word that the guests would be his special dinner guest. He said he has already ordered knowledgeable people to trace members of Negassa's family and would report later today or tomorrow, latest.

Isabelle was up ahead of everybody and had coffee brought to her courtesy of the kind coffee lady. She had also breakfast of *qinche and fifit*, supplied courtesy of the same good lady. The portion for Stefan and Rashid was being kept warm at the coffee shop, awaiting the arrival of the two gentlemen. Of such as these is the bounty of Ethiopia's traditional hospitality composed, especially in the rural areas of the country.

Stefan and Rashid found Isabelle sipping coffee and writing on her daily journal. They greeted her and especially Stefan, who was anxious of how she would behave, was relieved to find her in her usual cheerful spirit. She even gave both men a kiss each on the cheek. "Did you sleep well, Cherie," Stefan asked her and she responded with a smile, adding, "Yes, I did. Did you?" So, back to normal, *Insah'Allah*, or rather, *Al Hamdu Lilahi*. Stefan and Rashid were told about the breakfast awaiting them at the coffee house. They went there to eat it. All three were grateful for the hospitality and had relished the *Qinche* and *fitfit* supplied by a woman whom they had just met. This was indeed an encounter of a special kind, for which they were grateful. Of course, it was Isabelle's initiative and charm that brought about this special bounty.

Aman came up with an interesting idea. He told Isabelle and her companions that the Oromo of Arjo have a very enjoyable form of communal dance by the youth. He had asked the administrator if it were possible to arrange for a special exhibition by passing an order to call the young boys and girls for an exhibition of their proud dancing tradition. And the good man accepted the proposal and sent the appropriate order.

By eleven o'clock in the morning hundreds of young boys and girls, aged between thirteen and sixteen, were arranged in a parallel row, boys facing girls. By the time our group arrived at the scene, not far from the hotel, full of excitement, the ceremony had just begun. There were head dancers who gave some kind of signal and the boys and girls (each boy facing a particular girl) started facing, and bobbing their head up and down toward each other each one of them emitting a strange guttural sound with their faces almost touching each other as they emitted the sound. It was deeply sexy and it went on for several minutes before the head dancer gave the sign to stop. After some rest, the same exciting and sexy dance ceremony begins and they go on for several more minutes.

Our group would have spent the whole day watching and listening to that haunting guttural sound. The three of them took pictures and hopefully they also caught the sound. It was an unforgettable sight and sound and our heroes had a wonderful time. Isabelle thought this would be the crown of their trip, next to the discovery of the unmarked grave.

So, they had a good day. They went back to their rooms for a good afternoon rest and looked forward to an evening as guests of the administrator. Aman walked them up from their siesta and took them for arranged dinner. The administrator welcomed them with the usual bows and shook their hands with both of his hands. Isabelle expected the lady of the house to come for the introduction, but she was disappointed when she did not come to meet them. That event happened when they were duly seated at the table to eat dinner. She came smartly dressed in Ethiopian costume and bowed to the guests. She was much younger than they expected.

Whereas her husband was in his sixties, a big man with a protruding belly and double chin, she was slim and probably in her early thirties. And she was a beauty with an Afro hair style. Her skin color is copper brown and she had a line of tattoo circling her chin thus framing her oval face and high cheek bones. She had a rather long neck adorned by a small wooden cross hanging from a thin golden chain. She smiled shyly when meeting the guests and then withdrew to the kitchen, apparently as local custom demanded. The guests could not have enough of her; Isabelle in particular was curious to know more about her. So she asked to see her at the dinner table—custom be damned!

The host was more puzzled than embarrassed. Yet he could not refuse—it would be impolite and contrary to Ethiopian good manners. Stefan and Rashid were embarrassed, Rashid thinking "Ah, this damned feminism!" In fact, Isabelle's demand, far from being actuated by feminism, was a natural curiosity by Isabelle to know how such a beautiful young woman could end up married to such fat old man, old enough to be her father. Her mind had got thinking: Was it poverty that drove such a young woman to marry such a man? Was she forced into it by a needy family to curry favor with a powerful local grandee? Whatever it was, in Isabelle's mind, it was wrong. Not that she could do anything about it, but the curiosity and sense of outrage, drove her to demand to have her join the party. The husband could not refuse, yet his discomfort was visible on his face.

The wife came smiling shyly and stood at the door. "My dear," the host called his wife, "pull up a chair and come and sit side by side with our one female guest, Madam…[*Isabelle cut in Isabelle*]… yes Madam Isabelle."… He informed his wife with a wry smile, "she wants to talk to you." He looked askance at his wife who was hesitating. "Well, go on then, sit down by our guest, " he commanded, and the wife pulled up a chair and sat by Isabelle's side.

"Aman will act as interpreter, because I don't speak Oromo," Isabelle said, and Aman said he would be delighted to interpret, but that the lady of the house understands English though she is not fluent enough to speak it." Isabelle was delighted to know that the beautiful woman understands English and said: "Well then you will only have to interpret what she says to me," Isabelle said and saw the woman was smiling in agreement.

The strained behaviour of the husband was not lost on the wife. She saw her husband's uneasiness, and speaking slowly and diffidently, she said that she did not want "to stand in the way of the conversation between my dear husband and the dinner guests who have some important matters to discuss."

Aman interpreted what she said. The wife was looking intently at her husband as she spoke and he smiled with huge relief and pride in his wife, who it turned out was not only beautiful but wise. Isabelle then understood that she had made a mistake putting the poor woman in a quandary. In order to redeem the situation of embarrassment, she said she was sorry and perhaps the two women could talk after dinner.

The administrator sighed with relief and thanked Isabelle for her "understanding." That was an interesting use of a word—understanding—and Isabelle realised that that she had encroached on a delicate domestic affair, and was thus happy she was saved by the grace of a wise woman. Rashid, who never lets an interesting situation without making an appropriate remark, observed: "This woman is not only cute, but acute," and smiled at Stefan, who looked a bit at a loss.

The dinner conversation proceeded smoothly after the "cute and acute" woman left the dining room. Her husband performed his role as host and also told his guests that he has been briefed by the district's Chief of Police that his minions had identified two middle-aged men who claimed to be cousins of Dr. Negassa. The informants also said that both Negassa's parents were deceased decades ago and that his only sister died recently leaving a couple of daughters who are married and who live in Neqemte. He wished he could give more information, but at least a few relatives have been traced and positively identified thanks to our able Police Chief's efforts, he was happy to report.

Isabelle thanked the district administrator and asked if she could meet with the Chief of Police in order to obtain more information on where and how she could find the relatives. Aman intervened to say that he can look into it and report to Isabelle by the following day. The administrator thanked Aman for wishing to help and thus the dinner was successfully ended with a positive note.

Back to their hotel, the three protagonists put their heads together and considered what to do next. They depend very much on Aman to use his knowledge of the place and people to see if they can trace the two surviving brothers in Arjo. If not, then trace the two nieces in Neqemte…

…A few hours later, Aman came with the sad news that the two brothers were also deceased. So now they must focus on the two nieces, who are the daughters of Negassa's younger sister. The information was that they live in Neqemte. Accordingly, the decision was made to leave Arjo and head to Neqemte on the way back to Addis Ababa, to look for the two nieces.

They left Arjo early in the morning after six am. He had placed phone calls to the Administrator of Wollega requesting for assistance to trace Dr.

Negassa's nieces. Aman had inquired about their names and was told their names are: Chaltu and Demequ, aged thirty-eight and thirty-ix. Aman had implored the administrator to have the local district police as well as the local Orthodox synodos to use their influence to trace these two nieces, who are apparently the only surviving relatives of Dr. Negassa. Aman's appeal to the parental instinct as well as the regional sentiment of the Wollega authorities to trace the only surviving relatives of a heroic son of Wollega was very shrewd...

And it worked, for lo and behold, Chaltu and Demequ do indeed live in Neqemte. Chaltu is married to a teacher who works in the district office of the Ministry of Education, as deputy director. Demequ is married to a carpenter who works with the Evangelical Protestant Mission as a carpenter in building schools and homes for teachers. The two sisters lived near each other, and are proud parents of one boy each, both of them attend college in the same college in the Oromia Kilil.

The good administrator of Wollega agreed to inform both sisters about the visit to Neqemte of a daughter of their grand uncle, Dr. Negassa, and that she wanted to meet them. The news of Isabelle's arrival in Neqemte and her desire to see them, brought to them by the highest government official of their region, hit the two sisters at once like a thunderbolt as well as a drop of Manna from Heaven. They were excited, elated and at the same time confused, lost as to what to do and say. When Aman went to the home of Chaltu and repeated the story and that he brought their cousin Isabelle from Addis Ababa, Chaltu made a weak attempt at ululation (*Ililta*). She sent for her sister Demequ and when Aman repeated the story, Demequ did better *ililta*, so that the immediate neighbors heard and came asking what was the good news. When they were told the story, there followed a strong communal *ililta* that shook the neighborhood.

Our "tourists" arrived at Neqemte and checked in a hotel in the center of the town. Aman had gone to meet with Chaltu and Demequ and related to his guests about the general exultation and especially of the two happy sisters.

"Isabelle," Rashid cried like an announcer, in the manner the Angel Gabriel telling the surprised Mary the good news, said:" do you realise, my dear friend and sister, that you now have found two cousins?"

"I do, my dear friend and brother, I do. And I am happy beyond words," Isabelle replied with deep emotion. And Stefan walked toward

Isabelle and hugged her for a few seconds and silently kissed her on the front of the head. Kassa also congratulated her in his own calm and deliberate manner. He asked Isabelle whether she is ready to meet her cousins and can he go with Aman to fetch them. Isabelle told Kassa to give her a few minutes to consult with my friends. She then told her friends that she feels like celebrating the felicitous occasion.

"What do you think, dear friends?"

"Wonderful idea," Stefan said and Rashid seconded him, adding, "Why not celebrate in the hotel by telling the hotel manager the story and asking him to instruct his chef and other hotel staff to prepare a special dinner for a celebration." Rashid's practical suggestion was accepted and Isabelle told Kassa he and Aman could bring her cousins "for a celebration."

She said they can bring them after six in the evening. She also told Aman to go to the administrator's house and tell him she is inviting him to a special dinner to celebrate the discovery of her cousins. The invitation was for him and his wife, Isabelle said to Aman.

Aman suggested to add the area Chief of Police to the invitation, for he had played a critical role in tracing the cousins. Isabelle said that was a good idea and told Aman to also go to the Police Chief's house and tell him of the invitation, with apologies for the late delivery of the message. Aman said: "It shall be done, Madame" with a deep bow. Kassa, who was present, laughed quietly, amused by Aman's love of ceremony. The two had become friends from the start of the journey in particular the stay in Arjo, which Kassa enjoyed very much, especially the communal dance. He told Aman that the ETO where he has friends, should bring some of these dancers to Addis Ababa. Aman made fun of him asking him if he wants to betroth one of those beauties. "You are crazy," Kassa would say laughing. It looks that these two people have struck a friendship that will last a long time.

Meeting of Cousins

A little after six in the evening Aman and Kassa brought two tall and good- looking women in their mid-thirties, to the lobby of the hotel. Isabelle saw them walk elegantly and with dignity toward her. Then they fell on their knees one after the other. First, Chaltu fell on her knees and Isabelle raised her up and threw her arms around her. It was a touching scene in which two lost relatives found each other and expressed their emotion in tears. Next came Demequ who also fell on her knees, and again Isabelle raised her up and hugged her with the same emotional outburst and lachrymal commotion.

It was a touching scene affecting all present scene. Both the regional administrator and his Chief of Police had arrived at the hotel in time for the touching ceremony. The governor who is a deeply religious man, intervened to declare that what they were witnessing was God's grace manifesting itself in this happy reunion of sisters who had never met before. It is indeed worthy of celebration, but the celebration would be incomplete if we did not recognise and openly declare our witness to God's miraculous deed.

"Miss Isabelle, allow me to ask you and everyone present to lower their heads and offer thanks to Almighty God," and each lowered their heads and offered a silent prayer. After that the administrators asked everyone to join him in saying the Lord's Prayer together, as our Lord had taught us. And he said in a deep baritone voice the Lord's Prayer in Amharic.

Then they sat to eat dinner, some twelve people in all. They started as ten; then the husbands of Chaltu and Demequ joined them an hour or so after the start. Stefan and Rashid assumed the role of stewards on behalf of Isabelle and encouraged people to eat and also to drink wine and beer according to their choices. The hotel manager had asked Aman what kind of music the guests like and Aman consulted with Isabelle who told him to put any Ethiopia music. So a choice of good songs came on, including Tilahun Gessesse and Alemayehu Eshete, as well as old and modern songs by female singers like Aster Aweke.

It turned out to be an auspicious and most enjoyable evening. Above all, Isabelle felt happy and told Stefan that she felt as though she met her father's spirit in the person of her two cousins.

She sat between her two cousins, looking at each one after the other and speaking in English with a smile. As it happened, Demequ understood and spoke a little English, as a result of her husband's encouraging her to take night classes and to speak with visiting missionaries in English. So, she did her best to tell her sister what Isabelle said. When Isabelle asked her cousins about children, each said she had just one son. Isabelle had Aman to note down the names of the two sons and the address of the college where they were studying. At the end of the dinner, Aman did as Isabelle asked him and gave her a piece of paper on which he had scribbled their names and the name and address of the college where they were studying. Isabelle felt for the first time in her life that her life had new meaning. She couldn't wait until she got back to Addis and phone her mother and sister and tell them of what she found.

At the close of the dinner, the Administrator and his wife rose to go and apologized after offering another prayer of thanks to God and expressing their joy and congratulating Isabelle and her two cousins and their husbands for finding one another. A few minutes after the Administrator's departure, the Police Chief also asked to be excused saying he had some duties to attend to. He gave a smart salute and left.

About half an hour later, the two sisters and their husbands also begged to be excused. Chaltu insisted that the group must have a meal in their house. So did Demequ. Rashid made a joke about how funny it would be if the two sisters were to quarrel on who will entertain their cousin. In any case, he went on, tomorrow is a day of their departure so that much as he and his friends would have loved to be their dinner guests they must wait for another opportunity. Next year, Insh'Allah? He asked with a laugh. And everybody laughed. The two sisters accepted the inevitable but Demequ told Isabelle: Will come back next year? Isabelle said she hopes to come as soon as she can, but she will write as often as she could. She also said she will definitely visit the two sons.

Isabelle thanked the manager of the hotel and his staff for a wonderful meal and for their sensitive and generous service. Everyone filed out of the hotel dining room and said their goodbyes. And the three friends as well as Aman and Kassa went to their respective rooms for a good night's sleep.

Back to Addis Ababa

The following morning Aman and Kassa were up before everybody else and waited for the three to get ready so that they could take the bags to the car. The three lingered longer in the hotel restaurant enjoying breakfast consisting of scramble eggs, lots of toast and marmalade and orange juice and coffee. Isabelle asked if Aman And Kassa had breakfast. A hotel staff told her they did. So, she called Kassa to help take the bags to the car and the three of them entered the SUV and started their journey back to Addis Ababa Isabelle said, it is a long journey, and Aman thinks a one-night stay in Ambo would be good. "So what do you guys think?" They both agreed it is a good idea.

So off they went leaving behind three days and nights of adventure with some pleasing outcome. Isabelle gained a lot of invisible energy that Stefan noticed…

"It is as if I don't know her. She is like a totally different person," he confessed to Rashid.

Rashid, on the other hand liked her new self-full of energy and self-reliance. He told Stefan that when one feels fulfilled by a new discovery, a new job or a new insight based on self-actualization, it may be a little disturbing to us men. Such a condition in a woman you love should be embraced and got used to, not rejected or questioned in any way.

"These are my views in general, but as regards Isabelle, you need to find out carefully and with the kind of awareness mentioned, which I think you need."

"Thank you, my friend," Stefan said, and added, "perhaps I have taken Isabelle too much for granted."

"No, you have not. I think your relationship with her is wonderful. It is based on mutual respect, in which I have not noticed you taking her for granted, at any time that I have known you two."

"*Merci mon ami. Shukran*! [Thank you, my friend. Thanks (Arabic) "*Afwan, ya aKi.*" [You are welcome, friend] (Arabic)

[Introspection on the preceding exchanges

These kind of exchanges of views between the two men have become rather frequent since they ventured on this journey. If we take Rashid's views or insights as correct, and agree with him that Isabelle does not feel taken for granted by Stefan, then we may be surprised if he is proved by events to be wrong, or gratified and happy for all concerned, because it is an important ingredient among people engaged in any common endeavor.]

The journey from Neqemte to Ambo was fairly pleasant and uneventful. They arrived in Ambo around four o'clock and checked in the hotel by the hot springs. After checking in the hotel, they relaxed, swimming and enjoying the evening sun going down on the western horizon. They had dinner in the hotel and did some walking and chatting while walking about things that have happened as well as of things to come in the following days. Rashid was curious to know if his insightful remarks, offered as advice to

Stefan, had had the desired effect. So he paid special attention to what was exchanged between them. He noticed a certain degree of diffidence on the part of Stefan, wondering whether his own remarks that had been meant to help might have acted to induce inhibition in Stefan. Rashid tried jokes and told stories about his soccer career and some of the obstacles he had faced. Isabelle became keenly interested in Rashid's personal history from Sudan to his current successful career. Her trip to Ethiopia, the first trip outside Europe and America, had exposed her to different situations and different people with all that such different experience entails in terms of self-awareness and "growth." And Stefan was exposed to the same situations and people and experiences. Can there be differing effects on the mind of people who underwent the same experiences? Such questions and what their answers might be, occupied Stefan's consciousness through much of their journey to Wollega and especially the meeting with Isabelle's cousins.

The journey from Ambo to Addis Ababa was also pleasant and uneventful. They passed by some small towns of note nearer Addis Ababa. The best known is Addis Alem which is perched on a mountain and has a well-known Ethiopian Orthodox Church. Then there is the famous Holeta town (formerly a village) that was the headquarters of the first military school in Ethiopia that trained thousands of officers, including some who became illustrious Generals and guerilla fighters during the 1935-1941 Italian occupation of Ethiopia. One such officer was General Jaghema Kello, a native of Ambo and the Mecha district around Ambo. Jaghema Kello was the son of a regional Oromo Chieftain whom an Italian governor tried to compel, during the Italian occupation, to hand over local leaders who were Amhara. The wise old Chieftain pretended to obey the order, but quietly ordered one of his servants to bring him two small sacs, one filled with white *tef* (a local grain) and the other filed with brown *tef*. Then the Chieftain told his men to mix the two types of *tef* by pouring the content of one sac into the other sac. He ordered the man to mix the two with his hands. Then he ordered the man to pour the content to the floor. The two were thoroughly mixed. He turned to the Italian and asked him if he could separate the white from the brown one. The Italian said it is impossible. Smiling triumphantly, the Chieftain told the Italian, our people here are like this grain thoroughly mixed. I cannot separate the Amhara from the Oromo. He told him his own children are mixed Oromo and Amhara. Example of Oromo wisdom!

In frustration, but obviously impressed by the Chieftain, the Italian left in a huff.

Our touring party arrived in Addis Ababa in the early afternoon. Isabelle thanked Aman for his incredible assistance and paid him generously. She also tipped Kassa who as a regular employee was not entitled to compensation like an Aman. Both Stefan and Rashid had agreed from the beginning to leave financial matters to her, except the accounts were to be audited appropriately.

Beletech was happy to welcome them and was full of questions about how they fared in Wollega. Isabelle briefed her on all essential matters, including the fact that she found her two cousins and was ecstatic about that. She also told her about their two sons in college. Beletech said she knew the place where the college is located and offered to accompany her if and when she desires to go there to see them.

Chapter Twelve

ENCOUNTER WITH JUSTICE OFFICERS

After the long and tiring journey, the three friends passed a restful night and got out of bed in the late morning. Beletech left them to sleep late but at about eleven am, she knocked at each of their doors and woke them up, one by one.

She prepared breakfast consisting of a variety of fruits, egg and bacon and a choice of *qinche* and *fitfit*. They ate as much as they could and left the rest. They met at the studio to discuss their next steps. Isabelle, as always, led the discussion by asking Stefan what he thought. Stefan reminded them that they had a few days before the Minister of Interior's deadline, so he thought of seeing the Minister of Justice in the meantime and see what he might do to help.

Isabelle said she agreed as did Rashid. So they set out with Kassa to visit the Minister of Justice. The Ministry was a stone building built by the Italians, and was situated on the side of the Interior Ministry like a huge twin tower of stone. They parked the car on one side of the building and, leaving Kassa with the car, the three of them walked toward the entrance of the building. There were scores of petitioners lined up to gain entry to the building, but upon seeing these foreigners, opened up leaving a passage for them to enter the building. Two uniformed police stood at the entrance, one holding the door and the other watching over. The police let them pass.

Isabelle asked where the Minister's office was. One of the police, a younger officer, probably with some training in a Police Academy, said in English: "Go forward...there." He pointed to the right corner of the interior of the building where a few people stood waiting to be ushered in. An older man, a civilian officer, stood guard assisted by a young police officer. Isabelle told the civilian she and her companions wanted to see the Minister.

The man's face twisted in a wry smile and said in Amharic; "You need an appointment to see the Minister...

... "What is the reason for which you wish to see the Minister?" he asked, and a young man among the group waiting to be admitted translated the man's words into English. Isabelle thanked the young man and asked him to tell the officers that they have a delicate matter to discuss with the Minister. They cannot reveal it. The young man translated it to the office, who laughed a hearty laugh and said: "Everyone has a delicate matter to discuss with the Minister. "And why should I let in without knowing the content of your issues?" The translator rendered it into English but at the same time he was engaged in an argument with the civilian officer.

The civilian officer was a tall, one-eyed man of about fifty. Rashid whispered to Stefan that the one-eyed man, who seemed to be determined to win his argument, was probably a former guerilla fighter and a war-invalid. The young translator, who seemed equally tenacious in argument was probably a University graduate who is one of the thousands of unemployed youth. It was apparent that the older man resented the "superiority" feeling of the younger man. This attitude of resentment is a natural consequence of the sense of inadequacy and deprivation the older man felt because he was fighting in the bush while the young "upstart" went to school and continued his education.

Rashid addressed the older man using his little Amharic vocabulary such as "Wondime." He asked the younger man to translate for him as he spoke to the older man, assuring him that once the Minister met them, he would be glad that they came to him. When the young man translated Rashid's appeal, his face softened and said; 'it is my duty to guard my boss and one way to guard him is to find out what type of people want to see him. That was why I asked, what was the nature of your business with him."

Stefan intervened and asked the young man to tell the older man that they were at the Ministry of Interior a few days before and that they were allowed to see the Minister after they wrote a piece of paper saying why they wanted to see him. "The police officer was kind enough to take the piece of paper to the Minister.

As if hit by a tornado, the one-eyed man exploded and uttered a torrent of words which the poor young translator tried to translate…He could not keep up with him… "Why is he angry," Stefan asked. The young man translated some of the old man's words. The young man said:

"He does not like to be compared to the "stupid" police officer who lets all kinds of people to go in to see the Minister." Isabelle addressed the old man with a sweet smile and said, in defense of the police officer at the Ministry of Interior as an honorable gentleman… "He was sympathetic to my tragedy," she told the man, almost in tears.

"Why didn't you say so, in the first place? What is your tragedy? Is it a state secret, for Heaven's sake?" the old man cried with sympathy, the kind of sympathy that only a man who had lost limb can appreciate. Instantly, Isabelle jumped at the opportunity opened by the old man's little interjection, and said" "Thank you, Ababa!" The old man's smile was so bright and warm it could melt butter… *Ishi lijye* (yes my child)…and he asked Isabelle to tell him her problem. Isabelle seized on the moment and poured out her story with embellishment, to the utter astonishment of the man who immediately went in and came back within minutes to usher the group into the Minister's chambers.

Before going in, Isabelle shook the hand of the young man and thanked him. Give me your name and phone number when we come out, she told him, much to his happiness.

The Minister's chamber was a richly furnished large room with two windows and a veranda outside the window. Minister Abebe Hailu, was a middle-aged man of about fifty, who is slightly built and with grizzled hair and a shaven face. He had a ready smile and his eyes were large and a little bulging. Having shaken each person's hand, he motioned the three to take their seat in front of his desk. He rang the bell and told the policeman to order… ["tea or coffee?" he asked the guests.] All three said: coffee, and the officer left after giving a salute.

"So, what can I do for you?" the Minister asked, looking at Isabelle's face with a smile.

Isabelle told him the whole story. She even told him briefly about their visit to Arjo and their meeting with her two cousins. "What remains now, Your Excellency is to locate the unmarked grave of my late father." Isabelle wrapped up and turned to Stefan and Rashid asking them if there was anything more they wanted to add, and they said no.

The Minister reflected a little, turned his eyes toward the ceiling as if he was looking for an answer from there. After a few seconds, he told them that there are no legal issues to be worried about and certainly no political problems either. "This is simply a human story that needs to be treated purely on human or humanitarian grounds," he said…

…Another gaze at the ceiling…Almost oppressive silence…

Rashid interrupted the ceiling gazing…He said: "Your Excellency, I know nothing about the protocol regarding the claim of retrieval of a person's remains. Let us assume that the unmarked grave is found. Is there any legal or other problem in claiming the remains of Isabelle's father, given the story surrounding his death?"

"I don't see any problem myself. However, I recommend that you take this up with the government's Attorney General, who is our legal expert advisor…As for finding the grave, I will ask my advisors as to who would be the right person to help assist you. You need also to see the Chief of Police, who can look into the records connected with the death and burial of political prisoners. I suspect there must be people who can help trace the exact grave.

"For the rest, what I can do now is to place a call to the Attorney General's office and tell him that you would be going to see him, if possible, today or tomorrow." With those words of promise, the Minister closed the meeting and rang the bell summoning the police officer to usher them out.

They agreed to try to see the Attorney General while they were at it. "Why waste time," intoned Rashid." And so they told Kassa to take them to the office of the Attorney General. It was a twenty minutes ride from the Ministry of Justice. Unfortunately, they were told the Attorney General was not in, and his secretary told them that H.E. the Minister of Justice had called to tell the office about the matter and that his boss had been apprised of it. And he will inform his boss about their visit and asked them to come the next day.

The following day, they rose early in the morning, ate their breakfast and went to the Attorney General's office.

Upon arrival, they were ushered in immediately when they showed up and met the Secretary of the Office. The Secretary went in to the Attorney General's Chambers and came back smiling and pointed toward the door letting them in. They followed the gesture of his hands and walked in to behold a tall and dignified man of about fifty with a bushy hair and trimmed beard that encircled his mouth.

"Welcome to my Chambers," the Attorney General said with a warm tone. He had a tenor voice which contrasted with his tall and bulky frame. He shook each one's hand and pointed them to their seat in front of the desk. But he walked round his desk and sat in one of the chairs. He apologised for his absence the previous day when they had come to see him. Affairs of state," he said in a jocular tone. "Tea or coffee," he asked, and all three said coffee.

"Good," he exulted. "That is good for our economy, which is principally dependent on coffee, and we are told by the experts it will remain so for a long while." He ordered the three coffees and tea for himself shouting the order to the attending personnel, who was waiting for the order. "As you can see, I am a tea drinker, from my childhood in Harar," he said.

"Your Excellency, can I ask you where you studied law," Stefan inquired "Not Excellency. That is reserved for the political types. The Americans refer to their Attorneys General as 'General,' in conversations," so because I did my studies in America, I guess you can call me, "General," or just call me Abate, which is my given name—Abate Tessema. By the way, to answer your question, I studied my first law degree here in Addis Ababa at the Law School but went on to do graduate degree in law at the Law School in Yale University.

"That is a great school," Stefan said

"Thank you. I think so too …One of the great schools in America and one of the best in the world. Have you studied in America, yourself?" he asked Stefan.

"I have spent a year in Chicago, but did not study for any degree… "The coffee should arrive soon; so, we can begin, shall we?"

"So, tell me what I can do for you."

Stefan and Rashid both looked toward Isabelle, and she cleared her voice to speak.

"First of all, thank you for agreeing to see us so promptly. We are here to discover the manner of death and burial place of my late father, Dr. Negassa…" She gave him the rest of the details, including the information given to them by an Ethiopian scholar that my father was tortured to death during the Derg era. His body was buried secretly in an unmarked grave by unknown persons. We are here to find out where the marked grave is and to claim his remains for decent Christian burial."

"I don't know if I am the right person to help you in tracing the grave. By the way, I was a young boy in my mid-teens in Harar when your father was killed by the Derg. Like most of my generation, we were involved in demonstrations, protesting against the Derg government. So, although I never met your father, I learned about him, so he is one of my childhood heroes who fought for his people…

My business is the law—its application and interpretation. I can tell you off hand that you have the right to claim your father's remains. But the question of finding his grave is not one of law, but of practically going about tracing the steps that led to his death and burial. We know how and why he was killed. Obviously, he was a threat to the power of the military government and Mengistu Haile Mariam in particular.

Have you approached the Police Department?

"Not yet. But we will" Isabelle replied. "Is it possible for you to write us a letter stating that there is no problem, legally, denying the right of survivors seeking to trace their loved one's grave and to obtain the remains for a decent burial?"

"Absolutely, I can do that, and I will," he said and raised the phone receiver and told his secretary to come to receive an urgent instruction. The secretary came and his boss dictated the appropriate letter, instructing him to type it and bring it…

"Make a copy each, to the Minister of Justice and to the Minster of Interior. And, of course give a copy to our guests. Can you hurry it up and give them their copy on their way out?… Okay? Good." …

"We can now talk about the weather, or your life in Europe… As you wish," Abate said with a chuckle.

Then they talked about sundry matters, drinking their coffee and tea. Each one of the three told him about where they live and work. When he learned about Rashid's soccer career in Europe, his eyes nearly popped out of their sockets...

"My goodness!" he cried. I used to play in the first eleven in my school in Harar, in college and even in America at Yale. But I was not good enough to be in the Big League. But my interest..." he continued and cried again: "My God!...I am beholding a celebrity!"

A bit embarrassed, Rashid said: "You must have been a real fan of Soccer." He said it calmly hoping to calm their host's excitement before he goes out announcing it to the whole people in his office...He kept looking at Rashid like a teenager admiring a favorite star...

When he realised that he might be overdoing it, the Attorney General then calmed down and rose to bid the guests goodbye. And he wished them good luck.

They thanked him and left the way they came. Isabelle stopped to thank the one-eyed man, shaking his hand by both of her hands and said, "Igzer Ystiligne Ababa [thank you father], which pleased him immeasurably. Isabelle also thanked the young interpreter and took his name, which he had written on piece of paper. He told her the phone number belonged to his uncle in whose house he said he lived.

Isabelle thanked him for his help and promised to call him before she leaves Ethiopia. His name is Leggese Kebede. "Goodbye Leggese and thank you, again," Isabelle said, as she walked fast to catch up her friends, going to the Secretary's office to pick up the Attorney General's letter.

Armed as they were with a letter from the Attorney General, the group decided to try to see the Minister of Interior, though there were two more days before the deadline. They found the same police officer who kindly took a note for them as a result of which the Minister saw them. Unlike last time, the corridor by the Minister's office was crowded with petitioners. The police officer received them with a broad smile and, with his limited knowledge of English, he told them the Minister was too busy. "Tomorrow is better, "he said. Isabelle and Rashid were about to give up when Stefan said: "Let us give him the letter from the Attorney General and tell him a copy will be forth coming." "Isabelle knitted her brows and looked at Rashid's reaction. Rashid said, "I think Stefan is right." Isabelle hesitated, then said, "No, we better wait till the deadline arrives. We don't want to cross the Minister. I think we should leave," she concluded, looking anxiously at Stefan and Rashid. Stefan though the better of it and agreed with Isabelle, changing his earlier idea.

"We have only three days to go, anyway," Isabelle reminded her friends, and they agreed to leave. So they decided to go to the villa and rest or for each one attend their affairs like calling Europe or America. Isabelle had been wanting to call the Wyzanskis, and Stefan called his office in Brussels, a little concerned that things were running well, even though he had taken a chunk from his annual leave. Rashid called Dr. Ibrahim to brief him on developments. His uncle was out but Azeb answered the call and she asked specifically how Isabelle was. Rashid told her things are looking up in some respects, but he told her to speak to Isabelle herself and ask her to give her a report. He called Isabelle who came running when he told her Azeb was on the line. She took the receiver panting being short of breath from the short running.

"Hello Azeb," Isabelle cried and was answered by Azeb who was excited to hear her voice.

"How are you, Isabelle, and how is the project going?"

"I am very well, thank you, Azeb, dear. And the project is going well in many respects. I will email you to give you more details. Just for starters, we have now established from a reliable source what you mentioned that my father was tortured to death. But we have not yet been able to trace his grave. We have a couple of VIPs too see in the next three or four days. I will brief you after that. I also was able to trace two cousins in Wollega. I am very happy, and I will tell you more details and new developments as they happen. That should be enough for now...

...Okay, Azeb...bye for now...bye."

Stefan was at the studio talking to Beletech, who was brewing some coffee. When she saw Isabelle, she rose to greet her and Isabelle gently pushed her back to her seat. She scolded her like a matron of an elder sister, telling her not to keep getting up and bowing. "These Ethiopian manners!" Are you complaining about their charming manners? Stefan complained.

"No, but sometimes it is too much." She answered. "By the way, how would you like to adopt a young Ethiopian who has reached University level?"

160

"Do you mean adopt him like a father?" "Yes."

"Not at that age. I think it would be hard if not impossible to act as a guiding father to a twenty-year-old young man.".... "Why do you ask?"

"I was just wondering...I am too old to bear a child myself. So I was thinking adopting one of my nephews. But then, it would not be fair to the other nephew. That is why I asked you...Do you think it is crazy?"

"Yes, to tell you the truth, I think it is crazy."

Isabelle did not pursue the matter, but Stefan now was confronted with a knotty problem. The woman that he loved and whom he was thinking of marrying after the end of the project, is now entertaining wild ideas of adopting a twenty- year old boy, and expected him to do the same, perhaps as a condition for agreeing to marry him. He was immersed in deep thought, trying to find an apt quote from Shakespeare or Goethe, something like *"Woman, Thy Name Is Trouble!"* Or some such line, like using Dante's warning at the gate of Inferno: *Laciate ogni speranza voi che'entrate* ["Abandon All Hope ye who Enter!"]

He was articulating the line loudly and Rashid who had come close in a cat's walk, asked him: "Did I hear you saying something in Italian?"

"Do you know Italian," asked Stefan in fright.

"I learned Italian while I was living in Italy playing for one of the Italian

Big League teams, but then I left Italy and have forgotten much of it.".... "What were you saying?"

"It was a famous line from Dante's Inferno." "Why did you say it now?"

"Oh, no reason, just fancy."

Please repeat it. I love the sound of Italian.".... "Come on Stefan, don't be coy..."

"It is really nothing, just a line, part of a longer stanza. It goes:

*"Per me si va nella citta dolente...per me si va tra la Perduta gente*etc, etc...etc...And the most famous line, the most cited by school children is... *"Lasciate ogni speranza voi ch'entrate*! [Abandon all hope ye who enter].

Ye who enter through the gate to Hell, that is..." Stefan said in exasperation and walked away, leaving Rashid puzzled.

Rashid had a suspicion it had to do with the *woman thing, as* the young say these days. He walked to Stefan's room and found the door locked. So, after a light knock, he left to go to his own room and rest…

The puzzle, however, kept bothering him, especially now that Stefan locked the door of his room. He found Isabelle chatting with Beletech. "Can I join you, girls?" he asked and they both smiled their consent. So, he sat and listened to their talk.

"We are wondering whether an older person can adopt a twenty-year old boy?" Isabelle informed him, and Beletech said that in the culture of the Oromo it is called *guddi Fejja*.

"It is a form of adoption, including adopting an older person belonging to another family or even another tribe… The Oromo are an interesting people as my aunt Azeb always told me." Beletech said.

"Well, your dad was an Oromo, Isabelle and so you are an Oromo on one side. So what do you think? For example, you can perhaps adopt both of your nephews, or one of them, if you want and if you can, that is to say, if it materially feasible for a person living in Europe, France or Belgium in your case, to do it. What do you think, Isabelle?"

'Frankly, I don't know."

"I think that is a fair and honest answer. I was half afraid, in view of your understandable excitement at discovering your nieces and learning about their two college age sons, I wondered if you might be tempted to do adoption.?"

"Would you blame me if I fell into the temptation as you call it?"

"Blame you? Why should I, and what right do I have any way. It is your prerogative. Only?…" "Only what?"…

"Only, it requires deep thinking and thorough preparation materially to accomplish it."

"So, you don't think it is foolhardy?"

Foolhardy? No. Not in the least. Actually, it would be a heroic act akin to your father's leap into what to lesser beings appeared impossible. Unfortunately, he was beaten by a ruthless, determined and fast- acting adversary."

"My God, Rashid, I had no idea you were such a deep thinker, in addition to your unique sense of empathy that I have come to like and cherish."

"Come on let us not exaggerate."

"No, I am not exaggerating. I wish Stefan were here, who is like you a deep thinker."

"By the way, speaking of Stefan, he is behaving strangely. We had a short conversation about Italian language, and he went to his room. I tried to enter but it was locked. Unless he went out walking.

Isabelle showed alarm on her expressive face. "I will go and see how he is," she said and left.

She came back empty-handed so to speak. Did you try his room?'

Yes, I did. It is locked and there is no answer... What were you two talking about, anyway?

It was a very short conversation. When I joined him, he and Beletech were having a chat. I heard him say something in Italian. He said it is some quote from Dante about a writing at the gate of Inferno. Something about abandoning hope all those who entered the gate of Inferno.

Our talk was very brief. Then he got up and left. *C'est tout.* [That's all] *"Oui, mais c'est drole quand meme* [Yes, but it is really strange]

Not to worry, his stout German need for a walk or a hike must have impelled him to up and go. I would not worry.

"I hope you are right, Rashid...You are wonderful," she said touching his hand and rose to leave to her room.

Later in the day, they met at dinner and Isabelle said nothing to Stefan who appeared tired. Rashid noticed the cooling of relationship between the two. But he did not want to add to the problem. Yet he reckoned he must say something. So, he called Beletech and asked her if there is ice in the Fridge.

He said loudly so all could hear him: "We have much to feel good about especially following our Wollega trip."

No response from either Stefan or Isabelle. Rashid then realised something was wrong. However, he did not want to leave things hanging in the air. So, he went for the jugular.

"So, either one of you or both of you do not want to talk to me. And it is cruel of you to sulk without giving me a chance to explain whatever it is that I have done to you. I appeal to you both in the name of the god of friendship: If I have wronged you, please forgive me. And I want also to know what evil thing I have done.".…

It was Stefan who spoke first: "You have done nothing, Rashid. I for one, am sorry I went off in a huff and locked myself up in my room. That was rude and I apologise for it.".…

"Apology accepted," cried Rashid…

… "And Isabelle?".…

…I don't know what to say. It was really silly of us…I mean of me to sulk…Rashid you are a true friend and a real a noble African gentleman.".…
"And Stefan and I have some issues to resolve…all in good time."

"And meanwhile our work goes on as planned." Rashid said somewhat triumphant and proud of the ruse he used to achieve his objective of harmony among the group.

In view of the "strange" experience that had threatened the group's harmonious relationship, Isabelle proposed a brief period of break. She mentioned her reading somewhere about the historic medieval city of Harar and suggested that all three, or whoever wished to go should undertake a visit to Harar. "Such a break will do us good," she underscored with an imploring tone. Rashid said he had always wanted to see Harar and said he would like to go. Stefan also said the same. So, they considered a visit by car or by train service to Dire Dawa and then by bus to Harar. They asked Kassa about it and he volunteered to go with them as driver of rented cars, as needed, and as guide, because he said he knew Harar very well.

It was agreed that they would leave the following day by train to Dire Dawa and from there the following day to Harar where they planned to stay three days all in all.

By the time they returned from a charming sojourn in Harar and Dire Dawa, the three friends were refreshed and ready to resume their project of search for Negassa's grave. The deadline the Minister of Interior had passed by four days; so they went to his office confident that he would receive them immediately. They greeted the same police officer who saw them the previous week, and he welcomed them warmly. He went in to announce their arrival to the Minister who told him to bring them in at once.

The Minister greeted them with open arms, telling them that he had expected to see them a few days ago and was wondering what had happened to them. The welcoming ceremonies over, the Minister ordered the usual coffee and started telling them, assuming a grave countenance, that unfortunately, he was not able himself to help trace the grave as he had hoped. But he said he has given strict instructions to the Chief of Police to leave no stone unturned (literally and figuratively) to find the grave of the late Dr. Negassa. I have also received a letter from our Attorney General to the same effect, and I understand the Police Chief has also received the same letter. The letter gives us legal clearance to do our job without any doubt that the search is based on law, and there can be no obstruction of any kind by anybody, even if there might be people who might object for any reason whatsoever. So, the ground is cleared for a lawful search…

…The Minister paused for a moment and looking at Isabelle, he said: "Isabelle, rest assured that everything will be done to discover the remains of your illustrious and heroic father who fell into the hands of ruthless renegades who dealt a deadly blow to individual lives and the national interest. So, rest assured we will do all we can to help you in your legitimate quest."

The Minister showed rare emotion for a politician, which suggests that he did indeed know and respected Dr. Negassa. In wishing the group all the best and terminating the audience, the Minister rose, walked round the desk, gave Isabelle a warm hug and shook the hands of Stefan and Rashid.

So ended the ministerial audience. What remains now is pursuing the detection work by continually visiting the office of the Police and dealing with those involved in the search at two levels: at a professional level requesting how far the inquest had gone as well asking for details of what was being done by the police personnel involved in the search. The second level was personal and human, which involved contact, cultivating personal relationship with some of the key personnel.

[*Here begins the new drama involving a romantic interest on the part of the lead investigator and his interest in wanting to know more about Isabelle…to be developed… Also a description of the government's ideologues*(political cadres) *the mass line versus personal glory and love of worldly goods]* [Hence the FALLEN ANGELS]

Part

ISABELLE AND THE FALLEN ANGELS

Chapter Thirteen

ENCOUNTER WITH THE SECURITY ESTABLISHMENT

The Regular Police

The Police Headquarters in Addis Ababa is found in the area of Addis Ababa formerly known as Mexico Square, and earlier as Mai Chew Square. The HQ is a large compound spread out into different departments.

Isabelle and her friends arrived at the Police HQ in and went through the entrance leading to the office of the Police Commissioner. They were met by a uniformed officer who asked them about the reason of their visit. Upon hearing about the reason of their visit, the officer told them to wait and invited them to wait in the waiting room, which was a carpeted large room with several chairs. He went in to the office of the Chief and after some five minutes came out and beckoned them with his outstretched arms to come and follow him into the office. They entered into a large room adorned with pictures and maps of the city and the country hanging on the walls. On a large table to the left of the Chief's desk was placed a number of items including medals and insignia of various size and color, as well as pictures of recently martyred comrades and of champions of sports won by police teams. Remarkably, the Police Commissioner did not give a military salute to the guests; instead he stood ramrod fashion, extended his hand and shook each one's hand. Having done that and having asked the guests to sit down, he offered the customary tea or coffee and passed the order to the officer in attendance.

Commissioner Kebede Akalu was a man in his mid to late sixties, tall and with heavily built body and impressive bearing. He wears a khaki-colored uniform adorned with the insignias of a General's rank. When sitting in office, he does not wear his cap of the same color as his uniform; it hangs on a wooden stand to the left of his desk. His left chest is bedecked with various medals arranged along three lines.

When he speaks with a pleasant baritone voice, he exudes a fatherly aura and speaks slowly but deliberately in short sentences. Graduate of the nation's Police Academy, he has also attended courses ranging from six months to one year in Police Academies in Europe and America. He speaks English with sufficient fluency and writes with moderate competency. He reads books on law and matters concerning security. He also likes history and reads biographies of some world leaders like Lincoln, Churchill and De Gaul, and recently those of Mandela, Martin Luther King and Nkrumah. Once a week he teaches history to advanced classes in the Police Academy. He says he likes teaching more than bureaucratic work, though he recognizes the importance of office work. Some of his former students from his teaching at the Police Academy, remember his passion about the law and justice, impressing upon his students the key role the police play in maintaining law and order and protecting the lives and property of citizens, even at times placing their lives at risk.

When he heard the story of why our heroes traveled to Ethiopia, the Commissioner was visibly moved especially when Isabelle talked about how much she and her family hope and expect the Ethiopian people engaged in law and justice to help in recovering the remains of Dr. Negassa. He posed a few simple questions designed to clarify some points, like whether Isabelle's mother has ever made the same request before. Isabelle answered this was the first time the request was made. The Commissioner then said the floor was open and Isabelle spoke at length summarising the work of the group including what they had achieved that far like meeting with Isabelle's cousins in Wollega. He said how happy he was to hear that and that he hoped that this achievement will give some hope and solace to Isabelle's mother and the rest of her family back in France.

"So what exactly do you want my office to do to help," the Commissioner asked in earnest. Isabelle said she hoped he would use his power and the prestige of his office to cause a thorough and systematic search for people who might have been involved in the secret burial of her father in an unmarked grave.

"I promise you I will do everything in my power to do what you ask. I was a junior police officer stationed in one of the provinces when the Derg came to power and never moved from there until the Derg was overthrown. So I can only rely on evidence that may be available in the archives and from people who worked in the Department at the time, especially those who worked in the Prison System at the time."

"We cannot expect you to do more, Commissioner, and thank you for your earnest promise. I feel sure I can count on you."

Isabelle looked at her friends to see if they had anything else to say. Rashid said he had a couple of questions, and the Commissioner gave him his undivided attention.

Rashid repeated Isabelle's appreciation of the Commissioner's promise and posed his questions as follows.

"First, does the police department have the power and the institutional capacity to search for people who had been close associates or special agents of Mengistu—people who were at his beck and call to kill and bury in secret?"

The Commissioner shifted in his chair, showed a little hesitation and then speaking slowly, said:

"That is a hard question to answer. It is an important question that my people and I will consider seriously, but it is not a question on which I can give now an unqualified 'yes.'"

"And your second question?"

"Actually you have answered it in part. It is related to whether the police department can utilise the services of allied government institutions on this question of finding out who might have been involved in the killing and burial of Dr. Negasso's body."

"We can and will utilise the services of allied organizations of the government in performing our duties."

"Thank you Commissioner," said Rashid. Stefan indicated by facial expression he had no new questions or comments. Isabelle made a short concluding statement telling the Commissioner that her friends and she would come to his office or the offices of his assistants involved in the matter.

"I hope and trust that you and you people will not be sick and tired of seeing our faces again and again."

"First of all you do not have faces which one can be sick and tired of seeing," the Commissioner said, demonstrating that he has a sense of humor.

"Then it is our sworn obligation to serve all who come to us seeking justice.

So, please be assured of that."

Then the Commissioner rose and stretched out his hand, which all three shook one after the other. The Commissioner rang the bell and the attendant officer led the group out.

Urgent Meeting at the Ministry of Interior.

An Urgent Summons was issued by Interior Minister Berhanu Bogale, that took our group by surprise. It was a summons called suddenly while the three friends were visiting Adama. They had travelled there to visit Isabelle's nephews who are studying at a college in the Oromo capital city. Isabelle had made an arrangement to visit the two boys in fulfillment of a promise she had made to their mothers during her visit in Neqemte. The plan was to use the occasion to spend a few days visiting the fast- growing city of Adama as well as the area around it, including the Wonji sugar plantation and factory.

A message came to Isabelle by a special courier carrying a letter signed by the Minister of Interior calling for an urgent meeting of the senior personnel of all the departments of the Ministry. Addressed to the heads of the said departments, the letter urges all concerned to cease whatever activities they are engaged in, and attend the special meeting. The letter mentions that the main item on the agenda of the meeting concerns the request by Ms. Isabelle Negassa to retrieve the remains of her deceased father Dr. Negassa. A copy of the letter was made, which is attached to the covering note sent to Isabelle by the secretary of the Minister.

A police officer riding a motor cycle brought the letter to Isabelle, having tried to reach her at the villa and was told by Beletech that she was in Adama. The summons took all three by surprise and awakened anxieties in Isabelle's heart, which had lately been affected by waves of conflicting emotions. The appearance of a uniformed policeman in a motor bike carrying a message put Isabelle's mind floating around expecting a tragic message. She asked him: "Is everything oaky?" The young man who spoke good English said, with a reassuring smile: "Everything is okay, Miss Isabelle. It is a letter summoning you to a meeting with the Minister."

"Thank God," she exhaled. She read the letter and shared it with her companions.

"This is good," Rashid said.

"What do you mean? Why is it good," Stefan asked?

"Very simple. Let us look back and consider what has happened thus far." We have seen the Minster of Interior, the Minister of Justice, the Attorney

General and the Police Commissioner. And I have not forgotten the individuals we have talked to, like Dr. Zekarias. Let me also remind you how the Minister of Interior received us. How he got up from his desk, came around and stretched his arms emotionally to embrace Isabelle. What he said about her father and the promise he made to help us..." Rashid stopped probably for dramatic effect...

"So?" inquired Stefan looking at Rashid with screwed eye brows and forehead.

"So, he must feel frustrated that there has not been any result so far."

"Yes, but why call a meeting?" Isabelle wondered, looking at the content of the letter again.

"Well, if you are a very sympathetic Minister of Interior in charge of all the departments that have been called upon to come up with a solution to a simple problem, namely, trace the location of an unmarked grave, and you received no answer, what do you do?" Rashid queried and waited for an answer. No answer.

"You call all hands on deck, and give the Hell. The fact that he called them all to a meeting together suggests a shrewd tactical move—getting them on a competitive atmosphere. The person or department section that gets to locate the grave receives the reward of ministerial favor.... Do you see my drift?"

"I see you drift, but I am still puzzled," Stefan said.

"Anyway, get your things fast. We must go back to Addis," Isabelle implored.

The building complex housing the Security Division of the Ministry of Interior is another architectural monstrosity—a maze of divided two-floored structures spread out a large area. At the center of a compound is the main entry to the Director's office, and adjoining it is a large meeting room. A group of people, numbering about thirty were seated on the chairs placed around a large oval-shaped table. They were chatting informally when our heroes entered. All rose and turned inquiringly at the guests. Two from among the group came forward to introduce themselves. Presumably they knew about Isabelle and her friends. The two men, both in their thirties, shook Isabelle's hand first and then Stefan and Rashid shook the two men's hands. The two spoke one after the other, saying they had seen the guests at the Police Headquarters, going in to the Commissioner's office.

"He is a nice man," Isabelle said.

"The best!" one of them said in obvious admiration of the Commissioner. "He is our hero and he is a great teacher; he taught us at the Police Academy."

"Is he coming here?" Isabelle asked.

"Oh yes, and he told us to get here ahead."

After some ten minutes, the Police Commissioner and the Minister arrived together. Everybody rose and stood to attention as the two men took their seats at the head table in front, facing the audience. Two among the audience, uniformed officers, gave a military salute to the Minister and Commissioner, who motioned everybody to sit and took their seats themselves.

"Good afternoon everybody," the Minister greeted the assembled group with a broad smile.

"Good afternoon, sir" the audience roared back.

"Is everyone present? "the Minister asked. The silence answer seemed an affirmative answer.

"All right, then. You have all received the summons, I am sure and, therefore, I will make my introductory remarks very brief. The Minister

172

of State for Security is out of the country, but he is informed about today's meeting. I have discussed the agenda with him before his departure, as well as with the Police Commissioner. I have also, as you may know, invited our three special guests because the agenda is of interest to them. As you can see, we have made arrangements for simultaneous interpretation so that they can follow the process as it proceeds." [*the three had already put on the listening gear on their ears and an interpreter was sitting behind a glass enclosure on the front of the hall, and is visible.*]

The Minister pointed to the window of the enclosure to his right and the interpreter bowed her head and smiled.

"We will begin the meeting with a short prayer. Please bow your head," the Minister said and made a sign of the cross and began a short silent prayer...

"Thank you, gentlemen..."

"I called for this meeting because I felt that the requests for a speedy handling of the request by our dear guest, Isabelle, daughter of the martyr and hero, Dr. Negassa, has not been as well as I had hoped. Am I right?" he inquired pausing for an answer. When none was forthcoming, he continued: "the silence speaks for itself, doesn't it?"

A couple of hands went up and the Minister stopped speaking and gave the floor to one of the men. "With due respect, sir, may I make a short comment?"

"Yes, of course. That is why I called for the meeting."

"Well, sir, I beg to differ. As far as my department is concerned, our personnel worked day and night to find the grave." "But what was the outcome of their work?"

"With respect, sir, I was coming to that. Have you been informed about how many graves my people dug, and brought sacs' full of bones?... Evidently, sir, you have not been informed. The question is not lack of diligence on our part."

"What is the problem then?

"The problem is: how do we know to whom the bones belonged. Obviously, the Derg regime killed so many people secretly, that it is not possible to know which grave belonged to whom."

"Have you finished?" the Minister asked rather impatiently. "Yes sir."

"Thank you for your remarks. I find your bold intervention commendable. That I have not been informed does indeed support the point of your complaint. Is there any other question or comment?"

The Police Commissioner raised his hand and the Minister gave him the floor.

"Your excellency, I think we need to separate the issues. First, we need to make sure that the unmarked grave in which Dr. Negassa was secretly buried must be found and identified. Finding and identification are related but separate issues. The points raised by the previous question about the difficulty of knowing which bones are those of Dr. Negassa raised a technical question of how we a decision can be made. Fortunately, nowadays we can do that easily through DNA.

The Minister intervened: "Thank you, Commissioner, for that good point about the need to separate the issues. As you know DNA testing is an expensive process, and we are faced with many unmarked graves, which seems likely, given the nature and practice of the Derg regime. Besides, digging up the bones of unknown people is an unpleasant thing—unfair to the deceased and his or her survivors, and deeply disturbing from the ethical point of view."

There was an audible murmur among the audience signaling a feeling of distaste and discomfort. The Minister hit the table with the gavel and the murmur slowly disappeared. The Minister, turned to the Commissioner, brought his head close to the Commissioner's ear and whispered something and the Commissioner nodded his consent to whatever the Minister might have asked him.

"Gentlemen, let us not miss the tree being lost in the forest. The tree in the situation facing us is a metaphor for the need to focus on the search for the unmarked grave. The problem of having too many graves with the logistical and other problems it presents is a real one; I do not mean to underestimate it." He paused for a few seconds as if to collect his thoughts and continued:

"Let me remind you of the reason for calling the meeting. First it is to stress the importance of the case presented to us by a family member of a deceased father whose disappearance had haunted her and her family for over two decades, and she is demanding an answer from us as a government and as a people, an upright people."

Isabelle was seen taking out her handkerchief and dabbing her face and her two companions patting her back. And the interpreter was affected by Isabelle's reaction that she stopped her interpreting momentarily and asked for pardon saying:

"I can't help being affected by the story and Isabelle's reaction…I beg your pardon…Sorry, and I will now continue my role as interpreter and I promise not to interrupt again."

The Minister agreed with the interpreter, adding that she instantly went back to do her job. "And we must do our job…Now where was I?"…

…A number of voices shouted words reminding him where he was. "Thank you. Yes, I was saying that Isabelle Negassa is demanding for an answer and we owe her an answer as quickly as possible…She has waited over two decades, in other words, most of her life…"

Again, the Minister paused for some five seconds. And continued: "Some of you may have wondered why I took the decision to call for a meeting. Why did I give this matter such due attention? I hope that you now understand the reason. In an ideal world, giving such attention and due respect to a case like this should be attended to speedily. Dr. Negassa's case is special because he was a special person who gave his life for a cause. So that fact did induce in me a sense of special duty owed to such a man or rather his surviving family."

The Commissioner, apparently moved by the Minister's noble sentiments, decided to interpose with his own tribute to Negassa. "Your Excellency, I wish to add my own humble voice to what you just expressed. I never knew Dr. Negassa. I was a junior police officer in a distant province at the time of his involvement in the revolution and his disappearance. But I know people who were his comrades and they revere him as a martyr who offered his life for the ordinary people to whose interest he had dedicated his life—unto death." He stopped a while and then with a strong resounding voice said:

"Sir, and Ms. Isabelle, I give you my word as an officer and a gentleman that I will mobilise my people and set them to do what needs to be done to find the graves. It is probably necessary to do a bit of detective work to find people who might have been involved in the burial. We will do it."

There was an explosion of applause from the audience and standing ovation to a point that the Commissioner was embarrassed. The Minister applauded with the rest of the audience and rose to salute the Commissioner.

"Thank you Commissioner. And thank you gentlemen. Let us do our job and be proud of our work."

And turning to the three guests, the Minister said:

"Isabelle, I hope you feel encouraged. We cannot bring back you father, but we will honor him in performing our lawful duties and obligations… Go in peace!"

And she did. And the meeting was ended.

On the way to the villa, Isabelle felt a sense of relief even before the process of search was over. She told her friends that she has been fortified in her optimism by the eloquent words of the Minister and the Commissioner. I feel justified in having made the decision to undertake this search with you my two dear friends and brothers. I will never forget the favor you have done me…" And she stopped there as abruptly as she began…

Rashid, who is never lost for apt words, relevant to a situation, said: "That sounds like a farewell speech. Are you thinking of giving up?"…

"Ya… and leaving us out in the cold?" Stefan added a rejoinder.

Isabelle turned to Stefan first because she detected a note of desperation in his remark. Rashid's question had a comic quality to it even if his question was the same in content. But Isabelle has a good ear for sensing the tone of a statement or question. And there was a difference in the tones between Rashid's and Stefan questions.

The two waited for Isabelle's response—anxiously. She did not give a response and tried to change the subject. This provoked Stefan.

"Isabelle, you were asked questions by both of us. And you are trying to change the subject. I cannot believe that you are abandoning the project after the encouraging words by both the Minister and the Police Commissioner. Your behavior is bizarre to say the least. And your silent response to our concerned questions is worse than bizarre; it smacks of betrayal."

"Betrayal!" "Yes, betrayal.

"Who am I betraying?

"Your friends who have strung along with you because they believed in your just cause."

"But I did not say I am abandoning the project. You are jumping to a rash and unfair conclusion."

Rashid was seriously concerned about a potential breakup between the two of them and thought of a way of lowering the tension. He searched in his mind for an appropriate joke.

"Okay, you two. Stop this. I am ordering an armistice, to be fortified by a glass of whiskey?" "Let us go out and have some drinks in a hotel bar… Stefan, what do you say?"

"Damned good idea." Isabelle hesitated and Rashid put his arms round her shoulder and squeezed her, saying, how about a good old Johnny Walker…he goes a long way!"

She smiled and said, "damned good idea," and she smiled at Stefan who smiled back."

Their evening at the hotel bar did not last long and though the drinks helped them to get out of the "fighting" frame of mind, they were not completely freed of it.

The following day, Isabelle decided to go to Adama to resume the interrupted visit of her two nephews. She told her friends of her decision and told them they could join her or not. "It is up to you." Both decided to remain in Addis and visit friends or stay in the villa. So Isabelle arranged with Kassa to go to Adama for a couple of days.

Chapter Fourteen

ISABELLE AND THE EXTENDED FAMILY

She was raised by a European nuclear family. But she instinctively felt drawn to the idea of an extended family from which her father had come and by which he had been raised. As it happened, she and her sister had never been exposed to the African nuclear family. So, the appeal she felt toward the idea of an extended family presumably stems from her sense of loss of a father's love. Though she was raised in a nuclear family in France, the feeling of having been deprived of a natural bond with the missing father created an urge to seek it in an imagined extended family.

What had been in her mind for all her life came face to face with the reality of the extended family in the person of her two cousins. She could not describe the inexorable feeling of a sense of belonging she experienced when meeting her cousins. She could not have enough of them. The interruption of that special feeling she experienced which was cut short by her need to go back to Addis Ababa was frustrating. Hence her decision to visit the nephews. Her decision to visit her cousins' sons, her nephews, is an extension —a natural consequence, of what she felt in Wollega. Her snap decision to visit her cousins and its sequel of wanting to create a family connection with her nephews was part of a complex set of thinking and feeling born out of her decision to undertake the project of retrieving her father's remains.

When she came face to face with the reality of Ethiopia's social and political condition, especially during her visit to Wollega, she began some kind of self-examination whether the idea of retrieving her father's remains was realistic. And this process of self-examination was enhanced during her meetings with some of the government officials, and epically at the special meeting called by the Minister of Interior. The intensity of the emotional experience also led to some of her "bizarre" behavior.

Body and Soul: Isabelle's Dilemma

In addition to her preoccupation with the idea of the extended family and her wish to develop a special family relationship with her cousins and the two nephews, Isabelle was also conscious of a "spiritual vacuum" in her life. The need of a spiritual reorientation was dawned on her during the special meeting. It hit her like a flash of lightening, when the Minister was speaking, which was reinforced by the Police Commissioner's heart-felt remarks.

During the meeting called by the Minister and some time before, Isabelle had begun to re-examine her project of recovering her father's remains. But it was during her confession to a Catholic priest, following her "bizarre" behavior and just before starting her trip to Adama, that the self-examination assumed greater significance. One of the illuminating moments during the special meeting was the remark of the official who spoke about digging so many graves and not being sure whose bones belonged to Dr. Negassa. The significance of that point was reinforced by the Minister's remark about how costly DNA testing can be. Isabelle's self-questioning reached its highest level at that moment. The unfortunate aspect of this self-questioning led to her "bizarre" behavior, and her inability, or unwillingness, to explain it to her friends.

During her confession with a Catholic priest, the main point about the project was raised and Isabelle posed the question whether she was on the right track, spiritually, in insisting on recovering her father's remains. The priest told her that, while it is emotionally satisfying to do what she planned in the project, it is not necessary to recover the remains (i.e. the body) in order to do a memorial service for his soul. The body is dead, the spirit (soul) is with God. That revelation became a crucial fact in her re-examining her idea of the project. In this respect her main difficulty was the fact that she had involved two good friends to commit their time and energy to the project and its realization.

She agonized over this and she felt that to abandon the project of recovering the remains is like a betrayal of two good friends. That was her dilemma, a matter she must resolve soon after her return from her visit to Adama.

Meeting the Nephews

On the eve of the first visit to Adama, which was interrupted because of the Interior Minister's summons, Isabelle had found the phone number of the Adama University and talked to the Dean of Students of the University about her visit to her nephews. After the interruption of the visit, she had called the Dean's office to cancel the meeting and change it to another time. And just before her departure for the second visit she had called the Dean's office, with apologies, to have the two boys ready for the evening to meet with their aunt.

Isabelle arrived in Adama in the late afternoon. She checked into the Abebe Bikila Hotel and called the Dean's Office notifying them of her arrival. They told her the boys would be ready at six o'clock and wait at the Dean's office.

When she arrived the Dean of Students met her in his office where the boys were waiting. First, she greeted the Dean and then the boys, hugging and kissing them one by one. Their names are: Sisay who is twenty years old and Ibsa, aged nineteen. The Dean told Isabelle that the two boys were very good students and exemplary in their general conduct. Sisay is also a soccer star in the University and very popular among his student companions. Ibsa is studious, not particularly interested in sports.

The Dean then excused himself because he had a class to teach soon. Isabelle thanked him and took the boys to the hotel, where they had a sumptuous dinner. After dinner, Kassa took them on a tour of the city after which they had cappuccino at a café nearby to her hotel. She asked them what subject they found interesting and what they want to become.

Sisay said he wanted to become an engineer and Ibsa wanted to become a doctor. She encouraged them to do a lot of reading of fiction in English in order to improve their command of English.

They spent an enjoyable evening and it was past midnight when they left. Fortunately, it was a weekend and they did not have classes the following day. Isabelle fell in love with her two cute nephews; she could not have enough of them, so she decided to spend the following day with them touring the sugar plantations of Wonji, not far from Adama.

During their tour of the plantations, they ran into the manager of the company, who was curious to know who Isabelle was. When she told him who she was and why she came to Ethiopia, the man's fair- skinned round face changed reddish brown and he screamed: "It cannot be!"…He looked at her and at the two boys and said: "It is impossible!"

Isabelle cried: "what is wrong?"…

He said: "What a strange and wonderful coincidence!… I knew Dr. Negassa." "Where? When?"

"I was a young internee here as a third-year engineering student. He and a couple of his MEISON comrades used to come here to organize plantation workers, and I was a member of the local chapter of their party and used to meet with them secretly…Amazing!… What a coincidence!…What a blessed day!…And who are these boys? He said turning to the two boys.

"They are my grand nephews, the grand children of Negassa's younger sister."

"Well, bless your hearts!" the man said, and when he learned that they were studying at Adama University, he told them to apply for a summer job as internees at the Wonji Sugar Plantations. He got out a couple of cards and gave one to Isabelle and another to Sisay.

The name on the card was: Engineer Kumsa Debela. "I am also from Wollega originally. I am proud of Dr. Negassa, though I left the politics of Marxist revolution in favor of Evangelical Christianity."

Isabelle told him she was raised as a Catholic, though she had strayed from the Faith for many years, until recently.

"I am glad you returned to the Faith. We all have moments of doubt, but in the end what counts is coming back to the Faith." Turning to the boys, he admonished them: "I will not try to impose my evangelical faith on anybody, but I hope that you boys remain within the Christian Fold."

"We are Orthodox Christians, sir," Sisay told him.

"Good. After all, that is the Mother Church in our country and I believe there is going to be a revival in the Orthodox Tewahdo Church.

Personally I believe in the Ecumenical Movement, which the great Pope John VII started."

Kumsa said he was glad meeting Isabelle and the boys. He told the boys to call him any time and, bowing respectfully to Isabelle and hugging the two boys, left them.

"Wasn't that an incredible coincidence?" Isabelle exclaimed smiling at the boys."

Ibsa said: "God is Great. This coincidence is His Work."

"Amen," Isabelle said. So did Kassa, who also said he was a follower of Evangelical Christianity.

They returned to Adama and Kassa deposited Isabelle in the hotel and took the boys to their residence. Isabelle called the Dean of Students to thank him for his assistance and gave him a brief account of the day, including their meeting with the engineer. She told him about Kumsa's offer of Summer employment to the boys, which pleased the Dean.

Early in the morning, Isabelle left Adama. She told Kassa to be ready early in the morning because she needed to attend Mass at the Cathedral in Addis, if possible the second Mass, which starts at 11AM. Kassa said he will be ready at six AM, which would give them enough time to reach Addis an hour before the start of the Mas.

Kassa was a man of his word. He came a little before six and they left Adama at a few minutes after six, and arrived in Addis a little after eight AM. After Mass was over, Isabelle went to the villa and was on time for lunch.

Beletech welcomed her with a warm embrace and Stefan and Rashid gave her a warm if restrained welcome. Rashid told her that Dr. Ibrahim and Azeb called the previous night and sent their love. He said both Stefan and he gave them a brief account of what had happened thus far, including the various meetings they had.

"Azeb inquired about your trip to Wollega and Adama, and we gave her about the highlights of our activities," Rashid said.

"Did you tell her about my bizarre behaviour," Isabelle asked with an embarrassed smile."

"Oh yes, everything," he replied without hesitation and with a straight face, stealing glance at Stefan.

"I don't believe it," Isabelle said. "You are joking, of course," she told him in earnest, and he frowned and said, "Not at all. Stefan and I thought we owed them a duty to tell them the truth. After all, they have been so generous."

"Oh my God," yelled Isabelle and frowned at Stefan and asked him: is this true?"

"Yes it is," Stefan said with a serious countenance, and added: "Do you doubt Rashid's word?" as she collapsed in the chair in utter exasperation."

Rashid faced Stefan and asked him: "Shall we also tell her that we have decided to leave?"

"Absolutely. Why not tell her the whole truth…How do the lawyers put it?

…The truth, the whole truth and nothing but the truth, "Stefan said, and all of a sudden he burst out laughing, joined by Rashid."

"Bastards!" Isabelle yelled…But after a few seconds of pouting with a protruding lower lip on which birds could rest, joined them in the hilarity…

"I will pay you back for this, you SOBs!…Wait, just wait." The kind-hearted Rashid, and architect of the plan, pulled her up from the chair and hugged her affectionately. Following him, Stefan held her by the shoulders and facing her, said: "Fooled you again!"…Then in mock gesture of remorse, said "Sorry!"

"Go to Hell!" was her quick reaction, remembering the circumstances in which he had said: 'Fooled you,' before"

"Well, I have been there before," Stefan answered, being surprised at her bitterness. Once more, the sensitive and peace-loving Rashid was back to the rescue, fearful lest Stefan might take Isabelle's exclamation the wrong way and decide to leave the project. On a couple of occasions, during Isabelle's absence, Rashid's sensitive soul had detected in Stefan frustration and expressions of wish to leave. So, he suggested to Isabelle and Stefan a night out in the city. To strengthen his suggestion, he said he would call the Sudanese Ambassador to Ethiopia, an old friend of his, to help in finding a suitable place and join them for a relaxed evening. Luckily, they both agreed and they went out for a night out.

The Lalibela Night Club was packed with revellers, a mixed clientele of foreigners and citizens. Rashid's friend and Sudanese Ambassador brought with him three guests—two men and one woman—who sounded thrilled to meet our three heroes. To everybody's surprise, one of the two guests that the Sudanese Ambassador brought was a man by the name of Teshome. When Isabelle was introduced to the Sudanese Ambassador by Rashid and his guests, Teshome told Isabelle that he had seen her and her two friends at the Minister Interior's special meeting. As the partying went on with drinks and select food offered by smartly dressed waitresses, Teshome sat on a table with the other two guests of the Ambassador. He told Isabelle that he was deeply touched by the story of her father and that he would do everything in his power to help her in the search for her father's remains. The conversation went on back and forth with everybody joining in talking randomly with those around them.

It was when the other guests were engaged in conversations or when their attention was drawn by other guests that Teshome spoke to Isabelle in a low voice. He is a tall and moderately good-looking man in his mid-forties, with a closely cropped hair that was partly grizzled and a mustache that was neatly trimmed and tinted black. He has large eyes that are constantly roving to gaze at other people, especially women. And he is endowed with a deep and soothing voice that women found appealing.

Toward the end of the evening, a striking looking woman singer came on the stage and, while soft music was on, an announcer invited people to take their partners to the dance floor. Teshome lost no time before he rose and elegantly bowed and asked Isabelle for a dance. There was no chance of Isabelle refusing such an elegant man asking a woman for a dance in that deep, seductive voice. Isabelle rose and he took her into his arms and danced with her cheek-to-cheek almost immediately when they hit the dance floor. The music took a long time before it ended, but before the dancers had a chance to go back to their table, another tune was on and the dancing continued.

This time, Teshome had Isabelle completely embraced and they danced cheek-to-cheek throughout. On a couple of occasions, he broke from the embrace slightly to whisper something to her ears and she giggled loudly, raising fear and anxiety in Stefan's heart. Rashid, always the caring friend, kept gazing at Stefan and tried several times to engage him in small Talks, but to no avail. Finally, he got up and stepped to the dance floor, and tapped Teshome's back and asked: "May I have this dance now?" According to an unwritten custom, Teshome could not refuse.

He broke from the embrace reluctantly and Rashid took Isabelle into his arms. But no cheek-to-cheek stuff. Stefan has had enough torture. Instead of cheek-to-cheek stuff, Rashid talked about their business. Her response was one of despondence and irritation. And lo and behold, Teshome decided it was his turn and came tapping Rashid's back. Rashid released Isabelle. However, Isabelle said she was tired and headed toward the table where she found Stefan sulking.

"Do you want to dance, Isabelle asked Stefan and he flatly declined, giving Teshome another chance. When he asked Isabelle for a dance, she said yes and went to the dance floor with him. "I thought you said you were tired Isabelle," Teshome quizzed her. She did not answer him but put her cheek to his, which he accepted with immense surprise and pleasure.

"Are you staying long in the country," Teshome asked Isabelle, breaking from the cheek for a moment. She answered that she did not know…

"It depends on how fast I am able to complete my project," she added. "Meanwhile, if there is anything I can do to help, please don't hesitate to call. I will give you my direct phone number later. And if I may, I will call you at the Ibrahim villa"

Surprised that he knew where she was staying she was curious to know who he is.

"What exactly do you do in the ministry?' she asked him.

"I am director of Intelligence," said to her immense surprise. This man, she thought, is not just a good looking gigolo, but a high-ranking official heading a crucial department of the Security Establishment. "How mistaken I have been," she chided herself.

"Well, thank you, I will do that. I will take your card" She became curious how he was able to be the head of intelligence and asked him for his background. He said he had been a guerilla fighter and was a member of the Central Committee of the Fighting Front.

Astounded, "the plot thickens," she thought. "Have you heard of our Fighting Front?" "Not really."

"It is an interesting story. I will tell you about it, I hope."

By that time, his friend the Sudanese ambassador was rising to go with his other two guests. So Teshome broke the embrace and fumbled from his left inside pocket for his wallet and extracted a card and gave it to Isabelle.

They said good bye to one another and our three heroes walked silently to the parking area, got into their car, which was driven by Rashid and drove home without a word all the way. Even the supple Rashid was at his wit's end as to what to do with his two friends. They bid good night to one another and went to their respective rooms.

The following morning, they rose late, as they were late in going to be. Beletech knocked at Isabelle's door, wondering if there was something wrong. She knocked a few times and finally Isabelle answered in a groggy voice and opened the door.

"I apologise for disturbing you, Isabelle, but I was a little worried because you always rose early on weekdays. Today being Monday, I thought maybe you might want to awakened."

"It is quite alright, Beletech. Thank you for your thoughts and I will be down in a few minutes after I take a shower and dress up. Okay?"

"Okay. Did they tell you that Azeb and Dr. Ibrahim called from Geneva?" "Yes they did, thank you. I'll see you later."

Stefan and Rashid di not yet get up, but Beletech did not bother to disturb them. She had learned from Kassa that they took the car for a night out… Isabelle came about twenty minutes later and joined Beletech for coffee and breakfast in the kitchen.

Isabelle asked Beletech if she spoke to Azeb and Dr. Ibrahim. Beletech told her she did but there was nothing she could add to what Rashid had told her.

An hour or so later Stefan and Rashid came to the kitchen and said good morning to the ladies. The response was the usual perfunctory response with no additional small talk. But as usual, Rashid broke the circle of silence by asking Isabelle about what their next work was going to be. She told him, perhaps visiting the office of the Chief of the Prison Administration would be a good idea. She explained why: "I don' think it will be good not to do so, since we have covered all the departments of the security establishment."

"You are right. It would be bad diplomacy. I think Stefan would agree.

Here he comes, I'll ask him." And he did ask him

Stefan had just joined them sitting in a chair near Rashid away from Isabelle. When Isabelle asked him about her suggestion, he gave a quick and sharp response. He said that the Prison Administration was represented in the Minister's special meeting. So what was the use of wasting time, he asked gruffly. Rashid knew the reason why Stefan was being gruff and uncommunicative on the whole. He also knew that Isabelle knew. She spoke to him nonetheless.

"It would be a brief encounter. And it would be undiplomatic of us to omit the Department. After all the grave was dug and the body buried inside the prison or somewhere nearby."

Stefan suggested that Rashid and she could go and brief him of whatever they can find. "Alternatively," he added with a wry smile, "why not use the services of her new friend to find out if it is really necessary to duplicate what we have already found from the other departments of the security establishment." Isabelle knew whom he was referring to. But asked him nonetheless.

What new friend are you talking about?"

"The one you danced with all evening. Who else?"

"As a matter of fact, I might do that," Isabelle replied, and rose from her seat and walked away. Rashid gave up his usual mediation effort and, for the first time, he wondered whether he had done the right thing to get involved in the project.

He turned to Stefan and just gazed at him with a strange expression of dismay. He decided not to say anything. Stefan sensed his mood and tried to justify his behavior.

"I hope you are not going to condemn me for reacting the way I did. You saw what she was doing last night. Am I supposed to applaud her for dancing cheek-to-cheek with a man she had just met in a night club?"

"I am not condemning anybody, but I am sick and tired of this emotional see-saw between you two. In fact, I am wondering whether I did the right thing to join you in this project. I really am, Stefan."

Stefan did not respond. He too, wondered whether he had done the right thing.

Chapter Fifteen

THE "PROJECT" IN A LARGER HISTORICAL CONTEXT

(An Interlude)

We have seen that the "project" on which our story is based has reached a deadlock. A noble effort is in danger of ending, and a wonderful friendship is under threat of demise. What is involved is a complex set of circumstances affecting three people that have been bonded by noble ideas—ideas of personal devotion and sacrifice for the sake of others. Ideas also of the search for justice in the face of an obstinate reality. The beauty of the bonding of the three main protagonists of our story is that their ideas and actions constitute a *defiance* to that obstinate reality. Hence the title of our novel—Defiance.

At issue is a human problem involving primordial emotions of personal love and the hazards attendant to such emotions, as well as human foibles and pursuit of fugitive glory on the part of persons who regard themselves as beyond good and evil by virtue of their thirst for social justice in the name of which they can commit crimes. The execution of Dr. Negassa by the order of an unaccountable historical figure like Mengistu, was a horrendous act. In the context of our story, can persons (historical actors) with whom Isabelle and Stefan befriend in pursuit of a noble "project" be allowed to do what Stalin's commissars did, namely liquidate innocent human beings in pursuit of the requirements of the "project"?

Are any of them capable of committing such acts, or other acts that would seem to contradict the noble aims they express in their rhetoric like social justice or "the interest of the masses?

Let us put the question in the context of recent Ethiopian history. In the Ethiopian revolutionary firmament, there are two type of stars, or two main categories of veterans. First, there are those who were actively engaged in the armed struggle to change the imperial system. Then there are those who "struggled" from within as underground auxiliaries to "the real struggle."

This typology is complicated by the fact that the Emperor's government was overthrown by a popular uprising, which was, however, taken over by the military, called the Derg. Some commentators believe that though the Emperor was gone, the empire continued under the guise of military regime that spouted revolutionary rhetoric.

There has appeared a constellation of ideological stars both during the period of anti-imperial struggle, and in its post-imperial sequel, including the Derg era. The common thread running through the period—of both pre-and post-imperial revolutionary struggle—was the noble rhetoric of fulfilling the human obligations to "mankind." Such fulfilment of a human obligation is presumed, in the minds of the revolutionaries, to exculpate (or cleanse) them from crimes, including illegally eliminating supposed adversaries. *All done without due process of law. Tout est permis* (All is permitted.) In such ideology, there is no respect for law or justice as generally understood. Under the revolutionary ideology, the law is an instrument of "class struggle," not an abstract concept with moral content of right and wrong. In its extreme form, the justification of horrendous acts like murder, rape, pillage and dispossession of legitimately acquired property is rationalised under the controversial phrase: "The End Justifies the Means."

It is reasonable to wonder whether any unexpected or unsuspected feelings torment the perpetrator of such act as it torments Raskolnikov, in Dostoevsky's novel, Crime and Punishment? In the context of Ethiopia's recent history, does a similar psychological process of the commission of a crime torment the perpetrators, as it tormented Raskolnikov? Well, it did not torment Mengistu, who is answerable in the bar of history, as well as under Ethiopia's Penal Code, for committing horrendous crimes, any more than it tormented Stalin or Mao for their crimes.

We shall see in what way, and to what extent, these questions are relevant in the *denouement* of our story. In what way and why some (historical) actors may be involved in the project of our story will be the subject matter of some of the pages that follow.

Where Do We Go from Here?

From the foregoing disquisition—in an interlude, a break away from the narrative of our tory—we go back to continuing it. Two of our protagonists, Stefan and Rashid, had gone to the extent of possibly disengaging from the project to which they had committed themselves. They both expressed frustration arising out of the "emotional saw-saw" connected to Isabelle's conduct, especially with regard to her relation to Stefan.

The answer to the question whether they might carry out such "threat" will depend on Isabelle's response as to whether she values their friendship and appreciates their sacrifice of time and energy for the cause to such an extent that she would re-examine her own emotions and make an appropriate adjustment. It is interesting, especially, to find out how she will handle the new problem of her feelings toward the new character, called Teshome, that appeared, all of a sudden, to have captivated her. What price personal entanglement, in view of the need for cohesion and continued commitment to the project. Unless, of course, Isabelle is captivated by Teshome to such an extent that she might consider terminating the project. But that would mean the end of our story, which Heaven forbid! So, where do we go from here?

Let us consult with Stefan and Rashid.

It should be recalled that Rashid had acted as a mediator and bridge-builder between Isabelle and Stefan. Isabelle is obviously fond of him and thinks his services as valuable. So, it may be safely assumed that if Isabelle exerts enough emotional energy and feminine wile she may persuade Rashid to stay. It may also be safely assumed that Rashid is committed enough to the project and to Isabelle personally as a close friend, she will succeed in persuading him to stay.

The real hard question concerns Stefan. How emotionally wounded is he by her conduct toward Teshome? Can he consider it as a brief encounter, an ephemeral involvement that their long-time friendship can withstand, as it did with regard to his involvement with the late Dorothy Shaw? Is he man enough to remember his own misconduct for which she forgave him and let the "cheek-to-cheek" dance slip out of their deep-rooted relationship? Or is he so incensed by it that his ego cannot stand it, even if she forgives him?

Of course, all this assumes that Isabelle is still committed to the relationship with Stefan and that she is willing to forget Teshome. Let us consider what Isabelle has been up to since that fateful night at the Night Club.

To the surprise of her two friends and fellow travellers, Isabelle travelled to Bahrdar with Teshome without telling them. Actually, she left a note to them, which read as follows:

> *"Dear Stefan and Rashid,*
>
> *I hope you will forgive me for leaving suddenly to Bahrdar at the invitation of Teshome and his comrades in the government in the Amhara Kilil. It seems that there is a unique event going on there that Teshome thought might be of interest to me and the project and that we would miss it if delayed our departure by even a few hours. In fact, he had to use his private plane to get there on time. I will tell you all about it as soon as I get back. Meanwhile, let us use this break to iron out the creases in our relationship.*
>
> *Love, Isabelle*

She left the note care of Beletech and the two read it early in the morning.

To say that it was a surprise is to grossly minimise its impact on the two friends. They did not utter a word for a quite a while. And when Rashid spoke, it was a question in the form of exclamation: Private Planes!!

Then Rashid changed the exclamation to a question:

"Who is this man, anyway?… A former guerilla fighter who has no income other than the miserly salary of the government, and he owns a private plane, or probably a fleet of them.

I smell a rat, 'and I see it flying in the air,' to misquote one of my English teacher's lesson on mistakes in grammar.

Stefan, awakening from the shock delivered by Isabelle's stunning message, calmly said: "haven't you heard of the so-called fallen angels from among revolutionary heroes? Those who abandoned their original ideal of social justice, and the rhetoric of the greatest happiness to the greatest number, to be seduced by corruption, ill-gotten wealth and worldly pleasures?"

Rashid gazed at Stefan in wonderment for a moment and then said:

"Stefan, that is an insightful remark. Actually, I think it is a kind of revelation. I have indeed heard of such people, but I thought it came from the figment of the imagination of what you and I, in our college days, used to call the enemies of progress."

"Alas, no! It is as real as the price of eggs in China. Or is it the price of rice? I forget."

"From the sublime to the ridiculous!" Rashid exclaimed patting Stefan on the back. And then after a few seconds of reflection, and looking Stefan in the eye, he said:

"Let us talk about us: what the Hell are we doing here, brother?" Rashid asked in earnest.

"You know, brother, I was just asking myself that very question," replied Stefan with an ironic laughter...

Two days later, Isabelle returned from Bahrdar and called Stefan from the villa.

"Where are you, Stefan, dear?" she asked and continued, "I have been back for a couple of hours. I am bubbling with so much wonderful things and I rushed back to the villa and found you guys are away. Can you, please come and relieve me of this load of information that will make your head spin and your eyes pop out?... And where is Rashid? Is he not with you?"

"Rashid is in the Sudanese embassy taking care of some family matters. He should be back in an hour."...And he stopped there. No small talk. No: how was the trip? Or, what is all this talk about unique events, or welcome back... Nothing. Just silence, a silence more eloquent than words.

He was talking to him on the cell phone. He did not tell her where he was. What is more, he called Rashid and told him about her call. "I told her you are at the Sudanese Embassy and that you may be back in an hour. I am calling you not to come to the villa, but wait in the Embassy. I am taking a taxi and will join you there in about an hour. Okay?"

"Okay. What is going on?"

"Plenty, I think. I am coming and will talk to you soon."

At the Sudanese Embassy

Stefan arrived at the Embassy of Sudan, as he promised, after an hour and a few minutes later. The Ambassador was entertaining a large group of guests, many of them high-ranking Ethiopian officials and a couple of Sudanese members of the Embassy, plus some white men, Americans and Europeans by the look of them.

Stefan asked for Rashid when he entered the hallway leading to the salon where the large guests were assembled, almost of all of them seated in groups around sofas and chairs, and dining wine and liquor. Rashid came out from the salon and greeted Stefan warmly. He seemed a little tipsy.

"It seems your friend is having a big party," Stefan said.

"It is a send-off party to an American diplomat who is leaving after the end of his three year's term as the Councillor at the US Embassy. He has been a close friend of the Sudanese Ambassador. So, what is the story that brought you poste haste before Isabelle's arrival at the villa?"

"We need to find a quiet corner," Stefan said.

"Yes, but meanwhile you must join the party and have a drink. After a while most of the guests will be departing. There are a couple of people I want you to meet." Rashid said.

"Alright, but I also need to talk to you. It will take only a few minutes. We can go to a small ante-chamber, over there," he said, pointing to a small room not far from the big salon.

"Okay, let's sit there."

They sat on the chairs and Stefan looked Rashid in the eye for a while, and seemed lost for words, which is unlike him. Then he put his hands on Rashid's shoulders and began:

"Rashid, you and I have been friends for many years…" He seemed to hesitate but continued: "And I have enjoyed and cherished your friendship, as you know."

"And I have cherished your, my brother," Rashid responded with emotion…

"All good things come to an end…I don't mean to tell you this is the end of our friendship. Quite the contrary…On the other hand, the special commitment you and I agree to undertake in aid of a dear friend… and sister… is on the rocks. It has been foundering for some time, as you have witnessed."

"I know, and I have been ever anxious to help mend relations…But lately it became rather difficult."

"I know, and believe me, your sensitive and beautiful soul has been a great help. I cannot tell you how much I appreciate and value your untiring attempts to help mend our strained relationships…"

"I feel sorry to say that I did notice the strain which has become more intense lately…"

"On most occasions it seemed to work," Stefan went on, interrupting Rashid…" But lately, if I may put it this way, the magic seems to have gone…I don't mean the magic touch of your mediation efforts, but the original magic that existed and sustained my relationship with Isabelle."

"Don't give up, Stefan. The magic that kept you together can work again." "I don' think so; not this time…I decided to come here because I have the feeling that your Sudanese Ambassador may have the key to understanding the puzzle that has intrigued us… I think we should now join the party."

They walked to the salon where many of the guests were leaving. The Sudanese Ambassador rose and welcomed Stefan and asked him what he would like to have."

Stefan said: "Scotch, please. With mineral water."

The Ambassador called and told the order to the waiter, who brought the drinks and have them to Stefan.

"*Merhaba, ya Doktoor*!," the Ambassador said welcoming Stefan, whom he had met at the Night Club earlier in the week, and he introduced him to the guests, with flowery language of compliments about his academic credentials and "commendable work at the EU."

Of the guests who remained in the salon, about ten of them, there were three Ethiopian officials including Teshome who eyed Stefan with great interest particularly when they heard he worked at the EU.

"Real pleasure to meet you, Dr. Stefan. We were not introduced during our meeting at the Night Club," said Teshome and introduced his two Ethiopian colleagues as follows:

Dr. Stefan, I would like you to meet my two colleagues and comrades in struggle. They are: Brigadier General Aregawi Desta and Colonel Kidane Mekonnen. General Aregawi is a member of the Chief of Staff in the Revolutionary Army, and Colonel Kidane in my deputy in the Intelligence Department.

"Pleased to meet you gentlemen," Stefan said.

"We are honored to meet you, Doctor," replied Colonel Kidane, who sounded like a fast-talking and probably fast-thinking intelligence operative.

"If you have some time tomorrow, I would like to invite you to lunch in my house to meet Colonel Kidane and others, if possible," Teshome said, leaving out the Brigadier General's name, which Stefan found intriguing. But he said he would be happy, but tomorrow may not be possible. Then he asked Teshome: "Can I call you or email you tomorrow?"

"Certainly. There is no urgency, and I hope to hear from you tomorrow.

Here is my card," Teshome said and handed Stefan a card.

Rashid was listening with great interest. Both he and Stefan knew that Teshome had his eyes on Isabelle. Indeed, Stefan provoked Isabelle by telling her to consult with Teshome when she was talking about the need to visit the Prison Department. And they both knew that she had travelled to Bahrdar in Teshome's private plane, a fact that intrigued them immensely and raised red flags about Teshome's real interest, including possible shady business interests.

They waited until the guests left. Rashid had apprised his Ambassador friend that both he and Stefan were interested to know about Teshome, and he had said they need to wait until everybody else had left and that he would tell them about him and the other Ethiopian officials present among the guests earlier. So Rashid, who had drunk a lot of coffee to sober up from his earlier state of being a little tipsy, began the conversation in earnest by asking his friend, the Ambassador what he knew about Teshome.

The Ambassador also ordered some coffee and they settled for a long evening session of talk. The Ambassador had a gift of telling stories in an interesting way, and he is also obviously a born story teller and a man interested in many matters. He was suited to his position as Ambassador whose job is to collect intelligence about the country where he is appointed to serve the interests of his country. This means, among other things, that he collects intelligence about key personnel of the Ethiopian government like Teshome and the other two officials who were among the group of dinner guests of the embassy.

Before he began telling them about Teshome, he made an interesting point of historical significance. He told them that a large number among the top echelon of the ruling party, including civilian leaders, the military and security are involved in business monopoly, awarded to them by the government. They are awarded contracts and licenses for profitable business.

These leaders, many of them former guerilla fighters and their associates have become so corrupted that the public has coined a powerful name to describe them collectively. They are called *Yeqen Jiboch* (the morning hyenas). Among the literati in Ethiopia and elsewhere, they are referred to as "the fallen angels." This appellation is based on the fact that they had been considered as angels because of their heroic roles in liberating the public from oppressive governments. They have obviously been found wanting and thus lost the original positive appellation and awarded a pejorative one

—*Yeqen Jiboch.*

The Ambassador told them that Teshome was part of a cabal of former freedom fighters who have obtained monopoly businesses from the supply of cement for buildings of various type and in various places and supply of medicines and fertilizers without any form of competitive bidding as required by the World Bank and other international financial organizations.

With regard to Teshome and his interest in Isabelle, the Ambassador said that he had observed at the Nigh Club that he was interested in her. He has gone a step further in that respect by boldly inviting her to attend some special events in Bahrdar. He flew his private plane to take her to that event and it was the Ambassador's understanding that Teshome had scored a sort of victory in that romantic endeavor, not to call it battle. At that point the Ambassador thought first of all, he did not have details of Teshome's exploits, and secondly because it would be "undiplomatic" to go any further. He stopped to ask his guests if they had any questions.

With great hesitation, but deeply interested on having useful information on a matter of interest to him, Stefan asked the Ambassador first if Teshome was a married man. The answer was negative. He had been married for a few years but divorced his wife over accusations of his philandering. Stefan said that he regarded Isabelle s his betrothed and had plans to marry her at the end of their current project. He stopped there and waited to hear if the Ambassador might have information on Isabelle's potential interest in any romantic involvement with Teshome.

"I am afraid I cannot help you there, Dr. Schmidt, though I do appreciate your interest and obvious concern by the behavior of Teshome and their developing interest in each other, judging by his inviting her and taking her in his private plane…"

He paused a little, rubbed his forehead and continued, "Speaking of his use of aeroplanes, I know that the man has had an interest in that subject over a long time. So he developed a special relationship with the Air Force people and learned how to fly a plane…"

…Rashid was extremely anxious about Stefan's state of mind and disturbed that he inquired from the Ambassador whether Isabelle might be interested in Teshome. He was sympathetic and concerned about his friend, but disappointed at his abject behavior. He did not expect such a behavior form Stefan whom he liked and whose intellect he respected. Again, Stefan wanted to know if the Ambassador knew whether he has investments abroad. The answer was yes a lot of investment in China, Europe and the USA.

To add more to Stefan's inquiry Rashid informed the Ambassador that Isabelle may be interested in relocating her two newly- found nephews to Europe near her so that she can help their education. Her problem is she cannot do it financially. He asked the Ambassador:

"Do you think he might use that interest of hers in inducing her to become his lover?"

The Ambassador said he wouldn't be surprised if that happened. Stefan also added the fact of Isabelle's fascination with the African institution of extended family. This explains why she is interested in having her nephews close by her. Stefan even gave a psychological explanation for her fascination with the African extended family.

It is grounded, he said, in her sense of deprivation, with an absent father who disappeared from her life and was later killed.

The ambassador said that Teshome is a ruthless man who would use any means and dream up any scheme to attain his interests. His history of single- minded pursuit of power and the use of that power to acquire immense wealth by methods fair and foul is ample proof if one needs to provide proof.

The Ambassador was showing signs of fatigue and Rashid advised that perhaps it was time to end the encounter and meet again another time. The Ambassador thanked Rashid and saw his guests to the door...

At the Church of San Salvatore

The Church of San Salvatore, a relic of Italian missionary presence in Ethiopia, is located in what is popularly known by Addis Ababa residents as Leghar (*La gare*), the area of the first Railway station in Ethiopia. The railway was built by a French railway company—*chemin de fer franco-Ethiopien*—in a joint venture with the government of Emperor Menelik, early in the twentieth century. The advent of French commercial (and diplomatic) influence in Ethiopia, which preceded the Italian invasion by a few decades, was spearheaded by that railway, which introduced, or rather helped expand exponentially the export of Ethiopian products such as coffee and hides to the outside world.

The Church of San Salvatore is frequented by a large number of Catholic devotees every Sunday attending Mass. The devotees include French and Italian as well as Ethiopian Catholics. As it happened, Isabelle decided to make a confession and attend Mass a few days after her trip to Bahrdar, spending a weekend with Teshome, which had created a row between her and Stefan. She was waiting to make her confession session with a priest. She had made a confession on a previous occasion and was now waiting for another, when she heard someone call her name. She was pleasantly surprised to find it was Corrine, her classmate in language studies in Geneva.

"Corrine, what are you doing here?" Isabelle asked.

I was going to ask you the same question. *Ou lala!* What a wonderful surprise. Well, since you asked first, I will tell you first. I have been hired for a three- month segment interpreting at the meetings of the African Union.

"That is wonderful. Do you like it?"

"It is a change, and Addis is a beautiful city and is a center of many international organizations. So it is interesting. What about you?"

"I have come here for a special project." "How long are going to stay?"

"It depends on a couple of factors. Maybe a couple of months or a little longer."

"Well, I am staying at the Sheraton Hotel. Let us get together and talk about our good old student days. How about coffee now?"

"Now I am waiting my turn to see a priest for confession. But I will call you at the Sheraton maybe this coming weekend."

"Okay, I will wait for your call. *Au revoir et a la pochaine.*" "*A la prochaine.*"

Isabelle then walked to the confessional, where she waited for a few minutes and entered the priest's office. The priest arrived and sat inside and gave a welcoming sound indicating he was ready to hear the confession. The window of his confessor's small chamber was covered with a brown colored perforated cloth, such that the confessing person cannot see the priest but the priest can see the confessing person.

"Bless me father, for I have sinned," Isabelle began.

"Go ahead, I am listening," the priest said with a soft baritone voice. "Father, it is a rather long story and I may take your time for quite a while." "You came on time for confession, and it is my priestly obligation to listen to your confession, however long it may be."

"Thank you, father. I thought it was just and proper to tell you that, in case others may be waiting."

"If by chance your confession takes longer than the available time, we can agree to do it another time. And if that happens, we would continue from where we left of. Don't worry. Now, you may begin."

"I will, father. My name is Isabelle Negassa. My late father, Dr. Negassa who was Ethiopian, was married to my mother, Claudette, a French citizen. He was a leader of MEISON and was killed at the order of Mengistu Hailemariam and was buried by unknown persons in an unmarked grave presumably in the Akaki prison compound. I have come to Ethiopia to find out where he was buried and to retrieve his remains for a Christian burial so that my family can have closure to his tragic death..." She stopped to regain her faltering composure and control her quivering voice...

"Take your time. I understand your stress and will let you regain your composure."

His calm manner and soothing voice were reassuring and so she thanked him and resumed her narrative.

"That is the background of my visit to Ethiopia. I wish it were a pleasant touristic visit to admire this beautiful land, and to enjoy the wonderful hospitality of my father's gentle people. Alas! My visit is for a special project of discovery of my father's unmarked grave and reclaim his remains." ... Again, she stopped to recall her previous confession.

"Father, please bear with me. I have made a brief confession a short while ago, and judging by your voice, I don't think you were the confessor."

"You are right. I don't remember hearing your confession. In any case, I have been away and just returned after six months' absence. Please continue..."

"...I am here to confess and am seeking spiritual assistance for what had happened to me and my project. While the objective of my project may be noble, my human weaknesses have intervened to complicate matters..."

"In what way? What has happened to you, and what is it that you need spiritual assistance for? Do I detect distress and confusion?"

"Yes, father. I am going through a distressful condition, torn between two opposed demands."

"What are these two oppose demands?"

"I have been involved in a very good relationship with a man who has been good to me, and is personally involved in my current project. He is an important official of the European Union (EU) and was responsible for helping me to obtain an interpreter's job at the EU. He hopes to marry me at the end of this project. His name is Stefan and together with another good man, Rashid, they have been the rock on which I have learned to conceive and carry out the project."

"So what is the problem?"

"The problem arises out of my human weakness and attraction to an Ethiopian official who has been attracted to me, and to whom I am attracted, God forgive me..."

"Let me guess. And this has complicated the project's mission. Is that right? "That is right. There is more complication...I have two lovely nephews whom I want desperately to take to live nearby where I live and work. But I don't have the financial ability to do that..."

"Go on."

"My newly found Ethiopian friend is able and, I believe, willing to help me realise my idea of getting the boys to be near me and continue their education."

"Has this new friend said so?"

"No. Not yet, but he is willing to bend over backward to accommodate my demands."

"How do you know?"

"Woman intuition…Also hints that he has given telling me he has a lot of property in Europe and America, and even China."

"Did you raise the question of your wish to get your nephews to live and study near you?"

"Yes I did, and that was when he bragged about his property abroad—bragging I call it, but he said it in a subtle Ethiopian manner. That is why I spoke about woman intuition, if you see what I mean…

"Oh, I do…And I am awed by such intuition…" the priest said with a little hint of a chuckle. Isabelle hesitated and waited for his direction or command asking her to continue. When he did not, she began to feel worried…

"Can I continue, father?" she asked fearfully. "Yes, indeed. I was waiting for you to continue."

"Thank you for your understanding…His name is Teshome, this high- ranking government official, "she continued.

"Where does he work?"

"He is the head of a Division of the Security Establishment." "A military man?"

"A former guerilla fighter, turned high ranking security official…"

…Isabelle's voice betrayed some derivative pride, derived from her association with the man. Her intention was to impress upon her priest confessor that her attraction to Teshome was not a silly woman's fanciful and passing affair, but a serious undertaking. In addition to the matter of her nephews, she also told the priest that Teshome had promised to cut through all bureaucratic red tape and help her to discover her father's unmarked grave."

"Let me ask you. Are you sure this official is able to succeed in finding your father's grave, where others have tried and failed?"

"If he tries and fails, I will be satisfied to call off the search. After all, your fellow priest had actually almost persuaded me to give up the search by reminding me that in the eyes of the Mother Church's teaching, it is the soul that matters, not the corpse. But I had persisted in the search nonetheless in the hope that I may find my fathers' remains, which would help me and the rest of my family to find closure. But if we continue to draw a blank in the search, it would be time to call it off."

"Let us say, the man fails, but he is still interested in you, will this mean you will abandon the hope of marrying Stefan?"

"If Teshome proves his love to me by helping me achieve my aim of bringing my nephews to live and pursue their university studies near where I live, my answer to your question, father, is yes..."

"What you call love is a tricky matter, one on which you may not be able to place trust forever. Have you thought about that?"

"It has occurred to me, yes. But as I see it, and considering Teshome's willingness to do what I need and what my nephews' need, how can I doubt his love? I have to go with what he does now, and not worry about future change of heart."

"How about Stefan's love?"

"I will still regard him with warmth as my dear brother."

"Is Stefan's love weaker than that of Teshome? What does Teshome have what Stefan does not, in your mind?"

"Father, I feel that you may think of me as churlish for choosing Teshome over Stefan, but..."

"No," the priest interrupted, "the word is not churlish...It is opportunistic..."

The priest's remark hit Isabelle like a thunderbolt. She did not expect it, certainly not from a gentle-sounding man who speaks with a soft voice... She took time to respond, and did not quite know how to respond...

The pries must have understood her quandary. He cleared his throat and asked: "Are you alright Isabelle?"...

She said: "Yes, father, I am alright. It is just that I had not expected your remark."

"Why not? Because you don't think you are being opportunistic when you chose one man over the other?"

"Don't I have the right to choose a person who is ready and willing, *and able,* to help me?"

"You have the right to make a choice of one as against the other. But there is, to me as your spiritual counsellor, a moral issue concerning your history of relationship with Stefan. In this instance, morality essentially involves fairness. Don't you think you are being unfair to Stefan who has come all the way to Africa in pursuit of your objective, and was hoping to marry you at the end of the project?"

She paused a little and then said:

"If, forgetting everything else, I am to weigh the two loves on a weighing machine, so to speak, my love to Teshome weighs heavier…"

The priest sighed deeply and addressed her:

"Isabelle, we have come to the conclusion of your confession. And at this point, I want to tell you what we know as love is of two kinds: one is carnal love, or romantic love. The other is, to me as a priest, a higher and weightier love. I am going to ask you to read two passages from the New Testament, to help you make your decision. This is my last remark to you and the end of the confession. He gave her his final blessing and concluded as follows:

First, I want you to read the whole of *Chapter Five of the Gospel According to Saint Mathew.* **Second**, you need to read *the First Letter of Saint Paul to the Corinthians, chapter thirteen—all of it.*

The priest was heard stepping out of his office. The sound of his departing steps was heard echoing on the corridor. Isabelle left the confessional chamber and stepped out into the bright light of a sunny day.

Chapter Sixteen

ISABELLE'S DECISION AND HER FUTURE

As she left the area of the Church, Isabelle felt torn between two hard choices. Before she made her final decision, she decided to spend quality time with her nephews in Adama. So she went to the villa and asked for Kassa, but he was out on assignment. She didn't want to deprive her friends of Kassa's service and of the car. So, she rented a car for one week and drove to Adama by herself. Her sudden departure to Adama driving a rented car intrigued her friends, who still hoped her decision would be one they favored. They waited for her return hoping for a decision favorable to the project, which means against Teshome.

As she drove on the Bishoftu-Adama Highway, Isabelle went in her mind, through much of her confessional dialogue with the priest. She recalled his soft baritone voice and his gentle manner. She was also struck by his remarks concerning the morality of "abandoning" Stefan. She remembered the stern tone in which he admonished her when she asked him if she didn't have the right to choose a man who is willing and able to help her in her wish of bringing her nephews to live and study close to where she lived. She remembered his words about what he called the moral issue of her long history of relationship with Stefan and his hope of marrying her after the end of the project.

She replayed in the film of her mind his admonition citing scripture and her own attraction to a man who had her in thrall, but also a man who, according to her, would be of great help to her.

"Why shouldn't I go with a man to whom I am drawn?" she heard herself saying in a loud voice. "I am a free woman in the Modern Age, the Age of Women's Freedom?"

…A few seconds later, in an urgent wish to fortify her position leaning toward Teshome, she boldly voiced her views of the scriptures:

"I don't think the scriptures are against a woman's right to choose what she thinks is beneficial to her, for God's sake!" She yelled pounded the steering wheel, as though the steering wheel is in cahoots with the anti-women forces…

She arrived in Adama with her mind engaged in a silent debate, not yet resolved, though she is leaning one way.

She checked in the hotel and after a shower and lunch in the hotel restaurant, she placed a call to the college asking to speak to the Dean of Students. After a few seconds waiting, the Dean came on the phone and she greeted him and requested to take her nephews out for a short break of two or three days. He told her that would be great for the boys and that they are lucky to have an aunt like her.

The following day, she took the boys out to the countryside around Adama. They visited the Wonji Sugar Plantation for the second time and met with the manager whom Isabelle invited to lunch in Adama or Assela, a neighboring town. He thanked her but declined because of heavy workload and meetings he had to lead. Isabelle had a good reason to visit the manager; she wanted to reinforce the connection she had created for her nephews whom he had promised to employ during the summer break.

By day's end, they were tired and ready for an evening meal to be followed by a good night's sleep. During dinner at the hotel, Isabelle talked to the boys about her plan to get them scholarships in Europe near where she lives. The boys were so excited that they pressed her to tell them when she was going to do it. She almost regretted blurting out with the plan, fearful that they would be sorely disappointed in case she was not able to implement the plan. After all, she reminded herself that everything depended on Teshome's fulfilling his promise. So, she qualified her earlier statement by saying: "Now, don't raise your hope too high. It is still a plan, and we must not get excited before the plan becomes reality.

The faces of the boys dramatically changed from excited smiles to faces covered with clouds of disappointment. Again, she was forced to tell them not to worry. "I was just being cautious and wanted to avoid disappointment, just in case. I am sure things will work out. Just continue doing well in hour studies, behave well, as I am sure you will," she said…

"And I love you very, very much, my sweet nephews," she told them before she got up and entered the car with them to take them to their college quarters. They arrived some twenty minutes later, and they got out of the car. And she hugged the boys one by one and kissed each on the forehead. She got into the car and waited, watching them walk away slowly until they disappeared around a corner of the dormitory building.

She decided to do more touring by herself. She drove to Assela and checked in a hotel named after Ethiopia's athlete and Olympic champion, Haile Gebreselassie. When she asked the hotel manager, why the hotel was named after the athlete, he informed her Haile owns the hotel among other local enterprises. Apparently, the place is his home province. She became deeply interested by that piece of information, so she did more touring of the place, and decided to spend three more nights in Assela.

At the end of the third day, she drove back to Adama where she spent one night before she returned to Addis Ababa. She arrived in the villa where she found both Stefan and Rashid, as well as Kassa. She asked Kassa to take the rented car to the company from which she rented it. Kassa wondered whether she could drive the rented car herself and he would follow her with their own car and they would come back together in their own car. She agreed, but asked Rashid if he could accompany her in the rented car and come back together. He agreed and the two of them drove with Kassa following them.

No sooner had they started than Rashid rushed to hurl an angry set of questions at her" "What the hell are you doing, Isabelle? Where have you been? Why have you shut us out and gone on your own as if we didn't exist? Is this the way a friend should treat a friend? Is this our reward for being your true and loyal friends engaged with you in your noble project? Or have you forgotten all that?"

Isabelle could not answer him. She was surprised at the vehemence with which he posed the series of hard questions. This is a different Rashid than the one she is used to, she thought. And wondered how Stefan could behave if gentle Rashid behaves like this. The two of them must have talked a lot during her absence. She expected that naturally.

On their way back, Kassa was present driving the car, so they did not want to continue the conversation. They were quiet throughout the whole journey back, with Kassa only asking Isabelle about her Adama trip. When she told him, she had also visited Assela and stayed at the Haile Gebreselassie hotel, Kassa expressed surprise and told her he wished he had traveled with her.

"Perhaps we will all visit Assela together," She said "I hope so," Kassa said.

They entered the villa compound and Isabelle said, she will go straight to bed and wished the two good night and went up to her room.

Isabelle rose early the next day and went to the kitchen ahead of everybody. Beletech joined her for coffee and they were chatting about sundry matters when they were joined by Stefan. He shook their hands and told Beletech if she could be good enough to order from him a breakfast of the usual. The cook knows what that means. Beletech said, she would do that and left them. Isabelle gazed at Stefan's face with its withering look. She suspected this was the moment of truth. Nevertheless, she decided to be calm and await the moment when everything she expected to explode, judging by the look on his face. Stefan kept quiet, probably expecting her to start the conversation…

"…did you miss me?" she asked teasingly.

"Miss you?… Do you want a diplomatic answer, or the truth?" "I want the truth. I always do…"

"I do too, as you know…And to tell you the truth I did not miss you at all…"

"That is incredible…Not even for one moment?"

"If you want to continue skirting the issue by these silly and irrelevant questions, you can do so. But I don't find it amusing. It is not funny."

"So, what would you like to talk about?"

"Well, to begin with, where have you been and why did you keep us in the dark?"

"I did leave word saying I will take a break of a few days."

"Yes, but you don't think seriously that was sufficient, given the fact that things were hanging in the air...?"

"What things?"

"You ask me what things? Are you serious?"

"I am serious. I ask you what things were left hanging in the air?"

"We were facing the cross-roads and in the middle of that crucial moment, you had left us wondering what you were doing, suddenly going AWOL, flying to Bahrdar with your new boyfriend."

At that point, Rashid joins them and says: "Sorry am I interrupting something important?"

"No, this just an exercise in futility, a merry-go-round of fools," Stefan says with a quick laugh.

"Merry-go-round of fools? Did I hear you say?"

"Yes, Rashid. We are the holy fools who had rushed in where angels fear to tread," Stefan replied in an acerbic tone.

"Come, come, Stefan. I accept the appellation of a holy fool and don't mind being chided for rushing to tread where angels fear to tread."

"I know my dear friend; that is why we love you. But being rewarded with neglectful absence by a fellow holy fool was not in the bargain," Stefan told Rashid, as if to remind him that Isabelle had failed her obligations to them as a fellow "holy fool."

"Far be it from me to even attempt to remind you of the teachings of the Sermon on the mount, but didn't Jesus say: Blessed are those who hunger and thirst to see right prevail?"

Isabelle laughed a little and said: "He got you, there, didn't he? By the way, Rashid, who taught you about Jesus?"

"I had Jesuit teachers at school who tried everything to convert me."

Rashid also responded to Isabelle's remark, rightly fearing a worsening of a bad situation.

"I didn't mean it to be a battle of wits between the two of us," he corrected Isabelle...

He continued, "But I do believe that we were engaged in a valuable spiritual journey when we decided to help Isabelle retrieve her father's remains…"

He paused a little and continued: "We seem to have lost our way in the middle of our journey. There is no question about that, is there, Isabelle?"

Isabelle shifted in her seat and first scanned Stefan's face and then looked at Rashid with evident desire to give him a response to his serious question. She remembered the previous night's short talk with Rashid, which was mostly a tirade from him in a stern voice. This time's voice was softer, but the question was a serious one and must be answered.

"No, Rashid, there is no question…but it is I who lost my way…not you or Stefan."

"So, where do we go from here?"

"I have been reflecting on this very question all week during my tour of Adama and Arsi…I have also sought spiritual guidance from a Catholic priest at the San Salvatore Church…"

Stefan stirred from his somnolent state on hearing the last statement about spiritual guidance from a priest. He turned his gaze toward her. Rashid also looked at her with furrowed brows, expecting some decisive declaration of intent.

"I am waiting to see Teshome and speak to him before I tell you my decision," she informed the two men extending their agony. She didn't say when she was seeing Teshome or what decision she will tell him; she just left them on tenterhooks.

Stefan was heard saying *Scheize!* under his breath.

Rashid said: "I sincerely hope this does not mean waiting for Teshome for weeks on end."

"No, not weeks; days. He is traveling abroad and is coming back in three, or four days' time."

"Traveling abroad, huh. Was that why you up and went away without telling us?"

"I did leave word, Stefan. Don't exaggerate. I am not exactly enjoying this horrible agony."

"And have you thought about how this agony came about? Do you know who is to blame?"

"Stefan, I know my faults and am only human with all the human frailties, but you need to understand…"

"Understand what?"

"Understand that I am suffering, too. I am suffering from a pang of guilt on how I treated you and Rashid…Just because I didn't say so, doesn't mean I am not suffering of guilt, while at the same time trying to find the right solution?" …

…Rashid then asked if he and Stefan are going to talk to Teshome? "You have every right to speak to Teshome or anybody else."

"I want you to know, I have no need of talking to Teshome," Stefan told her. "What you do with him, or how you decide is your business. I am done worrying about that. I just want to end this charade quickly and properly. When I say end, it means including what we foolishly termed a project."

"It was not a foolish project. I may be foolish in dreaming it up, but it is not foolish," Isabelle responded to Stefan's unexpected statement. She was stunned by Stefan's remark. Her response betrayed a mind troubled by the prospect of terminating the search for her father's remains, a search that both Stefan and Rashid enthusiastically supported and spent valuable time and energy, taking leave from their own work.

Isabelle got up and walked away apparently in tears.

Beletech, who was sitting outside on a sofa, saw Isabelle walking in a rush, so she followed her, suspecting something was wrong.

"Isabelle," she yelled after her, "Is anything the matter?" No response. She heard Isabelle's bedroom door slammed closed.

Isabelle stayed in her bedroom all morning and Beletech knocked at her door around noon. She asked: "Is there anything I can do for you, Isabelle?"

After a few minutes, Isabelle came out of her room. Smiling diffidently and greeted Beletech, who told her that Stefan and Rashid said they will be out in town all day and will be back for dinner after six pm.

It became clear to Isabelle that the glue that had held the three friends—the noble idea of the project—was getting slowly unstuck. It became crystal clear to her that her two friends had given up on the idea and were thinking about going back to their respective work in Europe.

"I can't blame them, the dear men," Isabelle reasoned, "it was all my fault. And I expected them unfairly to stick by me even though the success of the project as originally conceived was doubtful. Despite the faltering and the doubts, they stuck by me, and I took them for granted."

Isabelle nursed her self-inflicted internal wound, but she no longer blamed either Stefan or Rashid, even though her behavior appeared to the contrary. But she was involved in quiet self-criticism, which was complicated by her attraction to Teshome. Indeed, if she were a religious devotee of self-flagellating cult, she would not have hesitated to flog herself with a lash, if it could ease the growing remorse that had been eating at her entrails, even though she managed to hide it.

Now that "the cat is out of the bag," and there is no more need to play hide and seek, she can and must tell them the truth and be done with it once and for all. She knows that telling the truth will hurt and it would mean the end of the project, there is no getting out of it. But Isabelle thought that she owed it to her friends to have it out in Teshome's presence, which was why she was waiting for his return from his foreign trip.

She waited until Teshome returned and when he did, she asked him to come to the villa for an important meeting with her and her two friends. She proposed three possible dates out of which he could choose one. It must be in the evening outside the working hours. The day of his arrival, Teshome called her and without beating about the bush, she told him about the important meeting, asking him to choose a day. He said what about tomorrow (that is to say, the day after his arrival). He was obviously in a hurry to see her. She asked him if she could consult her friends to ask them if they are free for that day. He told her to go ahead and get back to him after she consults her friends.

She got back to him a few hours later and told him that her friends agreed. "So, I will see you tomorrow," she said with a silly laugh and trembling slightly. She had obviously fallen head-over-ears in love with the man.

A Meeting with Teshome

The day of the meeting arrived. The meeting had been set to take place at seven pm at the Villa Ibrahim. Beletech was told about it and asked if she could arrange for a wonderful dinner. Beletech had a hunch that this was a really special occasion involving some kind of romance, so she gave it her best attention. The house cook was informed about it and Kassa

Was sent out to buy drinks (beer, wine, liquor, soft drinks, etc.). Isabelle inspected the kitchen and was satisfied that everything was going to be good. She also looked at the small cellar where wine and beer were kept.

At about five minutes to seven, Teshome arrived in a Mercedes, driven by a chauffeur.

The chauffeur got out, walked round the car, opened the door and held it for his boss to come out. Teshome got out of the car and walked toward the door slowly and deliberately. He was immaculately dressed in dark blue suit, a white shirt and red tie. He looked august as he smiled at the sight of Isabelle, who was herself well dressed in a green-colored, flowing African costume she had bought a few days before.

Teshome did not hesitate to take her in his arms and kiss her smack on the lips, a lingering kiss that denoted warmth and sent a message to all concerned, that this beautiful woman belongs to him, and to no one else!

Did she resist him in any way? Absolutely not. They walked arm-in-arm toward the salon where Stefan and Rashid waited. Both men stood up and greeted Teshome in a perfunctory formalism that did not hide its message. The message was: "You and your Mercedes can go to Hell!" They were there merely paying a courtesy presence in honor of the wish of their dear friend.

Isabelle was the one most ill at ease by the whole matter, and suddenly realised by the behavior of her friends, that she was humiliating them, especially Stefan. The truth is that she had been utterly absorbed in her new- found infatuation with this high-ranking, charming and wealthy Ethiopian official. There can be no doubt now that Isabelle Negassa has been swept off her feet by Teshome. Additionally, Teshome has promised her the world, including helping in funding the relocation of her two nephews.

To people who are still concerned about Isabelle's welfare, like her two friends, it should be a matter of great interest to find out from Teshome himself if what she hopes he will help her in funding her nephews' relocation and education is well-founded. For despite their disappointment her two friends are men who cared about her. This may be surprising, but even

Stefan, who is the one the most to lose in Isabelle's choosing Teshome over him, still cared for her.

Beletech brought a tray carrying a variety of drinks, and went around in the salon offering her guests, starting with Teshome. He took a glass of sherry, looked at Isabelle and raised the glass to her health and sipped from it. Both Stefan and Rashid took a glass of whiskey and added some mineral water. Neither raised his glass to drink to Isabelle's health.

Isabelle asked Teshome: "What kind of music do you like to be played?" "Any soft music will do, Ethiopian if possible," he answered with a smile.

And Isabelle beckoned to Beletech to come to her and whispered in her ears and Beletech bowed and went away. Within minutes the soft music of Aster Aweke came beaming softly.

After about an hour of staying in the salon drinking and chatting against the background of Aster Aweke's song, the party of four were invited to go to the dining room, and they all followed Beletech to the dining-room.

Isabelle and Teshome were seated side by side, with Rashid facing Isabelle and Stefan facing Teshome. For starters, before the main dish of a choice of Ethiopian Doro Wat and fried *Kitfo*, they were offered a choice of vegetable soup or spaghetti Bolognese. Teshome went for the spaghetti and Isabelle joined him. For second, Teshome chose fried *Kitfo,* and Isabelle chose *Doro Wat.* Stefan chose vegetable soup and *Doro Wat,* and Rashid chose spaghetti and *Doro Wat.*

They ate quietly, helping themselves to their choice of the variety of drinks. The most favored were Chianti wine and Ethiopian beer. The eating and drinking went on for over an hour, when Isabelle hit an empty glass of wine with a spoon, asking for attention.

"I am sure you are enjoying the food and the drinks. We could go all night enjoying this dinner. But I must intrude on this festive mood and remind us that we are here gathered for a special reason. As you all know, Teshome and I have been meeting and talking. The truth is that we have fallen in love with each other and this fact may impinge on the prospect of the project for which I and my two friends came. Teshome and I have talked about that prospect as well as other matters of great interest to me and members of my family.

At this point I would like to ask Teshome to speak and both Stefan and Rashid can pose questions to him.

"Teshome, would like to speak and are you willing to answer questions that may be posed to you by either Stefan or Rashid or both?

Teshome rose to speak, but Stefan said, "You don't have to stand, Teshome. Let's be informal." Teshome thanked Stefan and Isabelle and began his speech slowly, most of the time looking at Isabelle, but at times also at Stefan.

He began slowly with his soft seductive baritone voice. He smiled and said:

It all began with a dance one evening at the Lalibela Night Club. Although I had seen Isabelle in one of the group's meeting with the officials of our government regarding their project, I had not imagined that we would meet again. But, to my great surprise and happiness, we did meet. And we danced. Something pushed us into each other's arms immediately and we danced cheek-to-cheek. I think I looked into her eyes, and also delved into her soul. We clicked and were bonded both through physical attraction and emotional compatibility.

In the days following our dancing at the Lalibela, I could not put her out of my mind.

I called her a few times and I found out that she responded to my initiatives to meet again. Finally, I invited her to accompany me to go to a special meeting at Bahr Dar, which I think became the decisive moment when we wanted each other.

Bu then there was her project, about which I listened, with great interest, to her story and the reason for her coming to our country. It is a compelling story and I told her I would do everything I can to help her in achieving the aim of her project. I understand that Stefan and Rashid may ask me now.

Stefan raised his hand and asked: "Is it true that you promised to help her funding the relocation to Europe of her two nephews and help finance their education, near where Isabelle lives?

Teshome replied unhesitatingly: "the answer is yes."

Stefan asked: "Pardon me for sounding skeptical, but how do we know you will not change your mind tomorrow? Or next year, or the year after? I guess what I am asking is for some kind of assurance."

Teshome said: "Do you want an assurance in the form of written guarantee, legally sound-proof guarantee?"

"Yes. Exactly"… General laughter in the room.

"Satisfied?" asked Teshome in a triumphant tone. "Not quite."

"What now?"

"Well, there is the little matter of proof."

"Do you mean proof that I have enough financial resources to back up my promise?"

"Well, yes. You are perceptive." Sad Stefan half in irony, which was not lost on Teshome.

"Never mind the compliment, as long as you are satisfied." He said, and Rashid exploded into a fit of laughter, joined by Isabelle and Stefan. Perhaps it was the wine.

Actually, Stefan laughed for the first time in so many frightful days. Let us hope that all these augurs well for all concerned.

Part

5

TRIUMPH OF THE HOLY FOOLS

Chapter Seventeen

ENDING THE PROJECT AND REORIENTING ISABELLE

Now that an important objective of Isabelle's personal (family) interest has been satisfied, at the dinner meeting with Teshome, there remains questions on outstanding matters related to the original objective of the project. It concerns the matter of finding the remains of Isabelle's father. It is conceivable that having satisfied an important psychological need, Isabelle's original drive and determination might have been slacked, if not completely weakened.

The day after the dinner meeting in which Stefan forced (or induced) Teshome to make important promises, Stefan seemed to have been vicariously satisfied and had regained his former decisive mood regarding what remains to be done about the real object of the project, namely finding and recovering the remains of Isabelle's father. It was pleasing to behold Stefan and Isabelle laughing together and giving each other warm hugs. During breakfast the morning after the dinner, the three talked among themselves almost like the good old days.

Among the questions that were left unaddressed is whether Teshome's earlier promise to expedite the search for the unmarked grave will now pass muster. In other words, the cautious Stefan wondered whether Teshome is a man of his word and if his word carries much weight in the matter of searching for the unmarked grave? After all, Isabelle's belief in his capacity to deliver on his promise exercised considerable influence in her decision making, over and above the "love affair." Their discussion continued refocussing on the following:

What happens to the project if Teshome's promise proves untenable?

Taking the first question first, we need to recapitulate the events and find out what progress had been made ever since Teshome gave his promise. From the various meetings the project group held with officials of the government, so far there has been no progress in finding the unmarked grave.

Phone calls made inquiring into the progress in the search for the grave did not yield any positive result. Most of the unmarked graves had been dug and the remains (fragments of bones) have been registered with appropriate identification protocols, presumably awaiting DNA testing. Nobody knows whether DNA testing can and will be done. If not, the digging of graves would be meaningless. Certainly, the project and Isabelle herself personally cannot wait forever without any assurance of a meaningful outcome of all the efforts that might be made by the concerned government officials.

Considerably chastened as they had been by what came out of the dinner, toward the end of their breakfast discussion, the three friends felt comparatively sanguine. They accepted the reality of the way things were going, even though the ultimate object of gaining the remains of Isabelle's father had not been attained. Strangely enough Rashid was the one showing unhappiness that their objective was not attained. There was none of that jocular mood that defined his warm personality. Isabelle felt this and said in earnest: "Guys, I may have made a mess by falling in love. But please believe me that you guys are and will forever be part of my life." She said tearfully. "How can it not be? You know…You are dear to me. I cherish you…" And she let it all out in fits of sobbing.

Stefan gave her some tissue papers and walked round the table to hug her. The sobbing became louder. She tried to control it without success… She got up and left to her room, sobbing. Stefan followed her into her room. Thy stayed in her room about half an hour and came out together with Stefan's right arm round her shoulder. Her smile was one of embarrassment and Rashid cracked one of his old jokes, which pleased her immensely.

"Now you are back to your wonderful self, dear Rashid," she said.

"Don't push it, Rashid. You are tempting me to commit a crime by attempting to elope with Isabelle." Stefan joked.

Isabelle pulled Stefan's hand and put it in her two hands, looking at him the way a mother looks at an errant but beloved child."

The pathos of the situation was so affecting that the three friends got up and formed an embracing triangle.

"Just like the old days," Rashid said with a smile and all three shared a good laugh.

"Yes, except the old magic is absent," Stefan amended.

Rashid, always the pragmatist, reminded Stefan that there is new magic—a magic circle of an extended family—a magic in the form of a couple of wonderful nephews of Isabelle.

"We haven't met them yet, so we must and find out what can be done to make sure these new members of the extended family are introduced to the rest of the extended family. I mean Stefan and me," he said with a wink.

"What a wonderful idea," Isabelle exclaimed and rushed to kiss Rashid on the cheek.

"And who is a closer family to these kids, after Isabelle?" Stefan asked. "You, of course," Rashid answered.

"Right, as always, my friend. I just wanted to make sure."

A few hours following this exchange, Isabelle said that she would be glad to take her two friends to meet her precious nephews as soon as other outstanding issues were resolved. To begin with, they had to wonder whether it makes sense for them to wait for the lethargic pace of the investigation on discovering the unmarked grave. Isabelle was inclined toward giving up on the search for the unmarked grave, fortified in her belief by the authoritative opinion of the priest who said that the soul is what matters not the body. We are not engaged in an anthropological discourse on the appropriate disposal of the body in his birth place, the y seemed to be saying now. Our interest was to put closure to the need of Isabelle's family, which had suffered double privation of their father's life. When the three friends put their heads together and reflected on that felt need of Isabelle's family, they felt the need had been sufficiently, if not completely, satisfied. Isabelle, above all, felt that enough had been done.

In any case, it was abundantly clear that there was little chance of success, institutionally speaking, as was noted before. The digging of more graves did not make any sense to the fulfilment of Isabelle's original idea of recovering her father's remains. Teshome cannot be expected, from the nature of things, to help in this case, either. Rather, Isabelle should concentrate on causing him to work out schemes of getting her two nephews to gain entry into appropriate schools near where Isabelle lives.

Teshome's Promise

Out of Isabelle's friends, the one who was most skeptical about Teshome's promise is naturally Stefan. Naturally, because he was a rival for Isabelle's love and was beaten by Teshome in that invisible contest. Indeed, until the very end, he had hoped Isabelle would find Teshome unacceptable and thus leave him and get back to him (Stefan). Following his defeat, Stefan's honorable behavior toward Isabelle, demonstrates the degree of profound attachment he had with Isabelle, an attachment that goes beyond carnal love and borders on *Agape (*Charity*).*

As an extension of that profound attachment, Stefan was not interested in helping in Isabelle's reorientation from the search for her father's remains to the care of the living, to helping her adjust to the difficult new situation of adopting the difficult role of a mother to her nephews. In fact, in readjusting himself in his new relation with Isabelle, Stefan fancied himself acting in the role of an absent father to her nephews, a condition of which Isabelle is profoundly aware because she lived without the presence of a father. It will be remembered that one of the bones of contention in the tension that led to the fallout between Stefan and Isabelle was when she broached the idea of his role as a father figure in the future after marrying Isabelle. But all that changed and, just as Isabelle needed to adjust to a changed situation in which Stefan is no longer a lover and a future husband, Stefan was faced with a similar condition of the need to adjust from a lover to a loyal friend ready to act as a father substitute for her nephews.

Rashid and Stefan were drinking beer in the evening a few days after the tear-filled encounter of the three friends in a bar of a downtown hotel. Stefan asked Rashid what he thought of Teshome's promises. "I mean, what does your gut tell you?" he stressed.

"I don't trust him, but let's face it, she is head-over-ears in love with the guy. 'Ain't nothin' we can do about it."

"I know that, *ya majnun*! (you idiot) Remember, I am a victim of that situation."

"Ya, I know. I am sorry…Forgot…"

"I think we have had enough beer. Let's have coffee and walk a few miles. It will do us good."

"*Na'Am, ya ustaz* (okay prof)

They order coffee…They drink their coffee and leave the hotel and go out to the street, passing by The National Theater walking toward Leghar, the Railway Station, continuing their conversation with the fresh air restoring their sobriety.

"I think he will jilt her. Mark my words," Stefan suddenly says. "Do you think so?"

"I am convinced. You may think this is sour grapes, of which I have plenty mind you. But there are indications that the man is a philanderer, a corrupt official, used to getting away with murder. I don't mean literally. But you know what I mean."

"Yes, I do. I just hope for her sake that he may turn out to be what she needs. They are obviously in love with each other. I am willing to wait before I pass final judgment on the man."

"I hope you are right, for her sake, though I can't say I would be sorry if they fall out."

"That is my point. Your judgment is affected by personal bias…By the way, what if he asks her to move in with him in Addis Ababa?"

"Good question…If she accepts, that would change the idea of education of her nephews in Europe. So, she may not agree to relocate permanently to Addis…I don't mind confessing, that would be good!…Are you shocked?"

"Not really. It is a natural reaction of a person in your situation."

"Now a question, a hypothetical one…what would you have done in my situation?"

"To be honest, I really don't know whether I would have done anything different than what you have done."

"You mean accepting the defeat and adjust to live with it, as I have done?" "Yes, but don't get me wrong. I don't know whether I would have acted so nobly when she went out sobbing and you followed her and brought her back with your arms around her. That was beautiful, my dear friend."

"Thank you, Rashid. You are a true friend. I don't know what I would have done without your comforting friendship."

They reached the Railway Station and decided to turn and go back the way they had come.

Halfway on their way back, they heard a noise from a distance. Which kept coming nearer and nearer. They stopped for a moment and waited. The noise got close enough for them to hear the words. Repeatedly shouted, the words were in Amharic—*Netsanet*!—(freedom!).

Instinctively, they walked back and turned sideways to avoid confronting the mass of demonstrators that came nearer and turned leftward and continued along the highway leading toward Revolution Square, also known *Meskel Adebabay*, three kilometers away from where they were standing.

"I wonder what is going on?" Rashid wondered. "Freedom from what?" asked Stefan

"From Oppression, obviously… Dummy" Rashid chided. "It could also be Freedom from Hunger"

"That is too academic. You write a paper about it, you don't shout it as a demonstration slogan. When was the last time you were involved in a demonstration?"

"Oh…Eons ago."

"No wonder…Seriously, though, what do you think is going on?"

"I really can't say. Let us go back to the villa and maybe Beletech can enlighten us. It's time we went back, anyway."

Back in the Villa, "Isabelle must be having a special assignation with her lover," Rashid said, upon seeing the Mercedes parked in the compound. The two of them had taken the car, Kassa being on a short break. So they parked the car behind the Mercedes and walked into the salon, where they saw Teshome and Isabelle sitting on the love sofa.

"Welcome back," Isabelle shouted, and Teshome rose to greet the two and shook their hands. They exchanged the usual greetings and sat down.

Isabelle rose and began apologising for having to leave them; Teshome was also heading to the door with her. Isabelle said they were going out to a private party organized by Teshome's friends in his honor.

"What is the occasion?" Stefan asked mechanically looking at Teshome.

"I have been promoted to become head of Foreign Intelligence with a ministerial rank."

"Congratulations!" both Stefan and Rashid shouted. "Some friends actually are commiserating with me."

"Why? I thought you said you were promoted," Rashid inquired.

"Being appointed with a ministerial rank has political hazards in our current environment."

"What kind of hazards?" Stefan asked...

Stefan was curious to know what the hazards were, perhaps hoping in his heart of hearts that Teshome might be dismissed. He thought this could be a case of "being kicked upstairs."

After they left, Stefan said: "I don't know if you observed his facial expression. Something has changed, judging by his body language," he told Rashid.

"Perhaps Isabelle will enlighten us when she comes later." "If he lets her come tonight," Stefan said with a bitter smile.

Stefan's hunch was on target. Isabelle spent the night out, meaning with Teshome. The bitterness that had clouded Stefan's mood for some time after the cheek-to-cheek dance between Teshome and Isabelle, which had begun to subside, returned. He drank half a bottle of the whiskey left from the dinner last time, and went to bed dead drunk. Rashid tried to talk him out of the bad mood, but his efforts were rejected with some rude remarks uncharacteristic to him. So Rashid had given up and gone to bed earlier.

In the morning, Stefan slept late and missed breakfast, giving concern to poor Beletech. Rashid waited and had breakfast with Beletech whom he asked if she knew about the public demonstrations of the previous day. She told him: yes, it was on the news. To Rashid's question what they were demonstration about, she said that they were demanding freedom of the press and of movement, and demanding the release of political prisoners.

Rashid became curious and engaged Beletech in conversations over coffee. They were alone so there could be no fear of being spied on, so Rashid asked Beletech what her view of the government was. She looked left and right instinctively and told him in a low voice that the government was not popular. That it was dominated by one ethnic group, which angered the other ethnic groups who feel left out.

He asked her if she knew about Teshome whom she had seen during the dinner. She said she never saw him before and could say anything about him. She then turned the table and asked Rashid a shrewd question. She said: "I saw Isabelle with him. She looked happy, but also unhappy. Why was that?"

"Well, I don't know exactly. I think you can ask her directly; she likes you like her little sister. You can ask her as a concerned younger sister."

"Maybe you are right. I will ask her." "But don't tell her I suggested it, okay?"

"Of course not. In our Ethiopian culture, we don't ask personal questions, and we believe in silence as the best policy."

"That is a wise policy. Thank you, Beletech for all that you have done for us. You are wonderful and your aunt Azeb should be proud of you. I will tell her that."

"Thank you Rashid. You are a very kind man. I know how much you like Isabelle. It is obvious, and I think God will pay you back."

"How will God pay me back?" "By giving you a good wife."

"*Ya Allah*! You are so wise, Beletech. Thank you. I will get a good wife from Sudan, one of these days. But I have a girlfriend in England, a good girl."

"English?...No! Get a Sudanese or an Ethiopian girlfriend and then marry her."

Beletech heard the phone ringing and excused herself and went to answer the phone.

She came back with receiver and gave it to Rashid...It was Isabelle. "Hello Rashid. How are you and how is Stefan?"

"We are all well. How about you?" "I went AWOL, right?

"Well, we all do that from time to time..."

"You are just being kind. I am sure you were worried or angry or whatever..."

"Well, yes. Concerned is the right word..." "Is Stefan okay?"

"Yes, he is. He went out for a long walk. Are you going to join us for dinner?"

"Yes, I am coming in about an hour's time. See you soon." "Okay, see you soon."

Isabelle arrived around five in the afternoon. By the time she arrived, Stefan had been up and dressed in his Sunday best. Rashid teased him: "What is the occasion? You are dressed like a European diplomat."

"I thought perhaps, it might improve my mood. I have been horrid, haven't I?"

"Well, you were not exactly Mr. Prince Charming. But I understand you and do not deign to be judgmental. By the way, Isabelle just called and she is coming any minute now. She asked about you. I told him you went out on a long walk."

"You lied for me. Well, what are friends for? Thank you. See you at dinner," Stefan said and went up to his room.

About a quarter of an hour later, Isabelle came back the way she had left, in a Mercedes car, chauffeured by Teshome's driver. He accompanied her up the stairs and went back and drove away. Beletech met Isabelle and told her and everybody else dinner would be ready at six forty-five.

Isabelle stopped and kissed Beletech on the cheek and asked her if anybody called. She told her nobody called. She informed her, in case she did not know, that there had been public demonstrations demanding freedom. That was all, she told Isabelle. "And I will see you at dinner, Isabelle told Beletech, and went to her room.

The following day, early in the morning, Teshome arrived in his Mercedes and asked for Isabelle, who had not got out of bed yet. Beletech met him at the salon and told hm Isabelle was not up yet. He told her would she please wake her up. There is an urgent matter he wanted to discuss with her. So Beletech went up the stairs and knocked at Isabelle's bedroom door. After two knocks, Isabelle answered asking who it was. Beletech told her Teshome was here waiting to see her urgently. Isabelle put on her morning gown and came walking down the stairs. When Teshome saw her, he apologised, but he wanted her to come to town with him. She asked him: "Is everything okay?" He said everything is fine. Please get dressed and come down as quickly as you can.

Isabelle got dressed in ten minutes, looked at her face in the mirror and applied her lipstick on her lips lightly, picked up her bag and walked down the stairs slowly, somewhat worried by the sudden appearance of Teshome. She got into the car and he started driving; this time there was no chauffeur.

When they had driven a few miles Isabelle turned to Teshome with worry written over her face and asked: "Are you alright?" He said he was okay. There a few questions being asked about me and my new job.

"What kind of questions?"

"Somebody wrote a report about my connection with some foreign corporations and the boss wanted me to clear it before I start the new job."

"Are you safe? I mean are they going to arrest you or something?" "No. No. No. Nothing like that…"

"Then what was it that requires my presence? Did they ask you about me?" "Absolutely not. Isabelle, I am sorry I worried you. I just wanted to be with you, that is all. Your presence gives me a sense of security. Can you understand that?

"Yes I can. I am sorry, you just worried me that's all. I mean coming this early and driving your car yourself…"

"The driver is away on assignment. It happens from time to time. Do you feel alright now?"

She nodded and he asked, "Are you sure?" "Quite sure, thank you."

"Now we will have breakfast. What would you like for breakfast? We will eat at the Sheraton Hotel."

Back in the villa, Beletech informed Stefan and Rashid what happened. "Did you say he drove the Mercedes himself?" Stefan asked.

"Yes he did."

"Rashid I want to talk to you," Stefan called Rashid who was speaking to a visitor, an employee of the Embassy of Sudan. Rashid called back shouting: "*deghigha, ya ustaz*! (give a minute, prof). After five minutes, Rashid came to Stefan and asked him: "what was the matter?"

"The crook is at it again. He came early in the morning, asked for Isabelle, whom they had to wake up and literally drag out of bed. Well. I exaggerate. She was awakened and rushed out of her room. And he took her away driving his car himself…no driver. What is the saying you sometimes quote? "I smell a rat!"

"What is your suspicion? Why do you smell a rat?… It could just be love sickness, a kind of madness. Like, he couldn't be without her for one minute…

"…How is that as a possible reason for his sudden appearance and taking her away so suddenly and dramatically this way?"

"Could be. I don't know. I think the girl may be in danger." "So what do you propose we do?"

"We have to look for her."

"Where in his office or his house?"

"No, not in his house. But we can go to the Security Office and ask to see him. We have reason to go to the Security Office."

"I agree… Well, what are we waiting for?"…Let's go. I'll call Kassa."

They drove to town and headed to the Security Department. They entered the building and asked to see Mr. Teshome. They were told he was no in. Perhaps he is in his new office in the Ministry of Interior, they were told. When they asked where that is, they were told it is the old building off Churchill Road. It is the building where they had been to speak to the Minister. So, they drove down Churchill Road and turned right and got to the area where the Ministry of Interior was located. They asked for Mr. Teshome and were told he had not yet assumed his new function; the office was still occupied by his predecessor.

So, they decided to go back to the villa and wait for Isabelle's return.

Chapter Eighteen

TRIALS AND TRIUMPH OF THE HOLY FOOLS

The search for Isabelle had continued all day. Stefan and Rashid visited practically every office that might conceivably be connected with the work of Teshome. At his most desperate moment, Stefan imagined the worst possible danger, becoming despondent. Only Rashid's optimism kept him from sinking deeper into depression. Even Rashid was entertaining scenarios that included kidnapping and death. But no sooner had he imagined kidnapping than he dismissed it as inconceivable. For one thing, who would want to harm an innocent human being like Isabelle? And what would they gain by kidnapping her. She is not rich or powerful controlling wealth and people. She is not involved in local politics, so there is no possible political motive that could make anyone want to kidnap her.

So then, what? Why did Teshome come early in the morning and drive away with her? And where could he have taken her? Stefan started asking questions about Teshome: his history, connections, ambitions etc.

"Do you remember the Sudanese Ambassador's remarks about the group of former guerilla fighters who have formed a cabal of corrupt officials who monopolize business and amassed enormous wealth?"

"Yes, I do. What about them?" "Teshome must be one of them." "Do you think so?"

"I do, and the proof is staring us in the face."

"You mean his Mercedes car and his promise to do favors to Isabelle?" "Exactly."

"So what? What has that got to do with Isabelle's and Teshome's disappearance?"

"Do you also remember that the Ambassador spoke about another government official, a good guy, who was afraid of Teshome because of his power?"

"Yes, I remember. We met him at the party. He didn't talk much." "He didn't talk because of his fear of Teshome."

Stefan paused for a moment and said that he mentioned all this, including the fear of the good guy, because he has been worried from the get go when Teshome involved Isabelle in a "Faustian Bargain." Rashid was puzzled and asked Stefan to explain what a Faustian Bargain is. So Stefan told him the story written by the great German writer, Goethe. It is a story of Dr. Faust, a scientist and philosopher, who sold his soul to the Devil in exchange for power derived from science. So the Faustian Bargain is cited as a metaphor for an agreement or engagement with somebody, in which one sells one's honor for the sake of some interest.

"So, do you think Isabelle sold her honor for advantages promised by Teshome?"

"In some sense, yes I do."

"Well, I'd say most people do that, don't you think?"

"May be. But let me change the subject. What do you think of seeing the Sudanese Ambassador?"

"I was actually thinking about that. You mean to ask about Teshome?" "Yes. I thought also about asking him about the Ethiopian official who was quiet all the evening at the embassy party. He said later that the man was afraid of Teshome because he was powerful. I forgot his name, but we can describe him."

"A good idea. Let us go then,"

And they headed to the embassy and found the Ambassador was out; so they left a note saying they need to talk to him. Would he call them? By the time they reached the villa, it was past dinner time and Beletech was there, anxiously waiting for them.

"Any news of Isabelle?" Stefan asked Beletech, who told him Isabelle had been in for hours and was waiting for them. He exclaimed with his favorite German expression…

"Did you hear that Rashid? There we were, looking for her all over Addis Ababa and even worried sick, afraid something awful might have happened to her. And she is…(the German curse again!)"

"How long has she been here?" he asked Beletech. "About two hours," She replied.

Rashid was more calm and grateful she was well. "*Al Hamdu Lillah!* She is well," he breathed sitting down on the sofa.

Beletech asked both if they wanted dinner, and both answered with nods, with thanks and headed toward the dining room. After dinner they came out to the salon and asked Beletech if Isabelle had gone to bed. She said she did, but asked to be awakened when the two of them arrived.

"Shall we wake her up?" Stefan asked Rashid, who nodded in agreement. Beletech, who heard Stefan's question asked: "So, shall I wake her up, then?" And went up the stairs toward Isabelle's room and knocked at the door twice. When she heard the question: "Who is it?" Beletech said: "Your friends are here and want to see you."

Isabelle told Beletech: "Please ask them to come to my bedroom."

Beletech conveyed the message and the two went up the stairs and knocked at the door, and went in. They found Isabelle in her night dress, but was up and sat on one of the chairs. She asked her friends to sit down. "This is going to be a long story. If you prefer, we can talk tomorrow," she said, sounding unhappy. Both said, no she'd better tell them now, whatever it was…

"First of all, I want you to know that I feel terrible in putting you through so much worry. I didn't mean to. He said there was a new situation that he and I must discuss."

She stopped and was almost in tears when she continued…Again, she apologised, sniveling and blowing her nose…Her face looked haggard, as if she was deprived of sleep all night…

"Sorry, I need a bit of time to compose myself," she said, again tears running down her face. She blew her nose and continued: "I don't mean to keep you guessing. It is simple, really…"

"What is simple? Come on, tell us what it is," Stefan pressed her. "Would you like to wait till tomorrow morning?" Rashid asked.

"No, I will tell you now. The truth is that Teshome has been dismissed from his key position and was kicked upstairs to an office without any power..."

"Is that all?" asked Stefan with a ruthless tone.

"No, it is not." The point of his distress which he shared with me is that he has been informed from a reliable source that the top people are planning to arrest him, and have issued orders for him to hand over his passport," she said and sighed deeply.

Rashid instinctively turned his gaze toward Stefan who wore a smile that was difficult to describe. It was certainly not a smile of commiseration with Isabelle's distress. Nor was it one of satisfaction. For Stefan's love for Isabelle is deep-rooted and unconditional, one that would not involve happiness at her hour of distress, even if it did not involve commiseration. As for Rashid, he was obviously sorry to see her thus distressed because of the apparent changing fortune of a man he did not particularly like. The fact that his changing fortune affected Isabelle is regrettable, he thought. But we are still in the dark in what way that is going to affect Isabelle.

Stefan asked Isabelle: "What else did he tell you that has led to this distress?"

"He said, he would like me to go out of the country with him." "I thought they took his passport?" Rashid asked

"He has taken care of that and has people ready to take him out of the country, illegally." Isabelle said. She was almost trembling when she said that, not knowing what to do. She gazed at Stefan as if seeking a miraculous solution from him, and he just smiled and shook his head.

"What did you tell him when he asked you to go with him?" he asked coldly.

"I said I don't know if I could agree. I said I would seek the counsel of my friends."

Stefan looked at her with obvious pity and worry but pressed with more questions.

"Did he give you a deadline, like tomorrow?" "Yes, he did, and he was very firm about it."

"What would he do if you did not agree to go with him?"

"He didn't say what he would do. He expected me to go with him. He was firm about that."

"And to what country was he thinking of taking you?" Rashid asked.

"He said he has friends in Canada and Sweden who would arrange a visa immediately for him and for his wife. By the way, he also asked me to marry him."

"What did you say to that proposal?" Stefan asked.

"I said I could not answer him without consulting with you," she said pointing to Stefan.

"Let me guess. He was annoyed by that answer."

"Annoyed is putting it mildly. He was furious. Actually, I am frightened by the man," she said in a tremulous voice.

"Well, I wouldn't worry about that, "Stefan said. "Fortunately, we have embassies all three of us, that would give us protection, if necessary. The question is what do you tell him tomorrow."

"I don't want to see him alone. You two must come with me," she said, looking at one after the other, with an anxious furrowed brow...Won't you come with me?" she asked sounding desperate...

...What a difference twenty-four hours make!

From the emotional heights of a romantic involvement that promised paradise, Isabelle Negassa has come down to the reality of an ugly situation in which the lover now appears like the brute that the Sudanese Ambassador subtly described him. A "fallen angel" who once espoused ideals of the "mass line" and mouthed revolutionary rhetoric had descended to the depth of depravity and criminal enterprise...

Poor Isabelle, she was seduced by Teshome's physical charm and the mystique of the freedom fighter, who could do no wrong, later magnified by the magic of his promise of financial largesse to fulfil one of her dreams of embracing members of her extended family.

Stefan asked Isabelle point-blank a hard question:

"Isabelle, I am going to ask you a simple question which may be hard to answer. I want you to be frank for your own sake and for the sake of those of your devoted colleagues... Do you still love this man?"

"The truth is: yes, I love him, but I would not marry him in the circumstances, which is like an ultimatum or a threat."

"What if he tells you he will go without you, but wants you to follow him later, at your convenience?"

"To tell you the truth, I don't know how to answer that." Rashid changed the topic somewhat by saying:

"This man is under threat of arrest. Why? He must have committed a crime for which someone wants him to pay. Your lover, Isabelle, is probably going to be criminal on the run, a fugitive. What kind of life can you expect from him under such circumstances?"

"I have thought about that, Rashid. I agree with you. I would not want to be tied to a man who is on the run for crimes that may be subject to years of imprisonment and heavy fine."

"Are you afraid of him?" Stefan asked her. "Yes, I am, extremely afraid."

"You love him, but you are afraid of him!" Stefan's remark was cruel but true.

"Stefan, I know you judge me for disappointing you choosing him instead of waiting for you. But please understand. I did not plan it. It just happened, and I am suffering for it. I am willing to take whatever counsel you and Rashid give me."

"Including telling Teshome, you don't want to marry him?" Stefan asked "Yes, including that. But I don't want to be alone with him when I tell him that."

"Are you afraid he might harm you physically? "Yes, I am. He may even kill me."

"In that case, we need to take precautions, like warning our respective embassies and also notifying the security authorities," Stefan said.

And Rashid added: "Isabelle, are you okay with that, notifying the security authorities, I mean?"

"Yes, I am. Now you know why I looked distressed when you guys came in, to my bedroom," she said.

"Yes, we do," Rashid said

Chapter Nineteen

ON A KNIFE'S EDGE—RISKING LIFE TO SAVE A LIFE

The following day, all three friends rose early and met for breakfast. Isabelle looked much better. She was smiling and there was freshness and luster in her eyes. She reassumed her confident command of the situation by asking the first important question of the day:

"Are you going to ask for protection from the security people?" she asked looking at both Stefan and Rashid. "I mean not only for me but for all of us," she added.

"We have thought about that, yes." Stefan answered.

"Are you still worried about Teshome?" Rashid asked her with a reassuring smile.

"The last two nights, I have gained more insight into the character of the man. I had not perceived how ruthless he could be."

"He must have felt desperate after he became aware that he was under observation and perhaps even more than being observed," Stefan said.

In response, Isabelle said: "He did say that he has enemies among the top government leaders, and that they were after him."

"Well, it is time to go and talk to the security people," Stefan said, rising from his chair.

"Exactly my thought," Rashid said, also rising.

Isabelle rose and picked up her bag and all three walked out toward the parked car. They saw Kassa talking to a man about his age and height, who was wearing sunglasses. Kassa introduced the man to Stefan, first, then to Isabelle and Rashid.

"Dr. Schmidt, Mr. Rashid and Miss Isabelle, I would like to introduce my friend and colleague, major Assefa." Kassa said. He seemed a little embarrassed, so he explained something that was a secret to everybody except him and his superiors. Kassa said that he is a member of the Intelligenceservicesworkingundercover.Hesaidhehadfollowed everything that was going on and was equally concerned about Isabelle's safety and welfare as everyone had been.

"This is amazing!" Stefan said in astonishment. Both Isabelle and Rashid also expressed surprise.

"Were you assigned with a view to looking after us or spying on us?" Rashid asked, half in jest.

"It is part of my job to protect people from possible harm," Kassa said with a smile.

"By the way, I took the liberty of asking for an extra support from the people concerned. That was why Assefa has been assigned to help me. We are both appropriately trained and armed to do our job of protecting people."

"Well I'll be damned!" Stefan exclaimed. And Rashid proclaimed: "Oh Ethiopia, how full of surprises you are!"

Isabelle was silent for a bit and then said the most sensible thing of the moment. She said: "Thank you, Kassa. You have surprised everybody as you can see. But I say, well done and welcome! Your job in addition to the normal function of acting as our driver, has also included a special assignment to protect us. I say, May God Bless you!"

And Rashid continued:

"And Major Assefa, welcome to you too. Indeed, a special welcome. *Merhaba*! (Welcome)"

And Stefan added a practical point to all the exclamation and proclamation. He said:

"First of all, let us go into the studio and discuss what needs to be done." All followed him into the studio. After everyone had taken their seats, Stefan continued:

"I was wondering whether we still need to go to the Department of Security to apply for protection, now that Major Assefa has been assigned for our protection by them… Am I right?" Stefan asked.

"I was given instruction by the highest Security Authority to protect all three of you from any harm coming from anybody," the major said.

Stefan was tempted to ask the major specific questions but resisted the temptation out of concern that it may not be permitted by higher authority. But he decided only to delay the question, which he could raise quietly when he is alone. Stefan's concern was about Teshome's cunning and his wide network of connections. He did not want to be surprised.

Tackling a "Fallen Angel"

There was still the question of where and when Isabelle is meeting Teshome. According to her frightened and disjointed narrative, two things are known:

First, Teshome now knows he is a hunted man, and is desperate, and desperate people do desperate things. It is knowledge of these facts that prompted the Security Authorities to order extra security detail, in addition to Kassa. Teshome does not know about such security precautions, though he may know about Kassa being an undercover security agent. It is important that he does not know about Major Assefa's assignment until the very end. In other words, Major Assefa whom he must know, must remain incognito.

Second, Isabelle will be meeting Teshome, hopefully for the last time.

The two of them have not set up a time and place yet, and that must be done sooner than later.

Setting up the meeting will have to be done before the end of the day. If he does not call her, she needs to call him and set it up. All this assumes that he is not arrested in the meantime, or that he has not slipped out of the country, which is unlikely. Of course, when the meeting time and place is known, the security people must be informed. Major Assefa has the necessary communications facilities and it will be his task to inform the appropriate authorities on time. But Stefan thought Assefa may need reminding. He will remind him subtly when they are alone later in the day.

So now the question is: Do we wait until Teshome calls Isabelle, or do we take the initiative by Isabelle calling him? Isabelle, Stefan and Rashid consulted with Major Assefa and Kassa who advised that we wait for Teshome to call Isabelle. All the necessary and appropriate communications facilities will be arranged beforehand, a matter that Major Assefa will take care of.

As a highly trained, security personnel, Teshome will be on the lookout for any suspicious activities aimed at him, including what happens during his meeting with Isabelle. So, Isabelle needs to be warned and cautioned about this point. If he suspects that he is being watched, he may take desperate steps that might put her in danger. While it is important that she be cautioned not to give Teshome any hint that their meeting is being followed by anybody, she must also be made aware that she is undertaking a hazardous activity.

Stefan showed serious concern that Isabelle may be facing real danger in meeting Teshome. He even wondered whether it is necessary for her to meet him at all. Why not forget him and leave him to his fate, Stefan wondered aloud.

"But it is all up to you, Isabelle," he finally said. "It is your life and wellbeing, and you must decide yourself." Rashid expressed similar concern but was less worried. He did not believe that Teshome is capable of exerting such influence over Isabelle, who he said is a courageous and self-reliant woman. Let us give her the support and believe that she will do well, Rashid pleaded.

Finally, Isabelle calmly told her friends that she will be okay and that she will handle everything as carefully as she can.

"I may have behaved terribly last night, but I assure you I am out of the shock and will be okay. Stop worrying," she said with confidence. She looked at Stefan with a confident smile and said: "I know you are worried. Don't be. I know I will be okay. If the worst comes, I can take care of myself," she said, pulling out a small gun out of her right hip pocket.

"*Ya Salaam*!" Rashid cried...

"You didn't expect that, did you?" she exulted, gazing at Stefan's frowned face.

"No, I didn't. You are full of surprises," Stefan said and looking at Rashid, he added:

"It must be the Ethiopian in her!"

"I'll bet it is," Rashid said. Stefan watched Isabelle with a new perspective; he wondered whether the young woman he met many years ago had changed, becoming tougher. What a difference a few months make, he thought contemplating her transformed visage with a new insight. Well, he thought, it is just as well that she had become tougher, for she may need it in these uncertain circumstances.

Major Assefa asked Isabelle what the conversation had been between her and Teshome regarding the next meeting. "Did he say he would call you?" Isabelle said yes and so it was decided that they should await his call.

"What if he comes here unannounced and find us all assembled, and especially if he sees Major Assefa?" Stefan inquired.

"That is a good question," Isabelle said and suggested that Major Assefa leave and park somewhere nearby but stay in touch by phone.

All agreed and Major Assefa left quickly and drove his car out of the compound driving away a few miles' distance. Rashid thought of a new possibility. "Perhaps the situation is turning me to become paranoid but suppose that Teshome has dispatched one of his intimates to spy on Isabelle's movement."

"So now," Stefan said, "Major Assefa has left, and Kassa has been with us as Teshome probably knows. I don't think Teshome will come here; he will call Isabelle and tell her to meet him somewhere downtown…"

A few minutes after Stefan's remarks, Isabelle's cell phone rang. It was Teshome.

"Hullo beautiful woman! Sorry I am late in calling you. I have been busy. I want you to come to the place where we met last time, can you?"

"Hi Teshome. Okay, I'll be there in about an hour. Will you be waiting inside?"

"Yes, I will be on the lookout for you. I will take you back myself later, so you can dismiss the driver. The others may need his services anyway, right?

"Right… Okay, see you later."

She hung up and gazed at all three, including Kassa. She repeated the gist of what was said.

"He speaks of the place where you met last time. Where is that?"

"It is a house in the *Casa Incis* area, which he uses as his second office, when he wants to avoid people. I think the house belongs to him."

"Since Kassa will be taking you, he can lead us to it in case of need," Stefan said, already thinking ahead. "Right Kassa?" he asked and Kassa nodded his agreement.

"Major Assefa must be notified," Rashid reminded. And Kassa said he has his phone number and will notify him.

"Tell him also to notify his superior officers in the Security Department about the meeting place," Stefan said to Kassa.

Kassa asked if he should ask Assefa to follow him and Isabelle, and take Stefan and Rashid with him. Stefan said yes. "Please tell him we will count on him for assistance as it arises, and that we would expect it to be conveyed to us through you (Kassa).

"Hai Hai Sir! I mean yes, sir," Kassa said laughing at his mistake.

Isabelle left them with Kassa, and was seen making a sign of the cross, which had put in abeyance during her years of disaffection and rebellion against the Catholic Church hierarchy.

Kassa told her, when they were on their way that he noticed her making a sign of the cross. He told her that as an Orthodox Christian he used to make the sign of the cross also.

"It is like an insurance plan," Isabelle joked.

"I am afraid I have strayed from my family's Orthodox Faith. I feel the Church needs a revival for its youth to come back to it. As it is, it is not attracting the youth very much. Many of them have been attracted to the Pentecostal Faith.

By the time they arrived at the place of appointment, they had covered the issues of religious problems and of his firm belief that the Mother Church needed a breath of fresh air and a leadership that can attract the youth.

"Well, Miss Isabelle, I wish you well, and I am going to bring the others." And he returned to the villa and found the others waiting for him, ready to leave. They phoned Major Assefa and found him waiting for them in his car. They agreed to meet where Kassa will stop and park his car some fifty meters away from the house where Kassa had left Isabelle.

Stefan wanted to make sure that Isabelle was still in that house, just in case Teshome might have used that house as a decoy and taken her elsewhere. He asked Major Assefa if he could put on a hat and walk by the house to find out if Isabelle was in it. Major Assefa looked for a tennis cap and put it on as well as sunglasses and walked by the house slowly looking into the inside. He saw a man and a woman sitting side by side on a sofa in the veranda and reported this to Stefan. Satisfied that Isabelle was in the house, Stefan asked Rashid as well as Assefa and Kassa, who were in the same car, for their individual views as to what to do next.

"I mean we cannot just sit here in the car and may even be watched by Teshome's agents who would report to him. What do you think…all of you?" he asked.

Assefa said Stefan was right. "You think like a trained security officer, Dr. Stefan," he said with a smile, and continued: "I suggest that we disperse, like two in one care and two in the other car, and move our vehicles out of sight to Teshome's house, but in places from which we can see the house.

"Excellent idea," Stefan said. And they did as Assefa had suggested, with Stefan going to Assefa's car and Rashid remaining in Kassa's car. They kept watch of the house for any people going in and out of it. They must have waited a little under two hours when they saw a car coming out of the house. They all got themselves ready to see who was in the car. Assefa used his binoculars to see who was in the car. Meanwhile both drivers got the engine ready to start and follow the car. Assefa saw Teshome's head and Isabelle's beside him. He passed the binocular to Stefan who confirmed Assefa's report.

After the car passed both drivers started driving toward the same direction where the car had headed. They took care not to be noticed and kept a reasonably long distance from it. The car headed in a westerly direction toward the "Jubilee Palace" and turned right going northward past Hilton Hotel. Then it continued for half a kilometer and went into the Sheraton Hotel. Both Kassa and Assefa rushed into the hotel compound, but quickly left and looked for parking nearby. Once properly parked, Stefan got out of Assefa's car and joined Rashid and Kassa. Assefa also joined them and they began plotting what to do next.

"What do we do now?" Of all people, it was Stefan who asked instead of making a suggestion, which was the usual case. Rashid said: "You tell us ustaz."

"What do we do now? I am out of ideas or suggestions. What do you think, Major Assefa?"

"If you allow me sir, first of all, we need to find out if they have rented a room, which is likely. And which room they have rented."

"With what objective? To barge in there and catch them naked...? And cry: **Aha, caught you**!!" Stefan said laughing at his own question. They all joined him in the laughter.

"I think we needed that laughter, to tell you the truth," Rashid said.

"Yes, that was very funny, sir" Kassa said breaking out into laughter again. "I told you, we did need that laughter...But what is the answer to your question, Stefan?"

Stefan was suddenly getting nervous. Was he imagining the two of them having sex in the hotel?

He asked Major Assefa if he thought they had rented a room. Assefa said yes, very likely.

"Can you think of a way of finding out which room, Major?" "I will think about it, sir."

Rashid, who didn't see any point in finding out which room they are in, suddenly blurted:

"What the hell do we need to know the room for?"

"I just want to know. Do you mind?" queried Stefan angrily. His nerves were obviously on edge.

Meanwhile, Major Assefa said he may have a way of finding out about the room they rented.

"What is that, if I may ask?" Stefan pressed.

"Well, you see, sir, one of our undercover agents works at the hotel, and I know him well. I will go in the hotel and ask for him and ask him discreetly to find out if Teshome rented a room in the hotel and if so, which one.0

Chapter Twenty

THE DIE IS CAST

"That is great, Major. Go right ahead," Stefan said with eager expectation of a show down.

Rashid asked Stefan, after Assefa left to the hotel, why he was so eager to find out the room number. "Do you plan to go in there and rescue Isabelle from the brute?"

"Oh yes, I do. I am concerned of what might happen in a possible confrontation. That's all," Stefan responded gently

But the die is cast. Assefa may find out where the two of them are and what they are doing.

And Teshome, who knows who Assefa is, may not like it. Rashid was concerned with what Stefan might do, so he was determined to keep him in the car.

Assefa was gone for about fifteen minutes when gun shots were heard. Rashid literally kept Stefan by the arms and kept him pinned down. Meanwhile, Kasssa, bolted out of the car, drew his gun from its holster and ran toward the hotel entrance and went in.

Stefan made a strenuous effort to wriggle out of Rashid's hold, crying, "Let me go! Get off of me, Rashid…Get off, I say!"

But Rashid wouldn't budge; so, a struggle ensued in which Stefan used every trick to get out of Rashid's hold.

"Get off me!" "No!"

"I am warning you, I can be rough." "Really, and do you take me for a sissy?"

They continued struggling with Rashid holding tight with his arms around Stefan in a chokehold.

After another five minutes, gun shots were heard, several of them.

That gave Stefan a motive and an excuse to get out of Rashid's firm hold. He shouted at the top of his voice:

"Rashid, let me go or I will use my martial arts skill to strike you where it hurts.

"I am telling you: Let me go. Don't you understand that I must go and help Isabelle out of her captivity? Have you forgotten she is a captive of a cruel and selfish man? Please release me and let me go!"

When he got no response from Rashid, he shouted: "HO!…" and hit Rashid in the groin so hard that Rashid groaned with horrific pain and released Stefan from his chokehold.

Stefan moved to get out of the car and said in friendly apology: "Sorry, old boy; I warned you," and jumped out of the car.

As more shots were heard, Rashid managed to scramble out of the car and, summoning all his athletic force, got out and set himself to running after Stefan.

He couldn't catch him, so he jumped and grabbed his legs and brought him down to the ground.

But Stefan managed to break loose from Rashid's hold, got up and started running, with Rashid chasing him. Then suddenly, Stefan assumed an attack mode with arms stretched out for a Karate strike.

"Rashid, you are making a mistake; you can't stop me from going to help Isabelle. I will hit you hard," he said, and no sooner had he said these words than he leaped forward, twirled sideways and hit Rashid on the head with his foot, sending him down sprawling on the ground practically unconscious.

As he performed that Karate hit, Stefan had a flashback in his mind of the time when he struck the Trump follower with a red cap and MAGA written on it who was about to shoot him down before the Red-Head beauty by the name of Dorothy intervened placing herself in between them and taking the bullets on her chest. She had died and left a deep sense of guilt that must have been buried in his subconscious.

Now, Stefan entered the tragic melee, where Kassa had found Assefa badly wounded lying on the stairs. Kassa had tried to stop his bleeding and taken out a hand kerchief to block the blood. But it was too late. Assefa died. Meanwhile Stefan shouted to Teshome loudly challenging him, with Rashid following suit and standing beside him.

Then Stefan had cried, "Isabelle!" To which Teshome responded:

"Come up here, if you are a real man, and fired two shots toward Stefan, but missed.

"I will show you who the real man is, you bastard," Stefan said, running toward where the shot came from.

Teshome aimed his gun at Stefan and fired two shots hitting Stefan on the chest.

Isabelle, in desperation shot Teshome aiming at him from his back; and Teshome, though wounded on the shoulder, responded by shooting her point blank, killing her instantly.

At the same time, Kassa had crawled slowly toward a position of advantage from which he could see Teshome, and called Teshome who responded with firing missing Kassa. At that very moment, Kassa aimed two shots at Teshome, who was hit and fell over the bannisters crushing on the floor. He was dead.

Kassa ran toward where Isabelle had fallen; he knelt and touched her breathing. She was dead.

He then ran down toward where Stefan had been and found him dead too. He threw his arms in the air and shaking his head cried: "O Amlake!" "Oh my God!"

He was joined by Rashid who sat beside him on the stairs in a momentary daze, but hugging Kassa and then asked him to do his duty and call the authorities.

Kassa recovered from his daze and phoned the emergency number asking for an ambulance…

The ambulance arrived and the three medics ran upstairs, examined Isabelle's body as well as Teshome's. They brought a stretcher and took the two bodies down one after the other and placed them inside the ambulance. They also took Assefa's body to the ambulance and took the four bodies to the Fulwuha Hospital.

The hotel manager called the police to report of the incident, telling them that the dead bodies were taken by ambulance to the Fulwuha hospital. The Police sent a criminal law expert and a medic to investigate. When they found out the identity of the victims of the incident, they sent a team to take possession of the four dead bodies and took them in an ambulance to the Police Hospital for examination. Another team was sent to interview Kassa and Rashid.

According to the post-mortem exam of Teshome's and Assefa's corpse, the doctor had written his report in which it was reported that Assefa was killed from a bullet fired from Teshome's gun and Teshome was shot by two different bullets. One bullet had entered the body from the front and hit his chest going through his heart and thus killing him instantly. The other bullet entered his body from the back and hit his right shoulder. The conclusion of the examining doctor was that it was the first bullet that caused his death.

As to the second bullet that entered Teshome's body from the back, the examining doctor's conclusion was that it must have been fired from the back from a short distance. Upon examining the gun found in Isabelle's hand, the police concluded that the second bullet came from her gun. The doctor's report was made available to the public including the curious news media that started looking for survivors of the incident.

Two Weeks later

The news of the tragedy at the Sheraton Hotel had reached the curious local Media as well as the representatives of the international Press. Newspaper editors and website managers as well as government-owned radio and TV stations sent their agents and reporters hunting for the place where one of the survivors was staying, that was also the one place that they discovered was the meeting venue of two of the victims of the massacre—the Addis Ababa home of Yusuf Ibrahim, Rashid's rich uncle.

Hardly had the news of the shooting spree at the Sheraton reached the ears of the Media than they discovered the place where one of the survivors of the shooting stayed. They located the place and came swarming on the Villa Ibrahim. Their principal target was Rashid, and they peppered him with a series of uninterrupted questions for the better part of the day.

Rashid, true to character, answered all their questions with patience and grace, prompting one inquisitive journalist to complement him on his patience and willingness to answer all questions. He did not stop there…

"What do you do now, Mr. Rashid? Are you going to continue in your illustrious soccer career?" It was the BBC reporter who asked.

"Well, first things first. First, I have a responsibility. I owe it to my friends to deal with their remains—of Isabelle and Stefan, I mean. I have made the necessary arrangements to send the mortal remains to their respective places for burial by their closest relatives, one in France, the other in England. I have also another weighty responsibility to deal with other people…"

"May I ask who these people are?" asked the BBC reporter. "Certainly, it is no secret…"

And Rashid began telling the story of Isabelle's visit to Wollega and discovery of two cousins as well as their two sons who were studying in a college in Adama. He related Isabelle's intention to take the two students under her wing and send them to school in Europe. He said that he had decided to take care of the two boys, fulfilling Isabelle's promise to them."

"Do you mean you will pay for their education in Europe? Wouldn't that be costly?"

"Yes, it will be costly, but they are well worth it, and I am able do it. I have the financial ability to fulfill Isabelle's wish, *Al Hamdu lillahi.* "(Thanks be to God.)" I owe my sadly departed friend Isabelle, at least to fulfil her wish to take care of her nephews.

"Good for you. Mr. Rashid, good for you," cried one of the journalists. "Hear, hear," said the reporter of the BBC.

It was obvious that some, perhaps many of the media people assembled at Villa Ibrahim found it unbelievable to hear Rashid say what he was going to do. Some might have even suspected that there might have been some romantic entanglement between them, though she was betrothed to marry Stefan.

As if he suspected what might be going on in the minds of the curious media people, Rashid decided to explain, that his motives were honorable, purely the acts of a devoted friend.

He cleared his throat and addressing the assembled members of the media said:

"Ladies and Gentlemen, first of all I would like to thank you for your interest in the tragic events that occurred at the Sheraton Hotel...

... "I hope I have answered your questions. Before I close this meeting and proceed to attend to the business of preparing for the Memorial Services for my friends, Isabelle and Stefan, before their remains are shipped to their Final destinations, Insha'Allah," allow me to say a few words about our friendship, the bond of friendship of three people that brought us to Ethiopia on what can even be described as an adventure of the spirit, if I may put it that way..."

"You see, it was as if we were summoned from the grave—the unknown grave of Isabelle's murdered father..."

He stopped and asked a question: "How many of you have heard of the case of Isabelle's father who was an illustrious Ethiopian revolutionary and who was murdered by agents of Mengistu Hailemariam?"

The reporter of the French Radio Program, *Radio France Internationale*

(RFI) raised his hand to say that he had heard that Isabelle's mother had traveled to Ethiopia inquiring about the circumstances of his death.

Rashid answered, "Well, Isabelle's mother came to Ethiopia anxious to find out what happened to her husband. She went everywhere, spoke to anybody who might help, leaving no stone unturned, both literally and figuratively. But she drew a blank. Isabelle grew up hearing about all this and when she came of age decided to go deeper than what her mother had done and dig for answers. This was why I called our project an adventure and a summons from the grave.

"And as I am sure you all know by now, Isabelle lost her life in her brave attempts to find her father's grave. Her intention had been to recover her father's remains and take it to France to give it an appropriate burial. And she ended dying herself in the attempt.

You will agree with me if I say that this is a poignant ending of a noble search.

In conclusion, let me pay tribute to the friendship that brought us—Isabelle, Stefan and myself to Ethiopia on a noble project. Some of you might wonder at the unique bond of friendship that drew the three of us together. The story of our adventure in search of the remains of Isabelle's father, is the story of friendship itself, though there is the larger picture of migration on which the three of us had similar views.

I don't know how many of you know the story of Pythias and Damon in Greek myth. In that story, the Greek god, Dionysius condemns Pythias to death, but permits him to travel home to say goodbye to his friends and family, provided his friend Damon made a pledge for his return, on pain of getting killed in his place, should he fail to fulfill his pledge. When the fatal day arrives, Pythias had not returned and Damon was brought forth to be killed, never doubting that Pythias will yet appear. And he does at the last moment, apologising for the misadventures at sea that delayed him.

In the story, Dionysius is so impressed that he releases both men and begs them to give him friendship lessons. Dionisius wanted desperately to be close to Pythias and Damon, even though they told him he could not be their third friend.

"Our story is the story of true friendship," Rashid said with flourish One of the newspaper editors raised a question of how Rashid would manage his life with two boys without the help of a wife to act as mother to the boys.

"I am not surprised you raise this important question, and I was remise in failing to tell you that I have a life time partner in England who is a gracious lady and who will be coming to see the boys and join me in the adoption process. By the way, we will use the time-honored Oromo adoption system known as *Gudi-feja*, under which older people can be adopted. It reflects the Oromo genius of social organization.

I will end by saying, "long live the Extended family system of Africa including this wonderful process of adoption. And I thank you all for your interest and attention.

The End

ABOUT THE AUTHOR

THE BOOK FOCUSES ON THE CRITICAL AND PROBLEMATIC GLOBAL ISSUE OF MASS MIGRATION.

…It begins thus: "A Time Marked by Chaos in Government—widespread moral bankruptcy—corruption other threat of nuclear war and the phenomenon of migration creating political and social problems provoking conflict within and among nations.

Its three principal characters are united by a common objective of helping in the settlement of conflicts within and among nations. The central character is Isabel Nagassa, a young woman whose Ethiopian father was a leading revolutionary leader in Ethiopia, but her French mother is left fending for her and her younger infant sister while historical events happen in Ethiopia. Her father was eventually assassinated by the military government of Ethiopia, and she grew up missing a father that she adored and who was also adored by millions and respected by fellow revolutionaries in Ethiopia and Europe. When she and her two friends—one German social Democrat (Stefan), and another, a Sudanese (Rashid), a world-famous soccer star and fellow student and friend of Stefan agree to help Isabel discover her father's killers. The trio bond and make a pledget to set about a dangerous adventure of helping Isabel discover her father's killers and trace his hallowed burial ground. All kinds of substories occur, leading to a dramatic end in which some are killed.

The author is an emeritus Distinguished Professor of African Studies and Professor of Law at the University of North Carolina at Chapel Hill. His Memoirs, "The Crown and the Pen," relates the story of a man straddled two worlds—a progressive lawyer and Attorney General of Ethiopia's Emperor Haile Selassie. He thus struggled for justice within an archaic system bedeviled with imperial Court intrigue. He was banished to a distant province and eventually escaped to his native Eritrea, where he joined the armed struggle for independence. His Memoirs, and his novel Riding the Whirlwind (1993) paint a dramatic picture of a tumultuous life saddled with tension involving opposing ideas and forces. Out of Africa, he settled in America and began an academic life, writing over twenty books, including works of fiction. DEFIANCE…is his third novel. He was appointed to head the Constitutional Commission that drafted a new constitution of Eritrea.

Printed in the USA
CPSIA information can be obtained
at www.ICGtesting.com
LVHW090723120924
790746LV00002B/154